The Daybreak Bond

Also by Megan Frazer Blakemore

The Water Castle
The Spy Catchers of Maple Hill
The Friendship Riddle
The Firefly Code

The Daybreak Bond

Megan Frazer Blakemore

BLOOMSBURY
NEW YORK LONDON OXFORD NEW DELHI SYDNEY

First published in the United States of America in September 2017
by Bloomsbury Children's Books
www.bloomsbury.com

Bloomsbury is a registered trademark of Bloomsbury Publishing Plc

For information about permission to reproduce selections from this book, write to Permissions, Bloomsbury Children's Books, 1385 Broadway, New York, New York 10018
Bloomsbury books may be purchased for business or promotional use. For information on bulk purchases please contact Macmillan Corporate and Premium Sales Department at specialmarkets@macmillan.com

Library of Congress Cataloging-in-Publication Data
available upon request
ISBN 978-1-68119-479-0 (hardcover) • ISBN 978-1-68119-481-3 (e-book)

Book design by John Candell
Typeset by Westchester Publishing Services
Printed and bound in the U.S.A. by Berryville Graphics Inc., Berryville, Virginia
2 4 6 8 10 9 7 5 3 1

All papers used by Bloomsbury Publishing, Inc., are natural, recyclable products made from wood grown in well-managed forests. The manufacturing processes conform to the environmental regulations of the country of origin.

The Daybreak Bond

1

OUR VOICES DANCED UP INTO the sky like fireflies escaping a jar. We tramped through the woods away from Old Harmonie, giddy and edgy and loud. Theo had given up on keeping us quiet, and sometimes he even joined in with our singing.

The trees out here grew wild and magnificent, like something I thought only existed in fairy tales or my imagination. Thick-trunked hemlocks and pines with boughs that hung low and brushed our shoulders. Creeping bunchberry flowers sparkled over the ground, and moss cocooned the rocks. I still couldn't quite believe it was real. We were outside the fences of Old Harmonie. The plan to leave had been hasty and shaky, but here we were *outside*. Theo had lifted a map from Mr. Quist, and it had led us right to the train tracks that went into Cambridge. We were on our way.

"The Firefly Five!" I yelled into the night.

"The Firefly Five!" my friends called back.

That's what we called ourselves: Ilana, Julia, Theo, Benji, and me. We'd never been outside the fences of our town before. But Ilana was in trouble, so we went out to the wild world. Her ankle had a bandage wrapped around it from where Benji had cut out what we hoped was her only tracking device. She was something other than human—more than or less than, I still wasn't sure. She was a project of Krita, the corporation that ran the community where we lived. They wanted to scuttle her and we weren't going to let them. She was our friend.

It sounds much simpler than it felt.

But I couldn't let the confusion and sorrow weigh me down. I climbed onto a small boulder next to the tracks and watched my friends marching in a line.

A mosquito buzzed around my ear, then drifted down my body and landed on my ankle. I smacked at it, but it got away. The bugs out here were bad, and that was worrisome—insects carry many diseases—but as long as we kept moving, only a few of them landed on us.

I leaped from the boulder and landed clumsily, but for a moment it had felt like soaring.

"Okay, guys, so, this is the coolest, right?" Benji asked as he hopped along the tracks. "Here we are, out in the world, saving our friends. We're superheroes!" He ran and jumped with his hands out in front of him, trying to look like a flying hero. He tripped, though, and rolled forward with a soft *oof*.

"Benji!" I cried out.

He held up both hands. "No biggie. I've taken way worse diggers on my board."

Ilana walked over and reached out her hand to him. "Nice tumble," she said as she pulled him to his feet.

"It was a pretty great flip, right? I mean, if you're gonna fall, it's best to do it with style." He brushed himself off with his hands.

We made a single-file line and started marching toward the orange-green lights of the city. The tracks were set on railroad ties: thick, square slabs of wood that had grayed in the sunlight. Some still had their original brown color, and these oozed tar the way a sugar maple oozed sap. The smell was pungent and unfamiliar and gave me a headache. Between the metal cross-tracks were stones, most no bigger than a super bounce ball, but still big enough to roll your ankle. The tracks held down the growth enough to make the walking easier.

"The city looks close," I said.

"It's an illusion," Theo replied.

"Twenty-four point eight miles. Just a little bit less than a marathon. People run that in like three hours," Ilana said.

Then she glanced over at me and smiled. "But don't worry. You won't need to run it."

"Well, good," I said. "Because I would smoke you all. Even you, Julia!"

"Watch out," Benji said. "Mori Bloom is fired up!"

And I was. A week before, I never would've believed this was possible.

Ilana straddled tracks and walked with one foot on each rail. She stepped right over a tiny white starflower. I thought she hadn't noticed, but then she turned around and whispered to me, "Star light, star bright, first star I see tonight."

She didn't need to finish. We were all wishing for the same thing: Ilana's safety.

We walked on toward the glow of the city.

"All those lights," Julia said. "It's like a million people. At least."

"Two point seven million," Ilana said.

I shuddered. Nothing we had ever heard about the city was good. Fortunately, we didn't have to go into Boston proper. We were headed for Cambridge, a city just on the other side of the Charles River. Close enough to Boston. Dangerous enough. Scary enough. My mouth went dry as a garden before the rain.

Benji brushed against me as he caught up with Ilana. "I was wondering, what do you remember about Calliope?"

"Why?" Ilana asked.

"She wasn't actually there, you know," Julia said.

"Yeah, but she remembers it, and that's pretty cool. I was just wondering how detailed those memories were."

Ilana tugged at a curl. "I remember the cafeteria at my school."

"Was the food good?" Benji asked.

Theo punched him in the arm. "She didn't eat it. She wasn't there."

"I remember how it smelled. Like eggs. Fried eggs. But we never had breakfast there. Isn't that weird?"

"Your brain must have created a false connection," I said. "That smell probably goes back to something at the lab where you—" I stopped myself, but Ilana looked at me expectantly, almost hopefully. "Where you were born."

Ilana pivoted to face me. I tilted my head back to look up into her green-blue eyes, which flashed with anger. "I wasn't born. That's the whole problem. That's why we're out here on this silly walk."

I rocked back, surprised by her sudden anger. Theo stepped up between us. "Hey." His voice was low. "Mori's just trying to help you."

I knew what he was thinking. We all did. The truth was, we didn't really know what she was capable of, and whether or not something might glitch up her programming.

Ilana looked down at her orange canvas sneakers, the toes scuffed black from the tracks. "Sure. Whatever. Sorry."

I bit my lip. What if Ilana's functioning was somehow tied to Old Harmonie? We thought we'd gotten her tracker out, sure, but what if there was some deeper connection between her and the lab back at KritaCorp? It was possible, I imagined, that her whole operating system was linked to their servers and as we got farther away and the connection weakened, she might face more problems.

Theo brushed his hand through his hair. "We just can't do this right now, Ilana." We all knew what he meant by *this*. If Ilana glitched, we were done for.

If she *was* glitching, it could be related to the programming they'd given to her. They'd never seemed to get it quite right. I rubbed my arm. The bruise she had given me was mostly gone, but of course I still remembered her grip tightening around my biceps. The truth was, whoever had designed Ilana was smart. Really smart. And even they hadn't fully understood her. How could I expect to?

Stop, I told myself. The way my thoughts were spiraling, that wasn't really me, I had to remember that. That was the fear that came from being dampened. My parents had been trying to protect me, and so they'd taken away my bravery and made me afraid of everything. Just thinking about it started a red, angry feeling all over my body. I could feel it in my stomach and my head and the tight set of my lips. Who were they to change who I was? I had been bold and wild and that scared them, so they had made me fearful. I kicked at a rock. Angry was better than nervous, I decided. Anger pushed me forward.

"It's okay," I said. "We're back on track now. Let's just keep going."

"Good one, Mori." Benji laughed. "Back on track."

Theo grimaced. "We should be able to do it in less than twelve hours, so even with some breaks, we should get there by the afternoon. And then we find MIT and Dr. Varden."

"I still say that's a pretty weak final stage of the plan," Julia said. She was wearing a sweatshirt with reflective strips down the arms, and every once in a while they would catch the faint moonlight and gleam.

"Dr. Varden is still listed as a member of the lab. Professor emerita, whatever that means. It's in the Stata Center," Theo said. "Getting there will probably be the easy part."

"We'll find her," Benji agreed.

"She'll know what to do," I said. "She'll help us. She has to."

"That's the shaky part of the plan," Ilana said.

But I knew Ilana was wrong. Dr. Agatha Varden had founded Old Harmonie. She'd helped to design the ALANA project—the predecessor to the project that had created Ilana. But more than that, she'd been my great-grandmother's best friend. That's how I knew she'd help us.

"You cold?" Ilana asked me. "You can have my sweatshirt. I'm pretty warm, actually."

"I just want to get you there and get you safe," I told Ilana.

Ilana looked up at the sky. Her jaw was set in a hard line.

"She will help you, Ilana," I said. "I promise."

"You can't make a promise for someone else."

"I just know she will, that's all."

"She was Mori's baba's best friend. That matters," Julia told Ilana, with a bit of edge in her voice.

Ilana stopped walking. She pushed her fingers into her temples.

"What's wrong?" I asked.

Theo and Benji turned back to look at us. "You okay, Ilana?" Benji asked.

Ilana didn't answer. She closed her eyes.

I remembered the day in the pool when she had just shut down. "Ilana," I cried. "Ilana!" I grabbed her by the arms. "Don't do this again!"

She blinked her eyes open. "It's a headache. That's all."

I glanced over my shoulder at Benji. I wished I could telegraph my question right to his brain: *What if they had programmed her to stop? What if she can't go any farther?*

2

"THE NICENESS OF THE OUTSIDE world is actually a little disappointing," Benji said. "Like, I was expecting plagues of locusts and mind-sucking zombies and all that stuff."

"They might not be locusts, but these bugs *are* awful!" Julia punctuated her sentence with a hard slap against her calf. "Ha! Got you!" She held up her hand smeared with her own blood. "I am the slayer of beasts. If there were mind-sucking zombies, I'd save your life."

"I'm sure you would," Benji said.

"When I was little, and I'd hear about the bogeyman or monsters or whatever, I'd think it was someone from outside," I said.

"I used to have nightmares my parents brought me out

here and left me here," Julia confessed. "It was like this dark, burned-down landscape. No trees, no houses, nothing."

"But you could see the forest from Old Harmonie," Ilana said.

"But we couldn't really see beyond it," Julia said. "I'd have one of those nightmares and I could hardly sleep for weeks."

"And now here it is—all big, pretty trees and cool night air," Benji said, holding his arms wide. "Nothing scary at all."

"Except the bugs," Julia said.

"Except the bugs," Benji agreed. "Where's the danger? You can't have an adventure without danger."

"You'd better stop talking like that, Benji," I said.

"What?" he asked.

"I'm serious. If you jinx us—"

"There's no such thing as jinxes, Mori," Theo said.

"That's true," Ilana agreed. "If you see something as bad luck, that's just your way of seeing it. The universe doesn't care."

But not five minutes later, we ran right into our first big obstacle.

"What is that?" Julia asked. We all stopped short.

We'd come around a bend and then up a slight hill that had blocked our view of the city lights. We'd crested the top and now saw something hazy and pink shimmering in front of us.

"This makes no sense," Theo said.

"Beautiful things usually don't," I heard myself reply.

It was a lake. The rising sun was reflected across the flat surface of the water, so it seemed like we were being swallowed in a golden pink-and-red haze. I felt my breath go shallow at the beauty of the lake that appeared out of nowhere.

"This makes no sense," Theo said again in a low, quiet voice.

I knew he wasn't thinking about the sunrise or the steam off the water or the way it made me feel full of awe to the point I thought I might actually start crying. He was talking about how the train tracks ran right into the water, which lazily lapped at the rails.

"It's not on the map?" Benji asked.

Theo shook his head.

"How old is the map?" Ilana asked.

Theo spread out the creased paper and we all peered at it. "See, we're right here. There's no water anywhere. Just that river off to the west a bit." His voice sounded hollow.

Julia sighed. "See the copyright? This map is decades old."

Theo's face turned ashen, even in the pinkish light. "We can't," he began. Then he turned to Ilana, who was crouched down beside him. "I'm sorry. I didn't even think about how it might be out-of-date. I'm just used to maps that are always updated. I wasn't even thinking."

"It's okay," she said. She smoothed out the map with the palm of her hand.

"But now we have no idea—"

Ilana cut Theo off: "In a situation like this, there are always three choices: over, around, or through."

"Or back," Julia said.

I blinked. "No."

"Mori, just look at this lake: it's huge. We can't see where it ends. And without a map, we have no way of knowing how big it is. If we walk around, it could be miles and miles and who even knows where we would end up."

"I guess it's over or through, then," I said. I held my body as still and tall as I could, as if standing strong would make me feel strong.

"Are you honestly suggesting we swim? Or, what, build a boat?"

"We could build a raft," Benji offered.

"I'm saying that if we've come this far, we ought to at least look around before we give up entirely."

"Mori's right," Theo said. "Maybe there's another way across. Let's just split up and walk along the edge in each direction and see what we can find. Fifteen minutes out and back. That's it."

"Then we make a decision?" Julia asked.

"Exactly. An informed decision," Theo replied.

Julia twirled her braid. "Fine. But to be clear, building a raft is not actually an option."

"It wouldn't be that hard," Benji said. "We have access to plenty of wood. We'd just need to find something to hold it all together. Maybe some vines or—"

Julia narrowed her eyes at him.

"Mori, you can come with me," Theo said. "Benji, Ilana, and Julia, you go that way."

Ilana and Julia both hesitated, but then they headed off in the southerly direction, while Theo and I went north. We had only walked about five minutes when we saw a granite post with a plaque on it:

ALCOTT RESERVOIR

Drinking water area.

No swimming, boating, or fishing allowed.

No trespassing.

Underneath, the words "KritaCorp" were stamped in firm, capital letters.

"This is where our water comes from," I said.

"Of course," Theo said, and pushed his bangs from his forehead.

"But if this is our reservoir—" I began.

Theo interrupted me. "I knew the reservoir was east of Old Harmonie. What was I thinking?"

"It's not your fault. None of us thought of it either. None of us even thought to get a map."

"I'm guessing there's a lot we didn't think of."

He was right, of course. We'd barely had a shadow of a plan when we set out, so no wonder it was falling apart.

The bright sunrise was over, but the sky was still a dusty pink. My eyes were drawn to a shape by the shore: dull brown and arched toward the water. A tree that had toppled? Or could it be a rock?

Then the shape stood up.

I grabbed Theo's arm and pulled him to the ground. Perhaps it was the sheer shock of my forcefulness that kept him quiet. My glasses jostled off my face, but we were close enough, our cheeks against rough sand, that I could see his wide eyes. "Outsider," I whispered.

3

QUIET AS GARTER SNAKES WE slid toward a boulder near the woods. We peered around and watched the man. He wore a brown jumpsuit and on the back was a striped teardrop. He bent over the water again and scooped some out. It was hard to see what he was doing, especially since my glasses were dusty from their fall and I was too nervous to clean them. He separated the water into smaller containers. He paused. Then he turned and looked in our direction. I wasn't sure if I was hearing Theo's heart or my own, but it pounded in my ears and through my body.

"He sees us," I whispered.

Theo didn't answer.

The man turned back to the water. He picked up a bright

orange case and placed the containers into it. Then he put the case into a knapsack, slung it over his back, and disappeared into the woods.

We did not move. We did not speak.

A crow landed on the rock above us and cawed two times before taking off in a rush of wings.

"Okay," Theo said.

"Okay?" I whispered back. "How is this okay?"

"He's gone." Theo brushed the sand from his legs. "I think he must have been testing the water quality. We should follow him."

"No way!"

"He went back into the woods. Maybe there's a road out or something."

"No," I said again. "That man is an outsider!"

"You don't know that," Theo told me. "He probably works for Krita."

"Okay, maybe, but even if he does, any road out here is going to lead to outsiders."

"At some point in time we're going to be around outsiders, you know."

"I know," I agreed, though the very thought of it made me retch. I had been pushing the idea down since we'd first hatched the plan to get Ilana out of Old Harmonie. Outsiders were disease-ridden. And violent. At least, some of them were. That was one thing dampening surely helped: if anyone was too aggressive, it was dampened out of them. Exposure to outsiders was dangerous, especially out here, where they hadn't been through our decontamination procedures. "Of course we will. Just not yet."

He sighed. "All right. Let's go see if the others found anything."

I nodded, but it took a minute to get to my feet. That man in the jumpsuit might have been working for the reservoir, but all I could think of were the men in white jumpsuits who had come to scuttle Ilana.

Theo and I picked our way carefully back toward our meeting spot with the others. We crouched low and each of us looked over our shoulders in case the outsider came back. We glanced ahead, too—where there was one, there could be others. Still, we almost tripped over Benji, who sat curled in a ball at the edge of the water where the tracks disappeared.

"Where are Julia and Ilana?" I asked.

"Where were you?" he replied. "We said fifteen minutes!"

"How long has it been?" Theo asked. He checked his wrist for his watchu that wasn't there.

"You've been gone thirty-seven minutes. What happened?"

"How do you know we've been gone exactly thirty-seven minutes?"

"Where are they?" I asked again.

"I brought my stopwatch," Benji said, holding up a small round fob on a string. It had been tucked into his shirt. "I've had it running since we left. Anyway, we found a causeway. Julia and Ilana were exploring to see how far it went, but it seems to go across the whole way." He said it as if this information was inconsequential. His voice only rose again when he asked, "So, what happened to you?"

"We saw an outsider!" I exclaimed.

"A worker," Theo told him. "He was testing the water. We had to hide until he finished."

"Did he see you?"

"No," Theo said.

"We don't think so, anyway," I added.

Benji nodded. "Okay, then. It's just a little ways this way." He hopped to his feet and led us around a bend in the shoreline. The flat surface of the water and the light shining on it had camouflaged the walkway that stretched out over the water. It wasn't a bridge, exactly, since it was only a foot or so above the water level, but it was wide enough for us to walk two across if we wanted to. As we approached, Julia and Ilana were making their way back.

"As far as we can tell it goes the whole way," Julia said. "What took you guys so long? Did you find something, too?"

I shook my head and we told them about the worker.

"Well, this causeway provides no shelter, but it's our only way across, so far as I can see," Julia said.

"It would be a risk," Ilana added. "Perhaps this is where we should part ways?"

"Don't be a numb nuts," Theo said. "Like that's even a possibility. Come on."

"You know, I'm getting a little grumbly in my tumbly," Benji said. "Maybe we should grab a snack first."

"No. We need to go before the sun gets too high and before more people are out and about," Theo said.

"He's right," I agreed. "We can eat once we get to the other side."

"You're killing me, Mori. I thought we'd always see eye to eye on the necessity of snacking."

I smiled back at him. I was glad he came. With him here, things didn't seem quite so dire. He chucked me on the shoulder and led the way onto the stone path that went out over the water.

It was beautiful out there: surrounded by clear water that seemed to go on for miles. Occasionally we would see fish swim by below. A family of ducks swam toward the causeway and hopped up, but then, upon seeing us, dove back in the water with a splash, splash, splash. The mother led them away as fast as her legs could paddle her, quacking back at her ducklings, who struggled to keep up. I couldn't help but giggle.

"See, the outside world isn't so bad," Ilana said. "There are ducks."

But before I could reply, we heard the unmistakable purr of a drone engine.

"Get down!" Theo called out. "On your stomachs! On your stomachs!"

We dropped down.

The drone hung in the air above us.

"It sees us!" Julia cried.

"Be quiet!" Theo called back.

The drone danced in a slow circle above us.

I peeked up trying to see if it had a camera or some sort of a sensor. "What is it doing?" I whispered.

"It's looking for something," Ilana replied.

"For us?" I asked.

"Perhaps," she said.

"Come on," Theo ordered. "Crawl. Slowly!"

We did as he said, all of us on all fours creeping along the causeway. The drone still hung above us, its tiny motor purring.

Then, without warning, it darted. My heart leaped, then my stomach dropped. It had seen what it needed to see—us!—and now it was going back to report it to Krita or whoever, but, no, wait. It stopped out over the water and did another set of circles.

"What's it doing now?" I asked.

"Maybe it didn't see us?" Benji asked. "I mean, maybe it wasn't looking for us. Maybe it's just checking the status of the reservoir or something?" I wanted him to sound more sure of himself.

"We need to hurry," Theo said.

"Hurry where?" Julia asked. "That drone *saw* us. It doesn't matter if it was looking for us or something else. It saw us and now we're cooked."

"We're not necessarily cooked," Benji said.

"We're not?" I asked hopefully.

"If it's a monitor drone, it's just collecting data. It could be really rudimentary, not even images, but readings of some sort. Numbers. And then there's someone—a person or a bot—on the other end who's looking at them. We might not have even registered, and if we did, whoever is checking might not catch it. They might just think it's some sort of abnormality and send someone out here, but, I mean, it is possible they didn't see us."

"Okay," I said. I took a deep breath. "Okay. Then we need to keep going. We need to get across and find some cover before they send someone out here to check. We still have time. We can do this." I started walking. "Well, come on." I beckoned them to start, too. A big arm-swing. Too big. My foot came down on some loose rocks and I started to stumble, my arm-swing tipping me over.

My feet scrambled against gravel at the edge of the causeway. It happened in slow motion. It was like I was doing a cartwheel through honey. Over, over, over, and then down, with a big splash.

4

THE WATER WAS WARM UP top, but as soon as I sank below the surface, it turned cold. Something soft and slimy brushed against my ankles. I blinked my eyes against the sting of the water, and tried to get my bearings. The world was blurry without my glasses. All I could see were my own bubbles, rushing along beside me. Up. They were rushing up and if I followed them, I would swim to the surface. Just like in Julia's pool. I scooped my arms in a giant breaststroke, pulling myself upward. I started to move, but then the soft, slimy something tightened around my ankle. My momentum stopped.

I thrashed against the tugging, but that only made it tighter. I coughed. I didn't mean to. It just pressed out of me, and when it did, I breathed in, hard, a mouthful of water.

My vision swirled. *Up,* I thought. *Up, up, up.* But the more I moved, the more tangled I became, until it felt like both of my calves were wrapped in wet ropes.

I squeezed my eyes closed and then opened them again. Not ropes. They couldn't be ropes, but they could be plants, and water plants I could break. I reached down and tugged at them. As I pulled, the stems snapped, and my legs were free.

The weeds swirled around, ominous as eels. And then a gray human face peered up at me through the murk. I gasped again, sucking in another mouthful of water that made my lungs burn even more. I kicked hard, again and again, away from the face. I could still feel it looking at me, though, even as I burst out of the water, just as Ilana leaned over to dive in.

"Mori!" she cried.

Theo reached past her and grabbed my arm. She grabbed the other, and together they pulled me back onto the causeway. I couldn't stop myself from crying and shaking. I wrapped my arms around my knees to still myself, but just ended up rocking back and forth.

That face.

"Are you okay?" Julia asked. "Mori? Mori!"

That *face*.

Eyes blank, tight lips, gray skin.

I coughed. My lungs felt like they were being squeezed by a juice presser. I coughed again and spit out some of the brackish water.

Ilana crouched down next to me and put her hand on my back.

"There's something down there!" I gasped. "Something—something—someone!"

"It's okay," Ilana said, rubbing my back.

Benji held something out to me. "Your glasses floated up," he said.

I took them from him and shoved them onto my face. The camera whirred and they all came into focus, dubious expressions across all their faces. My words came between pants of heavy breath: "There's a person down in the water."

Theo and Julia looked down at me, frowning. Benji searched the water but shook his head.

"It had gray skin and empty eyes."

"It was just your imagination," Theo said. "You didn't have your glasses, so you could barely see down there and you were scared and you thought you saw something you didn't."

"No, you're not hearing me!"

"It's a totally natural reaction," Benji said.

"It's down there. Just wait. The weeds will move and—"

"Do you think you're okay to walk?" Julia asked, like she had decided it was better to just ignore what I was saying than to engage me. "We have to keep going."

"We're all under a lot of pressure and this is way intense, so it was probably just like a fish or maybe a reflection or something," Benji suggested.

"It wasn't a fish and it wasn't my reflection. You can't see your reflection when you're underwater. It was huge." I peered down into the water. "Huge and gray."

"What color hair did it have?" Ilana asked.

"What? I don't know. I guess that was gray, too."

"Was it moving?" she asked.

"Moving?" But no, it hadn't. Still as stone. "Stone!" I exclaimed. "Like a statue." Realizing I had not seen a real person but a statue of one calmed my heart a little. Still, it didn't make sense. "Who builds a statue under a reservoir?" I asked.

"I don't know, Mori. But I do know we need to keep going," Ilana said in a calm voice. She stood up and helped me to stand.

With each step, my feet squished and squelched. Water dripped off me and left a little trail. There was a face under there. A whole statue. I was sure of what I had seen. But then again, lack of oxygen can make your brain do strange things. Maybe . . . but, no, I knew what I had seen, even if my friends didn't believe me. Even if it didn't make sense.

Ilana walked close behind me. Close enough to grab my hand if I started to slip again.

We walked the rest of the way across in silence. We could see the drone in the distance, doing its little circles, but it never came back toward us.

"I don't think it saw us," Julia said. "It would have gone back to its base if it had, right?"

"Most likely," Benji said. "But it could just be a routine security thing for the reservoir. Periodic flyovers with someone back at headquarters to look at the feed."

"So what does that mean?" Julia asked.

"Well, I suppose it means that if there's someone watching the feed, and if they're paying attention and not sneezing or something, and they see us, then they'll send someone out."

"So it means we're hoping that the security guard sneezed?" Julia asked.

"We can't worry about it," Theo said. "We're falling farther and farther behind. We just need to focus and move." He glanced back at me. My clothes, my bag, and all of me was soaked. I couldn't move quickly even if I wanted to. "When we get to the other side, you can change, Mori. Do you have extra clothes, Julia?"

"Sure, of course."

"Good, so Mori will change, we'll get our bearings, and we'll keep going."

"Maybe we should—" Julia began.

"No," I told her. "I'm fine. We're keeping going. I'm not giving up."

"I didn't say I was giving up."

"Good, then let's go." I wanted to stride off confidently, leading the way, but the sound of my wet shoes sloshing every time I took a step wouldn't let me do that.

"Huh," Benji said. "On second thought, Mori, maybe I do believe you about the face."

Benji held my hand as I leaned out over the water. It was a little dizzying to see, like I had somehow been hung upside down above a city skyline. But there it was: a brick steeple with a cross on top. "It's a church," I said. "It's an underwater church."

"Very religious ducks and fishes around here, I guess," Benji said.

"It *was* a statue back there," I said as I straightened back up. I shielded my eyes from the sun. "A statue and now a church. What is this place?"

A crow made a slow circle above us as we stood out in the brightening sun. Water lapped at the causeway, and the underwater church seemed to shimmer.

Theo looked back over his shoulder, and then in the direction where we had seen the outsider working. "It's a mystery, but not one we can solve right now. We're more than halfway there, and, except for maybe that drone, I don't think anyone has seen us. But we have to keep going. We need to move faster."

"I can't run," I said.

"I might be feeling a little peaked myself," Benji said.

"I'll carry your bag." Julia reached her arm out to me. I hesitated, then shrugged my sagging, wet backpack off and gave it to her. Ilana took Benji's. They jogged but they might as well have been sprinting, since that's what I had to do to keep up. They didn't understand how Benji and I had shorter legs and for each stride they took, we needed to take two.

My feet pounded against the causeway and I just kept seeing that face over and over again. I felt my chest tighten as I realized what had happened: there had been a town here once. Now it was under a reservoir. And not just any reservoir—the source for most of Old Harmonie's water. Our reservoir took over a town. *We* had taken it over. What had happened to all the people who had lived there, I wondered, when the water swept through their town?

5

WHEN WE FINALLY CROSSED THE reservoir, my throat and mouth were parched. I crouched down at the edge of the water and scooped it into my mouth. It was cold and fresh and maybe a little bit earthy, but I didn't care. "It tastes so good," I gasped.

"Mori, stop! This water isn't clean!" Julia told me.

"It's our drinking water," I said.

"But they filter it first," she replied.

I kept drinking. I was still soaking wet, but all the same I felt like I couldn't get enough.

"Gross," Julia said, but within a minute Theo, Ilana, and Benji were right down beside me.

"I didn't even realize how thirsty I was!" Theo exclaimed.

"Seriously," Benji said. "Way parched. It's the Sahara in my mouth and this is my oasis."

"An oasis is an illusion," Julia told him, but as I slipped my glasses back on my face, I noticed her eyeing the water greedily.

"It's going to be a hot day," Ilana said. "We should fill up our water bottles now."

Julia sniffed, but she did fill up her water bottle. "If I get dysentery, you guys will never hear the end of it." Then she turned to me. "Come on. You need dry clothes."

We found a stand of trees to give us cover and she opened up her backpack. She pulled out a purple T-shirt and a pair of black running shorts. She held them to her chest while I wiggled out of my wet clothes. "I'm sorry I didn't believe you about the face," she said when my shirt was over my head.

"It's okay," I said, but I was glad the wet cotton was between us so she couldn't see my face.

"Are you stuck?" she asked. Before I could answer, she yanked the shirt off my head. I grabbed her purple one and pulled it on. It smelled like sunscreen. "Anyway, it's nothing like I expected out here, but a face underwater was beyond too weird, you know?"

I nodded.

"It wasn't a real person, though. You said it was a real person, but now you think it was a statue."

"There's a town under there, Julia. We flooded a town so we could have more water."

"It's not just for us. Everyone around here shares that reservoir."

"Maybe," I said, and swapped my shorts for hers.

We looked down at my wet shoes and socks. "I can give you clean socks, but I didn't bring any extra shoes."

"It's okay," I said again.

"Stop saying that!" she exclaimed. Her voice cracked. I froze. She rubbed her eyes. "Everything is *not* okay out here. The person, the drone, you falling in the water—all of this was a terrible idea!"

"We're going to make it, Julia," I told her.

"You can't possibly know that."

"I do."

"How?"

"Because we have to."

She sighed and bent over and picked up my wet shoes. "Come on. Carefully in your bare feet. I'll try to get some of the water out of these."

She led me from behind the trees and over to the others, where she sat down and pulled the insoles out of my sneakers. When she twisted them, a stream of water rained down.

Theo unfolded the map again. "Assuming the tracks come out on the other side of this reservoir, if we keep walking northeast through the forest, we should meet up with them again."

"Why not just walk the edge of the reservoir?" Julia asked.

I pulled Julia's socks on. They were knee socks with stars all over them.

"We've lost a lot of time already," Theo explained. "We need to make it up."

"But we don't know what's in the woods," Julia said.

"The forest is a whole lot less frightening than outsiders," I said.

"Mori and I know our way around the woods," Ilana said. "We'll be fine."

Julia glanced over at Ilana, but she swallowed whatever it was she was thinking.

"I guess we should get going, then," Ilana said. She went first, picking out a path between the trees and the occasional moss-covered boulder. Her feet were steady and sure as she marched along.

"Pillow moss," she said, and pointed to a patch growing in the shade of a tree. Just beyond it was a stretch of American pokeweed with bright green leaves and shiny purple-blue berries that were lovely and tempting, but poisonous. Maybe we did know enough to make our way through this forest after all.

"The good news is, if whoever was flying that drone saw us, then they would have been waiting here," Benji said. "So, I think that danger has passed. Smooth sailing from here on out!"

"Benji!" I said, my voice ringing around the forest. All my

friends turned to look at me. I lowered my volume. "I can't believe you just said that. You totally jinxed us. Again."

"Seriously, Mori, you can't possibly believe in superstitions like that," Theo said to me.

"I can and I do. Benji already jinxed us once."

"That lake was there whether he said anything or not," Theo told me.

I knew he was right. "Okay, but even if it's not really real, why chance it?"

Theo shook his head. "You're so smart about people and nature, but, man, when it comes to stuff like this . . ." His voice trailed off and he kept shaking his head. "Total nimwit."

Next to me, Ilana stiffened, ready to stick up for me.

"Wait," I said. "Let's go back to that part where you said I was super smart?"

I think Theo blushed a little, but we were all pink from being out in the sun over the water. "I just meant that you have a way of understanding—of seeing what's really going on in people. You see the truth. But there's no truth in superstition."

"I just think there's a lot about this world that we don't know," I said. "And when it comes to our safety, why chance it? Why tempt fate?"

"Says the girl who just drank duck-poo water," Julia said.

"Fate is just a story we tell ourselves," Theo said.

Maybe he was right. Maybe fate and superstition were just our brains' way of making sense of the world around us, creating a story to explain events. But still. It seemed a big risk to doubt it when your life was on the line.

6

"YOU'VE GOT TO BE KIDDING me," Theo said.

We stood at the base of the fence, which reached at least ten feet into the sky. It was topped with curls of barbed wire with rusty teeth like in a twisted shark's jaw. It made the fence around Old Harmonie seem like a garden decoration. We'd always been told that it wasn't the fences that kept us safe, it was us. This was a fence meant for safety.

The last of the trees put us in shade, while the sun dappled the ground on the other side of the fence. Sunshine and, of course, the tracks that we needed to find to get Ilana to Cambridge and to Dr. Varden. My feet felt like something was sucking them into the ground, and pulling me with it, and it wasn't just the water in them. "Smooth sailing," I muttered. "See!"

Theo dropped his bag and pulled out a pair of fierce-looking scissors. He stepped toward the fence, but Benji stopped him. "Wait!"

Theo hesitated.

"This whole thing could be wired up," Benji said.

"Like it will shock us?" I asked.

"No. Like it will send a warning back to whoever put it up. We could be surrounded in seconds by who knows what. The people running the reservoir, most likely, which, you know, leads directly back to Krita people. Best-case scenario, we get sent home."

I sank down to the ground and brought my knees up to my chest.

"Wait here," Theo said. "Julia, head down that way and see if you see any—anything." He started marching along beside the fence in one direction while Julia went in the other. Even Theo wasn't sure what could possibly help us.

"I just can't believe we've come this far and dealt with the reservoir and seeing the outsider and everything and now this. How are we ever going to find Dr. Varden? This whole thing is hopeless!"

Ilana looked down at me. "You're giving up already?"

"No, I just—"

Her face had the smile I'd grown so used to but had almost forgotten. It made her whole face dance. "It sounds a lot like giving up to me." She reached her hand out to me, then pulled me to my feet. "If I'd known I'd gotten involved with such a scalawag, I never would have agreed to come along."

"I don't think that's what 'scalawag' means."

Benji was leaning over next to the fence. "Stay here," he said. "I need to go get some rocks."

"A right scurvy maiden, then," Ilana said as Benji wandered toward the woods.

"That's definitely not what you mean. Scurvy is like a sickness. From not eating citrus or something."

"Did you pack any citrus?"

I looked down.

Ilana put her hand on my shoulder. "Come on, Mori. We knew this wasn't going to be easy."

"Having to cross a reservoir and get through a barbed wire fence didn't even occur to me."

"Escape and evasion aren't exactly in your wheelhouse."

She was right. How had I ever thought that I had what it took to get her to safety? I had never had to plan anything like this because everything had always been taken care of for me in Old Harmonie. The most planning I ever did was deciding whose house to meet up at in the morning. And my parents had made sure I wouldn't have the courage when they dampened my bravery. I should have known better than to try something so big and so important. "Maybe you shouldn't have let us break you out."

She glanced away.

"I just meant that I wish you had a friend who was—I wish I were better. I wish I could help you better." My voice cracked.

"Mori," Ilana said.

"I'm sorry," I croaked. "I really am. Back in Old Harmonie this seemed doable. But I'm just a natural, Ilana. I don't have all the—you know, all the stuff in my head that you and Julia and Theo have. Benji's naturally smart, but me, I'm just me and—" My words came fast and hard and choked me. I wiped hard at my eyes with my fists.

"Our heads are no better than yours, Mori. Trust me." Her voice was soft and low, right next to my ear. She put her arm around me and pulled me closer to her.

"I don't want to fail you."

"You're not going to."

"I think I already am." My breath caught in my throat and I coughed. "Right from the start, just by being me—"

She cut me off with a shoulder squeeze. "I need you, Mori," she said. "We're the Firefly Five. Between us we can work this out. But I—all of us, really—need you to be you and to believe that we can do this."

And then she hugged me again. Her arms were long, longer than my mom's, I thought, and when she hugged me it was like she was giving me a little bit of her strength.

"Okay," I whispered.

"What? I can't hear you."

"Okay," I said.

"Louder!"

"Okay!" I yelled. And then we broke out laughing. For a minute, it was like nothing had changed.

Then Theo came crashing back toward us. "What's going on? Why are you making so much noise?"

Benji returned carrying two round stones. "I don't know what's going on with them, but I will tell you this: they make terrible pirates. Also, you're all lucky I'm a genius."

Benji explained that the way the fence was built, only half of the wire that was twisted into the fence had sensors in it. "We just need to cut the other side. Here's the problem, though—you ever see those old movies where they have to defuse a bomb and they have to cut the right wires because if they cut the wrong wires, the whole thing will blow? And they have to wonder if the bomb maker used a logical system, or if the maker was trying to be deceptive and use an illogical system?"

"No," Julia said. Little beads of sweat were gathered on her upper lip, like dew on a blade of grass.

"Well, just imagine. And the fence is kind of like that."

"What are the rocks for?" Ilana asked.

"Ah, that's where my brilliance comes in. I don't want the fence to snap back and reconnect the wires or cross the wires so we can use them to hold the sections apart."

"Or someone could just hold the sides apart," Julia said.

"Maybe," Benji said. "Anyway, I'm ninety percent certain I know which ones to cut. But whoever put this fence up, maybe they're the deceptive sort."

Theo held the scissors out to him. "I trust you," Theo said.

So Benji cut the fence.

Nothing happened. No alarm sounded and no one appeared to arrest us or whatever other dark fate might await us. Benji kept cutting. Julia worked beside him, carefully untangling the links in the fence until there was a space big enough for each of us to crawl through. I went first, as usual, because I was the smallest. My gaze drifted up and settled on a sign:

OLD HARMONIE LIMITS

No Trespassing

Violators Will Be Prosecuted

• KritaCorp •

"We put up the fence," I said.

Theo looked where I was looking. "That doesn't make any sense."

"Old Harmonie doesn't come this far," I said. "I mean, we're outside of Old Harmonie by a lot. We left when we crossed over our fence. And we only have the one fence, right? Because it's not the fence that keeps us safe, right?"

"Maybe this is old?" Julia asked.

Benji shook his head. "I don't think so. Only the barbed wire is rusted. This looks well-maintained."

"If all this land belonged to Old Harmonie, we could have room for more people," I said. "Or farms. Mr. Quist was always saying how we needed to be more self-sustainable with food. We could've been doing it out here."

"There is the reservoir," Benji said. "That's probably what this fence is for."

"But all those woods between Old Harmonie and the reservoir? All that space?"

"It doesn't matter," Theo said.

"It does matter—"

"It doesn't," Theo said. "And we have to keep going."

7

IT WASN'T LONG UNTIL WE found the tracks again. They were shining in the sun, black with a patina of orangey green, like a little kid had drawn them and pressed too hard with too many crayons.

"It's about twenty-three miles to Cambridge. If we walk twenty-minute miles, that's eight hours of walking, give or take."

"Twenty-minute miles seems like a fast pace to keep up," Julia said, looking at me. There was a leaf stuck in one of her braids.

"I'll be fine," I said. But my heels were already starting to burn as blisters formed from my wet sneakers.

"If we do thirty-minute miles, that's close to twelve hours. It should still be light out when we get there, and that's what's important. I don't want to be out in unknown territory in the dark."

We all nodded in agreement. Going toward the city was dangerous enough—all the stories we had heard of it told of overcrowding, illness, and crime—but going there at night was a bit too much to even contemplate.

"Everyone packed sandwiches, right?" Benji asked.

We all nodded and Theo opened up his backpack and handed each of us a protein bar. "We have more than enough food to last us as long as we're careful. And as long as things go as planned from here on out."

"That's a big if," Julia said. "Plus, once we get there, we're counting on someone coming to get us and bring us home. The rest of us, I mean."

"We should have enough food to get home, too, if it comes to that," Theo said.

But if no one from Old Harmonie was willing to come to get us in Cambridge, then maybe there would be no home to come back to.

The protein bars were heavy and tasteless, but we chewed and swallowed them down. I took a deep sip from my water bottle.

"Water is a different issue," Theo said. "We don't know if we'll be able to find clean water along the way."

I took the straw out of my mouth. "They're just kind of dry," I said.

"I guess we should get going," Benji said. He stood up

and walked toward the tracks. We all followed him. They stretched out in front of us like a ladder to the sky. My shoes were starting to dry out, but there was no denying the blisters popping up on my heels and the balls of my feet.

The only sound was our feet crunching as we walked, the occasional smack at a fly. It seemed entirely possible that we could walk the whole way to Cambridge without even speaking a word to one another.

As we walked on, an embankment grew up around the tracks on either side of us, like we were sinking down into a valley. Then the fences appeared. Twisted, rusted chain links with corrugated metal pushed against them. They were festooned with ribbons that hung down in the still air. Old, tattered, and devoid-of-color ribbons were right up against shining new ones in purples, reds, golds—every color, really.

"Hey, Mori, you been sneaking out here at night? Making the world all pretty?" Benji laughed.

"Oh you know me, just leaving Old Harmonie every chance I get," I tried to joke. The air around us felt so heavy. It didn't help that the sun was on us now, burning our skin and making us sweat.

"If Mori did it, they'd be more ordered. And in the colors of the season, of course," Julia said. She had a smile on her face. It wasn't her real smile, but I was grateful for it.

"I wonder who did do it?" I asked.

"Whoever lives there," Julia replied. "On the other side of the fence."

We were quiet as if listening for voices or some other sign of life from the far side of the fence.

"Maybe they're like messages?" I said. "People used to tie yellow ribbons around trees to honor soldiers who hadn't yet returned from war. Maybe these are for people who have gone. There was a song about it that my baba liked to sing to me."

Julia walked up to the fence and rubbed her fingers over the ribbons. "Some of them look like they've been here a long time."

"Maybe friends do it," Ilana said. She touched her finger to a gold-and-purple ribbon. "There was this bridge in Paris and couples, like romantic couples, used to put padlocks on it as a way of locking their love together."

"That doesn't make sense," Theo said.

"It's symbolism," Ilana said. "Anyway, it got so heavy, they were afraid the bridge would collapse."

"What did they do?" I asked.

"I think they cut them off. Ribbons make more sense."

"They do," I agreed. "Locks might seem more permanent, but the ribbons are more sustainable."

"Like friendship," Ilana said. "Just kind of blowing in the wind. Easy peasy."

And with her, friendship had felt that way. She'd blown in like a warm breeze and we'd hit it off right away. We escaped into the woods together, creating our own world: Oakedge. We were growing a garden with plants from our neighbor Mr. Quist—I had some of the pea shoots in my backpack.

We'd climb up together into the split-trunked oak and survey our kingdom.

And then things had gone off course, so here we were peering through an old fence. It was mostly grassland on the other side and some expanses of black tar. But, off a ways in the distance, I could see some houses. "Look," I said. "There's an old bike over there." It was a faded green, and only had one wheel left on it.

"Creepy," Julia said.

"There's a scooter, too," Benji said. "And that looks like an old four-square ball right there." He pointed at something pinkish red and flat as a pancake. "It's like the place where toys go to die."

"Stop," Theo said. "Don't let your imaginations get away from you. There's a town up that way. We're gonna walk right by it. Probably kids play out here and these are just toys they left behind."

I slapped at a mosquito on my calf. Theo pushed his bangs off his forehead. They were sweaty and got stuck in funny spikes. "We shouldn't be standing here in this grass getting ticks or whatever. We need to keep going."

We hurried back to the tracks and kept walking along.

"I forget sometimes that the whole world isn't part of Krita," Benji said.

The fence got straighter as we kept walking, and instead of metal, there was a second fence. This one was made of wood, thick, with green plants in boxes up top, alongside the ribbons.

A sudden squeal stopped our feet. It was followed by laughter.

"Kids!" Benji exclaimed. He hurried up the embankment.

"Benji, wait!" I reached out to try to grab him, but barely touched the flapping tail of his shirt.

"I'm just taking a peek. There's a gap up here."

"We don't have time for this," Theo said. But he followed Benji up the steep hill to the fence. I hesitated. My heart felt like it was closing off my throat, *thump-thump-thump*.

"I'm open! I'm open!" someone yelled on the other side.

It *did* sound like a kid. I forced my feet to carry me up the hill to my friends. We crowded around the gap. On the other side of the fence was a neighborhood not too different from our own. Their houses all looked alike, though nothing like ours: three stories and long from front to back. Some had porches hanging off them, and some of the porches had potted plants or faded flags. And ribbons. There were ribbons tied on the bars around the porches and on the railings of the stairs and even around some of the streetlights. The town looked a little run-down, with curbs missing and the colors fading on the houses. But most of the buildings had window boxes with bright flowers, and the lawns were clipped neatly.

In the middle of the street some kids used hockey sticks to pass around a bright green tennis ball. One boy wore a black T-shirt with a yellow *B* on it. "McPhee has the puck! He's racing up the ice! No one can stop him now!" The boy lifted his stick and slapped the ball so it lifted off the ground and flew straight for us. It came in slow motion and horribly fast all at once.

Benji dropped flat on the ground. "Uh-oh!"

They pulled me away from the fence while Julia spun around and pressed her back to the chain link. Ilana slid down the embankment, then lay on her stomach looking up at us. Her eyes were wide and her mouth open a little bit, puffing out panicked air.

"McPhee!" someone yelled from the other side of the fence. "Get the ball! Back in play, back in play!"

"Hold up a second, why don't ya? I thought I heard somethin'!"

Closer. Closer. His feet clomped over sandy pavement.

I bit my lip hard. Theo held a finger to his lips.

"You heard your ego poppin', that's what ya heard."

"You heard your pants droppin'!"

More steps. It sounded like he was dragging his stick on the ground behind him, a cool *shrift-scratch* sound that went right up my spine.

A kid could do a lot of damage with a hockey stick.

"You heard your mama callin' her sweet baby home for din-din!"

What I could hear was the boy's breathing, heavy and

uneven. "I heard somethin'!" he yelled again. His weight pressed against the fence as he leaned up against it. I closed my eyes. I had never been this close to an outsider before. I could feel his breath. I could smell his sweat.

On the other side of the gap, Julia had her eyes squeezed shut. Her mouth, too, as if she were afraid to breathe out. I tried to hold my own breath.

"Maybe it's the Maynard strays, Tommy!"

"Yeah, Tommy, better step back before they bite your brains out."

Theo kept his gaze on the gap. His hands were in the dirt, ready to pull himself to his feet and what? Run away? Fight?

And then the kids on the other side of the fence started yapping and barking. Tommy, the boy, kicked the ground and muttered something under his breath before he spun around. "Quit your yappin', that's one more goal for McPhee's Boys and we're up three to two!"

Julia tapped my arm and nodded her head. We started to slide down the embankment with Theo and Benji behind us. It seemed impossible to move any slower or more carefully than we were, but still pebbles cascaded down the slope as loud as boulders in an avalanche.

Ilana helped me to my feet at the bottom and we walked back onto the tracks. We didn't have to say it. That had been a mistake—too close, way too close. Benji looked sick and even held his hand to his stomach as we walked on and on and on.

We were a hundred yards down the tracks before we spoke.

"That was intense," Benji said.

"Why do you always have to be such a numb nuts?" Theo asked him. "What were you even thinking?"

Benji didn't try to defend himself.

I was still holding on to Julia's hand. Ilana was on the other side of me. She reached out and gave me a pat on the back. "Deep breaths, Mori," she told me.

I tried to do as she said. I took a deep breath in and let the air out through my dry lips.

"They were so close," Benji said. "You could've reached out and touched him, Mori."

I shook my head. Never in a million years would I have stuck my hand through the fence to touch that strange boy.

"They're just kids," Theo said. "What exactly do you think they would've done to us?"

"Oh, like you weren't scared," Julia shot back. "I saw your face."

"With your eyes closed? Impressive."

"We were all scared," I said.

Theo gave half a nod.

"I know I was," Ilana said.

"Really?" I asked.

"Yes! They find us, and this whole plan is kaput." She reached up and pushed some of her hair away from her forehead. The sun was really brutal; it felt like my skin was cracking in the heat. Then the dirt that puffed up around us stuck to our skin. We looked like gray-and-brown ghosts walking down the tracks.

"Do you think they go to school?" Julia looked over her shoulder, though the group was long out of sight.

"Of course they do," Theo told her.

"They don't sound like they go to school," I said.

We were approaching a train platform. There was a small brick building, not much bigger than a KritaBus, with an overhang that shaded where people had once stood to wait for the train. We had learned about it in school. Commuters used to drive in their own cars from all the surrounding towns to the stations, park their cars, and then take the train into the city. When the diseases became more virulent, public transportation was a real problem, and there were times it was even shut down all together. This platform had a large, lateral crack; stubborn grass sprouted out of it.

"Their school is probably different, though," Julia said. "I mean, like it's probably the way it is in history books with big classes and rows of chairs and all that."

"I bet some things are the same, though. Like I bet some teachers are awesome and some are boring," Benji said. "Didn't Mr. Nussbaum used to teach out here?"

"Maybe they have all virtual school," I said.

"Like, they go into a classroom with a million kids and

then they have a remote teacher that they see on a screen," Julia said. "That would make sense."

"They probably still have to do the stupid fitness tests, though." Benji jumped up onto the platform and walked along its edge like a tightrope walker.

"Where?" Julia asked. "I didn't see any central buildings. No town hall, no library, no gymnasium. No school."

"We only saw the tiniest sliver. It's like if someone peered through the fence at Firefly Lane." Theo's voice cracked when he said the name of our street, and I think we all thought of home, so far away.

"I wonder if they have all the vaccines we do." Without thinking about it, I rubbed my hands on my shorts. Those kids were vectors, too, carrying disease from one person to another just like the flies we'd been swatting away.

"They must have some, right?" Julia said. "We send them out, so they must have them."

"Maybe we test ours on them," Theo mumbled.

"Very funny," Julia said. She turned back over her shoulder again. "It's not the way I thought it was."

"What do you mean?" Benji asked.

"I guess I thought it would be drabber. And sadder."

"Uh-huh," I agreed. "I thought everyone would be sicker."

"Why?" Ilana asked. "You said they get medicine out here. And of course they probably have even better natural immunity than we do—the people who survive pass on those genes."

"But they could still get sick," Julia said. "They don't have the precautions we do."

Ilana bent over and scooped up a rock. "Aren't there rules out here, too?"

"We can't force them," Julia said. "We encourage them, maybe, but no one is forced."

"It's not like they're stupid or ignorant," Ilana said. She said it slowly, like she was thinking out loud, but I got the sense she was just trying not to make Julia angry. That she knew exactly what she was saying. "I mean, it's not like Krita took all the knowledge and locked it up, right?"

The train tracks skirted around a black-topped wasteland—the old parking lot, I figured—and the sun blazed down even hotter. I never realized I could sweat behind my knees, on my ankles, between my toes. It even felt like my brain was sweating, squeezing out the moisture and giving me a headache. I took a small sip of water.

The sound of barking traveled over to us and I wondered if it was the coyotes we'd heard the night before or if they had gone to sleep.

"What do you think?" I asked Theo.

"About what?" Theo replied.

"About the kids. About how it is out here and back home?"

Ilana tossed the rock to Theo and he caught it easily. "I think we need to pick up the pace if we are going to make it to MIT by nightfall."

The chain-link fence continued past the platform. The other side of it was barren—no trees, no houses, nothing.

"It's kind of like Harmonie," I said. "I bet that fence went all around. I bet they quarantine sick people. They just don't have, you know, all the smart people we do."

Theo scoffed.

"What?"

"We don't know a thing about them. They could all be geniuses."

I thought of Tommy with the dirt smeared on his face and that strange accent that didn't seem to have any *r*'s in it. "I don't know about that."

"Don't be a snob, Mori."

"I'm not being a snob," I told him.

"You are being a snob," he said. "Because of how they looked. The way they talked. That's why you don't think they're smart, right?"

A tree root stuck straight out of the torn-up dirt. I didn't think I was a snob. I just knew that Krita brought together the smartest people they could, and the people left outside, well, sure, some of them might have talents and intelligence, but it wasn't the same.

Julia fell into step with me and hooked her arm through mine. "Don't listen to him. You're no snob."

"It's not your fault," he said. His voice almost disappeared into the sound of our feet on the stones around the tracks, the insects whizzing around the air, and even the distant barking. But I still heard him: loud and clear.

"Gee, thanks." I wished I hadn't said anything. Why had he even come?

"You only know what you've been told. You think it's so much better up in Old Harmonie, but you don't know what it's like to live out here. Not really."

"Leave her be," Ilana said.

"And you know what it's like?" I asked him.

"No," he said. "That's the problem."

"You don't make any sense." I ran my hand through my hair. Even my scalp was sweating. I knew we should just stop talking, that the heat was making us feel and say things that we wouldn't under normal circumstances. Our anger was a heat mirage, like the oasis, but if we acted on it, we wouldn't be able to undo it.

Theo seemed to feel the same way. His face was drawn together and he continued to speak in a low voice, looking more at the ground than at us or where we were headed. "None of this makes any sense," he said. "But here we are."

"If you didn't want to come, you should've said so back on the tennis court," Julia told him.

Theo chucked a rock over the fence. "I'm not saying I didn't want to come."

I ignored what he had said. "You were the one who asked me what was wrong. And you were the one that came up with the plan with me. So you had all sorts of time to say you thought it was a bad idea."

"You're not listening." Theo put both hands on the top of his head, his fingers laced together. It was like he was trying to hold his rage in.

And me, it was like I couldn't help but press and press to make him explode. "You've never really liked any of us, have you?"

"Mori." Ilana put a hand on my shoulder.

"You've never been kind to anyone but me, and I guess now that's over, too. Which is fine."

Theo's cheeks flared red. I remember what he had told me, that sometimes it felt like words were just spurting out of him and he didn't mean what he said. But somehow I knew that he meant these words, that he wouldn't erase them even if he could.

"In fact," I said, my voice rising in pitch and volume, "why don't you just turn around and go back? We don't need you."

Theo stopped walking. He hung his head and his fists fell down by his side. He might just turn around and start running back, and I realized that would be awful. Because we did need him.

"Come on," Benji finally said. "We have to keep going."

It was another moment before we started walking again. Ilana took the lead, and Theo dropped back behind us. Julia still had her arm looped through mine. "Theo's just being Theo. He doesn't really mean it."

"Maybe," I replied, and wiped sweat off my forehead. "I was afraid he really would leave. I don't think we can get there without him."

"He won't," she said. Then she nodded toward Ilana. "And she'll be okay. We'll get her there. I promise."

"And then what?" I asked. "It's all hinging on hope. This whole plan isn't really a plan at all. It's a wish."

"No. We'll get there and we'll get her help and then once she's safe, we'll come home." She held up her hand as if she knew what I was going to say. "She won't be gone forever. We'll know where she is, and maybe we can even send messages somehow."

"I don't want anyone to know where she is."

"Maybe we can do it somehow without them knowing. If one of the people there will let me use their computer, I could send a—"

"We don't know if anyone there will have a computer. We don't even know if it's there anymore. I shouldn't have gotten you all involved in this."

"You didn't. And I would've been mad if you'd gone—" Her voice was drowned out by the sound of dogs barking. It was like they had appeared out of thin air, a whole pack of them, pushing against the fence just up the tracks from us.

"Get!" Theo yelled, which only made them bark louder. A Rottweiler jumped its paws up against the fence and the whole thing groaned under its weight. Theo came up behind us. "Go. Not too fast. Not too slow. Don't make eye contact."

"There's a fence," I told him, still angry.

"If they all decide to jump, it won't hold them."

We stayed close together, moving past the dogs. I held my breath as we did, as if that would keep them from noticing us.

They ran along the fence back and forth, yipping and growling.

"Keep steady," Ilana said.

And then we heard the sickening creak as the fence gave way.

8

WE ALL STARTED RUNNING, TUMBLING down the tracks, bumping our elbows against one another. I could hear Theo's warm breath right behind me. "Go, go, go!"

The dogs thrashed toward us at an ever-faster pace. Their claws clicked against the rails. They breathed hard and snorted.

Ilana was strides ahead of the rest of us in minutes. She yelled: "Come on, doggie! Come on!"

"What's she doing?" I panted.

But by then the dogs nipped around our feet.

"Come on, dogs! Come and get me!"

"Ilana!" I yelled. "Stop it!"

A dog snapped just as my heel came up and caught it in the chin.

Whimper. Snarl.

Theo grabbed my arm and yanked me up the far side embankment, where there was another fence, this one low and dented. "Go over," he yelled.

"We don't—"

"Go over!"

The sound of the dogs was deafening.

I looked over my shoulder but didn't see any of our friends.

"Go!"

I shoved my toe into a link of the fence and heaved myself up. When I threw my leg over, my sneaker got stuck. Three of the dogs had followed us up the hill and one bared its teeth at me as it let out a low growl. It cackled at me like a villain in a movie. Just as it lunged at me, my foot broke free and I tumbled over to the other side.

Theo kicked at a second dog, then leaped over the fence and landed in a crouch by my side. The dogs threw themselves against the fence, but this one held. Theo's breaths came in heavy puffs.

I drew myself up to my full size, which wasn't very much, but it was enough. "Go away," I growled back at them.

And they did. Whimpering.

Next to me, Theo burst out laughing.

"What?" I demanded.

"Go away!" He mimicked my growl.

"Honestly, Theo." I pivoted.

He held up both his hands, which were stained red from

the rust on the fence. In the first moment, it looked like they were dusted with blood. "Come on, Mori." He laughed, and dug his water bottle out of his pack. "That was wild. I never thought I'd see you do something like that. Not in a million years." He held his water bottle out to me and I could see his hand was shaking.

"Right," I said. "It's about as likely as me breaking out of Old Harmonie."

I took the bottle from him and took a long sip. My mouth and throat had gone completely dry. Another long drink, and I tried not to worry where we would find water to refill.

He grinned and shook his head. "I'm sorry, you know. About earlier. I don't think you're a snob."

The fence had ripped a hole in the top of my sneaker, and I picked at a thread.

"It's just that . . . Well, there's so much we don't know. So much that's different than we thought out here. And Ilana. What else aren't they telling us?"

"Old Harmonie isn't some vast conspiracy."

"I know, it's just that—"

"Julia!" Benji's voice rang out, and Theo and I turned to see the Rottweiler standing above Julia, whose body lay across the tracks.

I leaped toward the fence. Theo grabbed my shirt. "Mori, wait."

I shook him off and climbed back over the fence, then scrambled down the hill. I sprinted toward Benji and Julia.

I could hear feet behind me and I really wasn't sure if they were people feet or dog feet. My eyes were trained on Julia like lasers. I saw nothing else. I ran with both hands in front of me and when I got to them I pushed the dog so hard it fell over. When it stood up, it growled low and guttural. "Go away!" I yelled. My heartbeat shook my body. The dog growled. "Go away!" I yelled again.

Ilana strode past me, right at the growling dog. "Yeah!" she said. "Go away!" She took a decisive step toward it, and it turned tail and ran.

I dropped to my knees next to Julia. Her eyes were wide in her ashen face. It looked like she had fallen in red mud. It was not mud, though. It was the flesh of her leg where the dog had taken a huge bite.

9

"HOLY CHEESECAKES!" THE VOICE CAME from behind us. I whipped around and there was the kid who had come so close to finding us before. He had bright blond hair—almost white in the sun—and flashing blue eyes that seemed more curious than menacing. The faces of his friends surrounded him. They were about our age, three girls and a boy. One girl had red dots all over her skin. Next to her was a tiny girl who looked at the ground and picked at her own fingers. "That was so bananas," the boy went on. "Like on a scale of one to ten, it was a ninety-nine. The way you all chased the dogs off like, *Rawrrrr! Go away! Leave our friend alone!* Not bad. Not bad at all."

"Shut up!" I yelled. "Shut up unless you're going to help us!"

"Well, that's a fine how do you do," the boy said. McPhee, they had called him. Tommy McPhee.

But one of the girls was already jogging down to us. She crouched next to Julia. "The good news is those dogs aren't rabid. They're just mean." She pulled down Julia's sock and revealed the mangled flesh on her calf. She kept talking as she examined the wound. "It's wastelands between here and Lincoln. Chemical dump. Only the dogs live there, getting meaner and meaner each year." She pressed on Julia's leg and blood oozed out around her fingers. I swayed up against Ilana. "It might not be as bad as it looks. It's just really bloody right now. We'll need to get it bandaged up and we can get her home and clean it."

"Okay," I said. "Okay, how far is it? Can we carry her?"

"I can run back and get a wagon," the other boy said.

"That's probably a good idea," the girl who was crouched over Julia said.

"Hey," McPhee yelled after the girl. "Whose gang is this, anyway?"

"Not now, Tommy." The girl held two fingers on the inside of Julia's wrist. She turned back to Julia. "My name is Naya. I'm not actually a doctor or nurse or anything, but my big sister is an EMT and I've helped her study and practice—"

Tommy McPhee scoffed at that. "Playing the victim doesn't count as helping her practice. All you do is lie there."

"I pay attention," Naya said to Tommy, then turned back to Julia. "Anyway, I'll bring you straight to her and—"

"No," Julia said.

"What?" I asked.

"Anywhere we go, we aren't safe. Leave me here."

Naya looked at each of us but didn't say anything.

"We aren't going to leave you here, Julia. No way," I told her.

"If we get caught, you know what will happen. It's just a little cut. I'll be fine. You guys keep going, and this future ambulance driver will, you know, patch me up. And then tonight I'll go to the hospital or whatever they have out here."

"Out here?" Tommy said. "Where are you all from?"

"No," I told her, but even as I said it, I knew she was right. As soon as we got outside doctors involved, our journey was over. "We aren't going to leave you behind."

Ilana crouched down next to Julia and looked at me. "Julia's right. You can't leave her. But I can go. It's just a straight shot from here, right?"

"Ilana, don't you start being ridiculous, too," I said. "I can only deal with one of you at a time."

Julia laughed at that, and I thought Benji was laughing along, but then I realized he was crying: big, fat, sobbing tears.

"I'm not sure what you all are arguing about, but we need

something clean to wrap her leg," Naya said in a firm voice that made me think I could trust her.

I opened up my backpack and dug out a sweatshirt that was still damp from my trip into the reservoir. "It's relatively clean," I told her. "It's kind of wet, though."

"That's fine." With ease, Naya ripped the sweatshirt into shreds and began carefully wrapping them around Julia's bloodied leg. Julia winced but didn't say anything.

"Here's what we're going to do," I said. "We're going to go back with these people and clean up your leg and maybe have the EMT look at it."

"Mori—" Julia began.

"I said maybe. We'll see when we clean it up. And then we'll see what state you're in and if you can keep going or not. And if you can, we'll all go. And if you can't, then we'll figure it out. But no one is going or staying alone. You got it?"

"Got it," Theo said in a soft, steady voice.

Benji nodded in agreement, and, after a moment, so did Julia and Ilana.

Tommy marched up closer to us. "This is all well and good, but I ask again, where are you all from? And why can't anyone know where you're going?"

Theo and Ilana lifted themselves up to their full heights, which made them tower over the boy. He didn't want to, I could tell, but he rocked back. "Where we're from doesn't matter," Theo said. "What matters is that we are on our way somewhere and no one can know, so you all can't go blabbing your big mouths."

"Hey, I dig it. I don't have a big mouth."

"Oh, yeah?" Theo asked. "Then how come we could hear you for miles down the tracks talking about your amazing hockey skills?"

Tommy blushed, and the girl with the red dots laughed. "They've got you pegged, McPhee."

"Shut up, Amnah," Tommy said. "Anyway, you all don't need to tell me where you're from. It's as clear as if it's written on your faces. You lot are from Old Harmonie. And that means if you want our help, you're going to have to pay."

The boy came back with an old, red plastic wagon. One of the wheels wobbled to and fro. "It's not exactly a deluxe ride," he said. "But it'll do."

"Thanks, Ethan," Naya said.

"I can walk," Julia said, but none of us believed her.

I twisted my fingers together while Ilana and Theo and the oldest-looking of the outsider girls—Amnah, the one with the red dots all over her brown skin—lifted Julia and placed her somewhat gently into the wagon. Julia winced. This was going to be a long, long ride for her. I wished I could trade places, that I could be the injured one in the wagon, that I could be the one to take on all that pain. I had the most experience with it. I knew I could cope.

Ilana took the handle of the wagon and started to pull. Theo had to bend over and push it up the hill. I jogged along next to her on one side, and Benji was on the other.

"It's going to be okay," I told her. "We'll get you help."

Julia closed her eyes and tilted her head back. "It's really hot out today," she said, her voice sounding a little groggy.

"Are you thirsty?" Benji asked. He shrugged off his backpack. He had the kind with a water sack built right in so you could drink out of it through a tube. Still walking, he placed it on her lap, and she grabbed the mouthpiece and drank deep.

"Not too much," Naya said.

"Why not?" Amnah asked. The small girl trotted along beside her, watching with wide eyes but never making a sound.

Naya didn't answer right away and in the silence I thought I heard the dogs again. My heart strained against my chest.

"It's just best to do everything in moderation," Naya finally said. "Especially when there's a serious injury involved. We probably shouldn't even be moving her, actually. I mean, probably."

"Not a serious injury," Julia mumbled.

I wondered if she could be going into shock. It was a phrase I'd heard before. Julia had even said she thought I'd gone into shock when I was attacked by the yellow jackets the first time we'd tried to go into number 9 Firefly Lane. But I still wasn't a hundred percent sure what it meant. I checked her lips to see if they were turning blue or anything.

Theo and Ilana got Julia and the wagon up next to the tracks where the ground was relatively smooth.

"We can cut across the lot," Tommy said, and pointed to the flat blacktop that we could see shimmering in the sun ahead.

"But that will bring us in right by Flannery's," said the small girl. Her voice was so soft, I wasn't sure she had spoken. I peered over my shoulder to look at her, but she was looking out toward the horizon. The sun cut across her face and I noticed a thin red scar that stretched over her cheek. Why hadn't it been erased, I wondered.

"It'll bring us in *behind* Flannery's, and don't you worry, I have a plan for that," Tommy said.

"It's your plans that get us into messes like this," Amnah said. I racked my brain trying to think of what those red dots on her face could be. Not chicken pox—I knew what those looked like. Measles weren't quite right, either. The dots on this girl's skin were like volcanoes with white lava erupting out of them. I was going to have to do my best to keep away from her—and definitely wouldn't let her touch Julia again.

"Are you sure this person can help?" Theo asked.

"Yes," Naya said.

Ethan, the boy who'd gone to get the wagon, said,

"Trudy's the best. She'll fix this girl right up. What did you say her name was again?"

None of us had said our names, and none of us answered the boy.

Tommy stopped walking. "Halt!" he cried out.

Theo straightened up, but Ilana kept pulling the wagon.

"Halt!" Tommy said again.

"You're not ordering us around," Theo told him.

Tommy's body stiffened, and I thought maybe he and Theo would get into a fight—the fist-punching kind, not the yelling kind—but then Tommy said, "Listen, I'm Tommy McPhee. You know Naya. And that's Ethan. She's Amnah, and she's Mouse. They're sisters." He pointed to the red-dot girl and the quiet one. They didn't look much alike as far as I could tell. "That's all of us. McPhee's Boys."

"We're not McPhee's Boys," Naya said.

"Yeah, well, you got mad when I called you McPhee's Girls."

"That was because—never mind, we need to get this girl to Trudy," Amnah replied.

Ilana was pulling away from the rest of us, the wagon, *chuck-chucking* over the rocks. Julia moaned, making my stomach twist. We needed these people. So I said, "I'm Mori. That's Theo and that's Benji. Julia is the one who—she's the one in the wagon, and Ilana is the one pulling her."

"And where are you going?" Tommy asked.

"Cambridge," I said.

"Mori!" Theo exclaimed.

"And that's all we can tell you, so now can we please keep going?"

Tommy clapped his hands together. "Sure we can."

Theo jogged to catch up with the wagon, and he took over from Ilana, who put her hands on top of her head as she kept walking.

Tommy fell into step with me. I noticed his sneakers had no laces even though they had eyelets. Did they have no shoelaces out here? We would have to send them some when we got back. If we got back.

"I was only joking about making you guys pay," he said. "I mean, if you wanted to throw a little moolah-moolah our way, I wouldn't say no. But we'll help you no matter what."

"We don't have any money," I said.

"What? But you're from Old Harmonie. You have swimming pools full of money."

"Geez, Tommy, give it a rest," Ethan said.

"He thinks your streets are paved with gold," Amnah added. "And that all you eat is ice cream and caviar."

"I don't know what caviar is," I said, trying to keep an eye on Julia. She didn't seem to have passed out. I quickened my pace.

"Anyway, all I'm saying is that I was just joking," Tommy said. "This is fun. This is an adventure. We don't get many adventures in South Concord."

"This isn't an adventure," Theo muttered.

"So we're going to come in behind this pub, Flannery's. And there's lots of people there—"

"But it's not even ten o'clock in the morning," Benji said.

"So it will have been open for an hour," Tommy replied. "This is what we're going to do. We're going to get another wagon. And we'll put Mouse or someone in it. You're pretty small compared to those giants," he said to me. I realized then that he was shorter than me by a good three inches. Only Amnah was taller.

"What's the point of the second wagon?" Benji asked.

"That's the genius of the plan!" Tommy said. "We'll pretend we're having a race. We'll have a bunch of us around each wagon pushing. All of you can have your heads down, and anyone who sees us will just see a pack of kids."

"They won't notice we're from outside?"

"Outside where? Outside South Concord? There's always kids coming and going—cousins and second cousins and friends from before. We just don't want them to get too close a look at you and start wondering. A curious adult is a dangerous thing."

"I guess that's an okay plan," Benji said.

"It's a brilliant plan! Right, Mori?" Tommy asked.

Up ahead, Theo and Ilana switched off again pulling Julia. "Sure," I called as I ran up next to the wagon. Julia was curled over her knees, her cheek bouncing on them as she rolled along. Her face was white and glistening like unnatural clay.

The blood from her leg had soaked through my shirt, making the cloth a strange magenta. It was all so bizarre, like one of those plays they made us watch, the kind that were supposed to awaken our artistic sensibilities but mostly just made us giggle. I wanted to tell her that, but her eyes were squeezed shut and I doubted that she would even be able to hear me.

10

THE LAST OBSTACLE BEFORE SOUTH Concord was a ravine. "We call it the moat." Tommy laughed.

"There's no water," Ilana said.

"Come back in the spring."

"I don't think we'll ever be coming back."

Tommy laughed again, and Theo said, "We can't take Julia down in the wagon. We'll need to carry her."

So Ilana and Theo lifted her out of the wagon and made a chair of their arms. I walked behind them just in case—though what I expected to be able to do, I don't know. If she fell back, I would just fall with her. I could feel myself shrinking with my sheer uselessness. Smaller and smaller until I was like a snail hiding in its spiral shell. Why had I ever thought I would be able to get Ilana all the way to Cambridge?

A whirring sound came from behind us, then a blur of red, black, and yellow. It was Tommy, riding the wagon down the incline toward the ravine. It crashed and he tumbled out. "Bananas!" he yelled.

Theo muttered, "That kid is questionable."

And I felt smaller still. Down to a microorganism. "It'll be okay," I said. But my tiny voice made no sound.

Tommy righted the wagon by the time we got down the hill and dragged it up to the flat part on the much smaller upward incline on the other side. Ilana and Theo placed Julia back in the wagon. Julia left a slash of her blood on Ilana's white T-shirt.

Theo grabbed the handle and pulled the wagon to a gap in the fence where the other local kids were waiting. There were buildings that backed right up to the fence for as far as I could see. We were near an alleyway, and I got a glimpse of some more of the town. Faded banners hung from the streetlights and there was a little convenience store with a statue of a pony outside.

"Ethan went for the other wagon," Tommy explained. "When he gets back, we can put the plan in motion. It really is a good plan. I mean, I come up with a lot of stellar plans, but this one takes the cake. Sincerely."

No one replied. None of his friends, and none of mine. He turned and held on to the chain-link fence, looking down the alleyway.

"What's your fence for?" I asked.

"You have a fence, don't you?" Amnah asked me.

"Sure, but—" I started to say that's because we had something to protect, but then I realized they were the ones we were protecting it from. "I just didn't realize every town has a fence."

"Not every town," Naya explained. "It's mostly because of the dogs."

"That makes sense," I said.

Julia murmured something through gray lips. "It's okay if I don't make it as an athlete," she said. "It's okay."

I crouched down next to her. "It's not okay."

"My chances weren't so great anyway. You know most of them come from the warmer Kritopias. Or outside." She rubbed at her eyes.

"You're going to be fine," I told her. "We're getting you help."

She closed her eyes tightly. Beads of sweat dotted her forehead.

"Does it hurt terribly?" I asked in a low voice.

She nodded and winced. "But don't get any ideas," she said.

I wanted to ask her what she meant, but then Ethan came back with the other wagon. We pushed Julia in through the gap and then Tommy said, "You, get in the other wagon."

"Me?" I asked.

"I figure maybe you're right and we should take

precautions. I like taking precautions. So we should probably hide as many of your faces as possible. Mori, you get in the wagon, and you"—he pointed to Benji—"push from behind."

I climbed into the wagon. The bottom was full of old leaves, and a strange insect scurried out from under them and disappeared through a tiny hole. "Okay," I said. "I'm good."

"Amnah and Mouse, you're on that team. Take them to home base and we'll meet you there."

"Wait—" I started to protest.

"On your mark, get set, go!" Tommy yelled.

And we were off, rolling at a terrible speed down the alleyway. Every bump we hit sent a shock to my bones and I knew it had to be a hundred times worse for Julia. "Slow down!" I yelled, but my voice was drowned out by our wheels on the pavement and Tommy's whooping and hollering.

When we burst out of the alleyway, both wagons veered right. I felt like I was going to tip out onto the pavement. I tried to look over my shoulder for Julia, but she was lost in the crowd of kids around her wagon. So I tilted my head back and tried to concentrate on the sky. That just made me feel sick. And then we were turning again. Away from Tommy's whooping. Away from Julia.

Mouse held out a water bottle to me. Her hair was reddish and spun out above her head like a cloud of tiny corkscrews. She closed her eyes and took a deep breath. When she opened her eyes, she looked at the bleached-out grass to the left of my sneaker. "Drink," she said. Her voice was so soft, I thought maybe I had imagined it. Like maybe it was the wind blowing through the trees. Another deep breath. "But slowly."

I glanced over at Benji. Had he noticed the way she wouldn't look at me? He just shrugged. I took the water bottle from her and tried to peek at its contents, but the plastic was opaque. I didn't really feel like I had a choice, though. My throat was parched like I hadn't had water in years—had never had it. I wanted to gulp it all down, but Mouse put her hand on top of mine, telling me to slow down without words.

Amnah looked over her shoulder. "We need to get them inside."

Mouse chewed on her lower lip. It was chapped and cracked at the corner.

"It's work hour almost," Amnah said.

Mouse took her hand off mine and nodded, so I took another sip.

Benji put his hand on my shoulder. He was sweating more than I'd ever seen him. When he breathed, his skin pressed in around his cheeks and his collarbone. I tumbled myself out of the wagon. "Benji!"

He held up one hand. "All good," he panted.

"Your inhaler? Do you have it?"

He nodded and I yanked his backpack off his shoulders. The pack was full of different tools and devices, most of which I didn't recognize. But there, at the bottom, was his inhaler and spacer.

"Put your hands on your head," Amnah said, and my body stiffened. Was this a holdup? All I had in my hands was the inhaler. "Put your hands on your head and breathe slowly."

Benji did as he was told.

"Well, go on! Give it to him," Amnah said to me.

So I held the inhaler up to Benji and when he put his lips around it, I squeezed.

"It's gonna take time for your breath to come back, but we gotta get up," Amnah told him. "Can you climb?"

"No sweat," Benji said, though he was, in fact, dripping with sweat.

Amnah looked both ways before leading us down another alleyway alongside a giant triple-decker house whose siding was green with mold. Back beyond the building was a lawn no bigger than the entryway to our houses, and squished up against a fence was an oak tree with a rickety-looking tree house in it.

I had always wanted a tree house in our backyard. I could read there, and sleep in it in the summertime. Of course, my parents had said it was far too dangerous, and anyway, it wasn't allowed by the building code.

There were boards nailed into the trunk of the tree for a makeshift ladder. Mouse went first. Then Benji. I waited until he was all the way up, but again, what would I have done if he fell? I certainly couldn't catch him. Amnah came behind us, closing the trapdoor.

"I just don't normally run that much is all," Benji said. He had his hands back up on top of his head.

"Keep you behind closed doors up there, I suppose," Amnah said. The red bumps on her skin were shiny and angry.

"It's not like that at all," I said.

"What Mori is trying to tell you," Benji began, then stopped to take a few deep breaths. "Is that you happen to be sitting with the dopest skateboarder in four counties."

"Dopest? Like stupidest?" Amnah asked.

"No, like cool." Benji picked up his inhaler and took another puff. I watched his skin. He didn't seem to be sucking it in so hard, but I still wished we had all gone to see the EMT. Why had they separated us, anyway?

The walls of the tree house were covered with posters. Some were for movies I had seen, but others were totally unfamiliar, like one with a giant, feathered monster peering down at a city that was held beneath a birdcage. I turned away from that one. On the far wall was a big map. I crossed over for a closer look. There was a big red circle around South Concord. Then lots of little *x*'s marking other spots. I didn't pay attention to those. I concentrated on the big green area marked "Old Harmonie, KritaCorp." Between there and the tree house was a blue rectangle—the reservoir.

"You've come a long way," Mouse said from a seat by the window, her voice like a puff of air. She looked at a stack of sketches on the table, paging through them while picking at her fingers again. The ends were all red and raw.

"Yes," I said. And then the air went still and heavy between us all. We had nothing to say to one another. Even Benji, who could fill just about any silence, looked uncomfortable.

There was a bookshelf tucked in one corner, but it didn't hold any books. One shelf had what looked like a bunch of circuit boards, another had battery packs, and the top had motors and lights of various sizes.

"Whoa!" Benji exclaimed. "Is this what I think it is?" He held up a small black box.

"I guess that depends on what you think it is," Amnah said.

"A Nyetalift?" He spun it around in his hands.

"Doesn't work," Mouse said, still looking at her drawings.

"You should send it back, then," Benji said. "'Cause these things are way cool. We have one in our tech lab at school and Theo and I programmed it so that when someone got close to it, it would levitate their hair."

"That was you?" I asked. My own hair had gone straight up and one of the boys from over on Serenity Drive had said I looked like the world's saddest peacock. A few days later he had come up to me all full of apologies, and I realized now that maybe his parents had dampened his cruelty so he wouldn't tease anymore. He'd been overly sweet ever since.

Mouse shook her head. She raised her eyes to peek at Benji. "I didn't buy it."

"You stole it?" I exclaimed.

Amnah exhaled slowly. "Really?"

"What? If she didn't buy it, then she must have—"

"Made it," Amnah interrupted. "She made it herself. Duh. Though I'm not surprised that theft was the first thing an Old Harmonie kid would think."

"I just—" I began. The truth was, I had never heard of anyone making their own Nyetalift. It was a device that created a field that allowed things to levitate. Mostly kids just fooled around with theirs, but they had some cool innovative possibilities. Julia had used one in a project to show how you could redesign the run-up to a high-jump bar so that people would get greater vertical lift, and then how the athlete could use that to better execute the jump. The idea was that athletes could use it while they were training to really perfect their technique. The school had bought a new one just for that project. No one had even suggested that she try to make one herself.

"What's not working about it?" Benji asked.

"It doesn't hold the field. Things go up, but they fall right down." Mouse held out one of her sketches to Benji. It was covered in numbers and notes.

"Huh," he said. "It should work."

Mouse agreed by nodding.

Amnah picked up a knot of loose wires. She began untangling the wires, coiling each one up so it wouldn't get re-tangled. "You should know that Tommy McPhee has a history of doing incredibly stupid things, and I think this is just about the stupidest."

My breath came quicker as I felt my chest tighten. What exactly was Tommy doing? Had this all been a plan? "What do you mean?"

"Helping a bunch of Krita kids. I bet he thinks the president of the company is going to thank us. Invite us up there for a big parade, maybe even let us stay. Ha! We all know that's not going to happen."

I looked over at Mouse and Benji. Neither of us told them how far up Theo's mom was in the Krita corporate ladder.

Mouse said, "Tommy wants to be a hero."

"Some hero. He gets us into more scrapes than I can count."

Maybe that's what I was doing. Trying to be a hero. And look what had happened. Julia had been bitten by a dog. "Is there a hospital nearby?" I asked.

Amnah shook her head, disgust smeared across her face. Mouse nodded. That cool silence descended again. It was almost like Amnah could summon it. "How long do you think it will take?" I asked.

"Hopefully not too much longer," Amnah said. "I mean, it's not like I've got all day to sit around babysitting you two."

I went and sat next to Benji, who put his arm around me. "It's okay, Mori," he said. I could feel that his breath was still coming all ragged. Mine, too.

The wind blew through the tree house, rustling some papers on the floor—comics, it looked like—and bringing with it a foul, smoky smell. I wrinkled my nose and Benji coughed.

Amnah started wrapping the wires again, tugging them around her fingers, then sliding them off.

"What are you hoping to do with the Nyetalift, anyway?" Benji asked Mouse. "Little science fair experiment or something? I've got a pretty dope plan for one, if I can ever convince my parents to get me one. Of course, if you figure out how to fix yours and send me the plans, then I can make my own. Totally rad."

"What would you make with it?" Mouse prompted. "And don't say hoverboard."

"Totally a hoverboard!" Benji said. "The last frontier of science. The one problem that no one has ever really solved, right up there with the cure for the common cold."

Mouse laughed at this. "Well, I'm working on an assistive walking device for senior citizens."

"Holy cow! Really?"

"Why is that so shocking?" Amnah asked.

"It's just really ambitious," Benji said.

"We have ambitions out here, too. You didn't get a lock on that."

"That wasn't what I meant. It's just—"

"Save it," Amnah said. "Not interested."

"Amnah," Mouse said in a soft voice.

Amnah scowled and looked out the window.

Benji turned back to Mouse. "It's a much better use of the technology, I'll give you that. Although I do think senior citizens might enjoy hoverboards, too."

Mouse smiled and Benji picked the plans back up.

"Hey, have you tried connecting this port to the one over here?"

She nodded. "Yep. No go."

She rustled through the papers and showed him something else.

"Got it," Benji said. "Did you ever think about—"

Before he could finish his question, she showed him another diagram.

Benji nodded. "Right, of course, because of the weight."

She smiled and nodded.

"Oh! So then that means, if you could shift the center of gravity forward—"

"Nope."

He took the sheet of paper from her. "Huh," Benji said.

"Huh," Mouse agreed.

And Amnah just kept looking out the window.

11

THERE WERE THREE QUICK KNOCKS on the trapdoor, followed by two slower ones. Mouse leaned over and pulled the lock out of the door, then lifted it up. Tommy's face appeared. "It's bad," he said.

"Where is she?" I asked.

"She's at Naya's. She's still bleeding and she's not real coherent all the time. Trudy gave her some painkillers and those seem to be helping a little. Anyway, she needs to go to the hospital, but she won't go. Said you all were on a mission and she wasn't going to be the one to mess it up."

"I'll talk to her," I said.

"Go for it," Tommy said. He climbed back down the ladder, and I followed him. Benji and Mouse came and then, after a moment's hesitation, and with a great deal of grumbling, Amnah came, too.

We walked back down the alleyway. There were dandelions growing out of the cracks in the pavement, bright yellow ones that reached for the sun.

"So, are you?" Tommy asked. "On a mission, I mean. Or is that just the fever dreams talking."

"She has a fever?"

"Probably." He shrugged. "Her body's going into fight mode. She's bound to get hot. But are you on a mission? What kind of a mission? You happen to have stumbled upon one of the a-number-one mission planners, so you're pretty lucky."

"Who?" I asked. I concentrated on my feet, putting one in front of the other. It felt like the alleyway had stretched and no matter how many steps we took, we didn't get any closer to Julia and my friends.

"Me," Tommy said.

But Amnah said, "Mouse."

"She's just saying that to rile me up. And because they're sisters. But there's no hiding the truth. I know what's what. You tell me what you all are up to and—"

"Are we almost there?" I asked.

"Just up here," Tommy said.

It was another one of the triple-decker houses. There were three mailboxes on the outside wall, and when Tommy pushed open the front door, there was another heavy door to our left, and stairs going up.

"Trudy and Naya live on the first floor, thankfully," Tommy said. He knocked three times on the door and while we waited I tried to figure out what he meant about Naya and Trudy living on the first floor. Did they live without their parents?

Naya opened the door and, after hustling us inside, bolted the lock on the door. We had a lock like that on our front door, but never used it. We had even forgotten to lock it during the outbreak.

"Wait, does more than one family live in this house?" I asked.

Amnah just shook her head as she walked by.

"This is actually a really sustainable use of space," Benji said. "Building up instead of spreading out. I'm surprised we don't do more of this."

I didn't like the idea of another family living above or below me. Would I hear them stomping around? Would they hear me?

"She's in here," Naya said.

As Naya pushed open the door, I braced myself. Julia was lying in bed, on top of a coverlet with tiny pink flowers. The pillows were pink, too. My sweatshirt was gone from her leg, and instead her leg was wrapped in white gauze. Her face was gray as stone dust. Ilana paced beside her, tugging at one of her curls. Sitting on the windowsill was an older girl, maybe sixteen or seventeen. Trudy, I supposed.

The room was silent as a coffin.

I dropped to my knees next to Julia. "I'm so sorry, Jules!"

Julia shook her head. "I'm fine. It's nothing. I'll be back balling in no time."

"We need to go back," I said.

"No way," she replied.

"Julia."

"No. You don't know—you don't know how far we've come. You can't go back."

"You need to go to the hospital. They have one here."

"I agree," said the girl in the window. "I've taken an oath, you know."

"The Hippocratic oath is for doctors," Tommy said. "You're a junior EMT."

"I thought you said she was an EMT. No junior about it," Ilana said.

I was still looking right at Julia. She wrinkled her nose, then shook her head. "No way," she mouthed.

Theo said, "Mori's right. You need to go, Julia. If you don't get that treated, it might not ever heal properly." We all knew what that meant. After all, who was Julia if she couldn't run the fastest and jump the highest?

"And when I do, they'll know we're out and where we are and we'll have to go back. All of us."

Ilana stopped pacing.

The sun poking through the window blinds stabbed at us.

"You have to go, Julia," Ilana said. "You can't stay—not because of me."

"Maybe now would be a good time for you to tell us what's going on?" Tommy said. "So we can actually help you all."

I considered the kids from this strange little city. Amnah didn't look ready to help us one bit. Tommy seemed caught up in the adventure of it all. The mission. But Mouse looked like someone I could trust. "It's complicated," I said. "I'm not sure if you could even understand. If out here—"

"Ilana got in some trouble," Theo said.

"It's nothing dangerous," Benji said. "I mean, what she did wasn't that kind of trouble."

"She just broke a few rules is all," Theo said. "And she has, um, some family in Cambridge, and we all thought it would be better if she got out of Old Harmonie for a while and—"

"That sounds like a load of bull," Amnah said. "Stinks like it, too."

Julia pushed herself up so she was sitting with her back straight. "All I have to do is make it a few hours to give you guys a head start. Then I'll go to the hospital. I'll tell them you went in a different direction."

I got onto the bed and slid closer to Julia so our hips were touching. I leaned my head next to her and our hair—the exact same color—flowed together.

"That was the bravest thing I've ever seen," she said.

"I'm not brave," I told her. "We both know that and we know why."

"I know I saw you running at that dog like in that River and Zane movie where Zane is stuck on that hostile planet and River comes in with her blaster blasting—your face looked just like hers."

"I wasn't thinking, Jules. I just reacted. I don't know if that's the same as being brave."

"If it's overcoming a dampening, I think it is." She shifted her body and winced.

"Julia, you realize what could happen, don't you? Even if this, this junior EMT can fix you up a little, I mean, even if she's very, very good, the longer you wait to get treatment for that leg, the worse it will be."

"I know."

I couldn't look at her, so I looked at our legs. My right was next to her left—that was her good one. Next to it was her torn-up one, the blood already starting to seep through the bandage. "You've had your thirty percent, Julia. They'll patch you up when we get back, but what if that's all they'll do?"

"Then you'll be able to keep up with me, Mori." I knew she was trying to joke, but her voice sounded hollow, and when I looked at her face, the smile was pasted on. "What choice do we have?"

The sobs hitched in my throat. I tried to push them down, but I couldn't stop them. "I'm sorry, Julia."

"Hey," she said. "You guys never really needed me on this trip anyway. You have Theo to navigate, and Benji to fix any technology problems. You're the heart and Ilana's the reason. I'm just the tagalong."

"That's not true," I told her. "You're strong and smart—"

"Okay, well, on the off chance that any tough math problems come up, I'll bet that Ilana or Benji can solve them. Not as fast as me, but you know, it'll be all right."

"We need you, Julia, you know that. *I* need you and I forced you to come because I was being selfish and—"

"You didn't force me to come."

"Then why'd you change your mind?"

Julia tugged the blanket up over her waist. The whole room seemed to quiet and disappear so it was just Julia and me. "Remember when we threw the basketball into Mr. Quist's yard?" she asked.

"Of course." Ilana had gone over to get Benji's wayward shot and ended up squishing Mr. Quist's prized cucumbers.

"We wrote him that note and nobody wanted to sign it. Nobody wanted to get in trouble. But then you came up with that Firefly Five thing and we were all in it together. We all did the cleanup. I mean, I know you and Ilana did most of it, but we all showed up and did the job together. We took responsibility."

Tommy was hunched together with Benji and Ilana. The girls sat together, talking, too. Their voices were a gentle hum in the background. Still, I leaned closer to Julia and lowered my voice. "So that's why you came along? To take responsibility together?"

"Sort of," she said, but she shook her head. The thing about Julia is, sometimes it takes her a while to say the things that truly matter—the things at her heart. And you can't rush her, because if you rush her she can say the thing she doesn't mean. Maybe that's how she and I had ended up fighting so much this summer. She tossed a braid over her shoulder. "I was thinking about the people who built Ilana. I was thinking how they all worked together on this project, and when it started to go wrong, they didn't really take responsibility. They just tried to shut her down, to hide their mistakes. And that's like the exact opposite of what they teach us. When you make a mistake, you have to own it."

"I see," I said.

"I made some mistakes this summer, Mori." She kept her eyes on her lap as she spoke. "I was jealous of Ilana and I didn't give her a chance. I was short-tempered with you. I broke your dad's phone. I got my latency early. I was mean. I don't know if what I did caused any of the problems with Ilana. I think about that day on the treadmills—"

"That wasn't anyone's fault," I told her.

"Maybe. Anyway, I made a lot of mistakes and I'm not going to be one of those people who doesn't own her mistakes." She glanced toward Ilana. "And I'm not going to let them—" She shook her head. "I'm just not."

"Okay," I said. "I can see I'm not going to change your mind."

"You're not."

I turned to the group. "We are going to leave Julia here long enough for us to get a head start."

"Let's say six hours," Tommy said.

"Two," I said.

"Mori," Julia said, shaking her head. "In two hours, you won't even be six miles from here."

"Well—" Tommy began.

"Six miles is plenty," Theo told him.

"Two hours, then. Unless she takes a turn for the worse," I said, staring right at Naya. I trusted her. "If something goes wrong, like her fever goes way up or she starts throwing up or something, then take her right away to the hospital."

"I will," Naya said.

"Take my stuff, Mori. All my extra clothes and food. I wish we had the same-size feet, I'd give you my shoes."

"Mine are dry now," I told her, and I picked up her backpack, tightening the straps so it fit my smaller frame.

Benji took supplies out of his backpack. “I’m staying with Julia,” he explained, handing the tools and extra food to Theo. He reached out and put his hand on Ilana’s arm. “You understand, right? I mean, I’d go to the ends of the earth for you, home fry, but I need to look out for Julia, too.”

“I know,” Ilana said. She threw her arms around him and hugged him close. And then I wrapped around him, too. He made an *oof* sound, but I knew he felt warm and safe because, for that one moment, I did, too.

“We should probably get going,” Theo said.

“Right, okay, so, of course I have a plan,” Tommy said. “Let me lay it out for you.”

“Can you lay it out while we’re walking?”

Tommy’s face fell. “Well, part one is in motion already: Julia stays here with Naya and Benji.”

“And part two?” Amnah asked.

“Mouse and I sneak them out of here and get them to Cambridge.”

“That’s a terrible plan,” Amnah said.

“It’s not a terrible plan. You just haven’t heard the whole thing.”

“In the history of plans, it ranks in the lowest percentile,” Amnah replied. “Right next to their big scheme to break out of Old Harmonie. Who breaks out of Old Harmonie?”

“Let’s focus on the getting *us* out of *here* part,” Tommy said.

I grabbed on to Julia's hand and squeezed it tightly. "See you soon," I said.

"Yeah," she said. "See you soon."

There actually wasn't much sneaking involved. Trudy and Naya's street hit a dead end at a cemetery. All the gravestones were flat on the ground and their shiny surfaces reflected back the sun in a dizzying manner. The benefit came from the high hedge that encircled the burial ground. We walked right along it and around to the other side of the cemetery and to a brick wall.

"Where are we in relationship to the tracks?" Theo asked. "That way, right?"

Tommy shook his head. "You're not going by the tracks. No way."

"What do you mean?" I asked.

"The tracks curve down south and then come back up and around to get into Cambridge. It's a good eight to ten extra miles."

"We have a map," I said. "Can you draw the route on it?"

"Nah, we're not gonna draw it for you," he said. But he said "draw" like "drawer" and I wondered if maybe they just didn't understand *r*'s out here.

"Is this about the money?" Theo said with a sigh. "Because we really don't have any."

Tommy's smile spread across his face so wide, I thought his face might split in two. "No!" he said merrily. "Mouse and I are going to take you. It's going to be fun."

"Me?" Mouse asked.

"Yep. I need you," Tommy said.

"No way, McPhee," Amnah said.

"But I really do need her," Tommy said, and then, as if the matter was settled, he began climbing the wall. He dug his fingers and toes into the mortar between the bricks and scurried right on up. He stood at the top with his back to us, staring out into the distance.

"What do you think you need her for?" Amnah called up.

"For the car, of course," Tommy replied, and then he disappeared, jumping over the edge.

Mouse turned to Amnah before her sister could say anything. "I'm going."

"Why?"

"Because they need our help."

"What's Krita ever done for you? Those jerks stole our home. They said you weren't good enough—"

"They aren't Krita. They need our help and I'm helping them." She set her lips firmly together.

Amnah didn't say anything. She just glowered. But she got down on one knee so that Mouse could get a boost. Mouse climbed first onto her sister's raised knee, then onto her shoulders. Amnah stood up then, and Mouse, like an acrobat, stood on her shoulders so she could reach the top of the wall and pull herself up.

"Not a bad trick," Ilana said.

Amnah still didn't say anything. She climbed up the wall, too—not as easily as Tommy, but she made it, and hopped over. A moment later Mouse hopped down, too.

"We'll lift you up," Theo said. "We can each take a foot."

It was a wonder they didn't drop me. They were strong enough, but as they each lifted me by one leg, I had to keep my body perfectly straight or else wobble all over the place. I reached my hands up and grabbed the warm, rough bricks. My knees banged against the wall as they let go, but I managed. Maybe that's the way it is with obstacles when you really need to get someplace. Maybe you always find you have just enough to get past them.

12

"THE PEOPLE'S REPUBLIC, HUH? THAT'S where you're going?" Tommy asked as he walked backward along a narrow, rutted path. There were some shaggy bushes on either side of us, pricker bushes, by the look of them, the kind that tear at your skin.

"We need to go to MIT," Theo said.

"Right smack dab in the center of the People's Republic. The new C-Town. Land of the Lost."

"What are you talking about?" Theo asked.

"He means Cambridge," Amnah answered. "He just likes to seem smarter than he is and he does that by trying to sound like he knows all about the world." Amnah scooped up a rock and tossed it at Tommy's feet. Tommy skipped out of the way.

"I am smart," he said. "Smart enough to go to StepUp Charter."

Amnah scoffed. "I wouldn't boast about that."

"What's StepUp Charter?" I asked, wishing I could tell him to turn around and just walk forward, safely. The sun blazed, and I wiped my hair from my forehead.

"Only the best charter school in Massachusetts. Run by Krita, of course. Pipeline to Old Harmonie. So what's it really like up there? Is it true that everyone gets their own place and robots to do the cleaning and the cooking and when you don't like your clothes anymore you just pop them in a machine and they're reworked into something new?"

Ilana marched along the side of the tracks, her feet *clomp-clomping* on the mix of sandy dirt and grass. I glanced over at Theo. "Not exactly," I said.

"Told you," Amnah said.

"Well, you must at least have some of that," Tommy said. "Or, like, all the coolest video games. Like before they even get released anywhere else? I mean, have you seen *BotFist Eleven*? Is it bananas?" As he spoke he veered off to the left. This trail was even more faint, and passed under a huge tree. Just as we stepped out, a drone flew overhead.

Theo grabbed my arm and pulled me to the ground. I landed hard on my elbow and winced, but managed to swallow my cry. Ilana crouched in the bushes. "Okay?" she mouthed.

I nodded.

The others stopped in their tracks and stared at us. Tommy's mouth was even open a little. Who cared? We stayed right where we were until the drone flew off. Theo stood up first. He reached down and helped me to my feet. I brushed the dirt off my chest. It was sort of a losing battle, considering how dirty I already was.

"You never seen a drone before?" Tommy asked slowly.

"Of course we have," Theo said. "We just didn't want the drone to see us."

Tommy rubbed his chin. "Um, yeah, there are a lot of drones out here. You're not going to be able do a nosedive every time one breezes by."

"We'll do what we need to do to stay out of sight. They can't find us until we get Ilana to MIT."

"Who can't?" Mouse asked.

"And why is this all hush-hush anyway?" Tommy asked.

"They said Ilana was trouble," Amnah said. "I think they all are. If you ask me. Which you didn't."

Theo stood in a wide stance, perfect posture. "The less you know, the better."

Amnah smirked at that, and Tommy held up both his hands. "Ease up, why don't you?"

"Let's just keep going. What is it you needed to show us?" Theo said.

Ilana walked up beside me. She put one hand on my shoulder. "I'd really like to get going, if you don't mind." Her words were kind; tension strained her voice.

"Sure, sure," Tommy said. "It's right up here."

The path led to an old, cracked road. We walked along that for a short way. Tommy started walking faster, and Theo jogged to catch up with him. Amnah and Mouse were right behind, so Ilana and I were at the back together. "You doing okay?" I asked.

"I guess." She looked back over her shoulder. "I just keep thinking that we should have stayed with Julia."

"Benji's with her."

"I know, but—"

"I know," I agreed. "But we need to get you to Dr. Varden."

"Mori," she said. "What if Dr. Varden doesn't want to see me? She's the one who scuttled me the first time, right?"

"That wasn't you," I told her.

She looked straight ahead. Her profile was etched against the sun and I could see a drop of sweat on her temple.

"That wasn't you," I said again.

"Maybe," she replied. "But Dr. Varden might not see it that way. And then what? Or what if it's like going to see the Wizard of Oz? We follow this yellow brick road and then we get there and it turns out she doesn't have any power at all?"

I didn't know what to tell her. I didn't have another plan for us. If Dr. Varden didn't want to help, then we were pretty well stuck. Ilana couldn't go back to Old Harmonie, and I wasn't about to leave her outside alone. "You know what we'll do? We'll go to Oakedge."

"Oakedge isn't real," she said. "It's a mirage."

"No, it's real," I told her. And to prove it, I swung Julia's backpack around and held it by one strap while I used my other hand to dig inside to find what I had stashed there. I pulled out two perfect sweet pea pods and handed one to her.

Ahead of us, Tommy jogged down a slight hill toward a fence. He pulled open the gates. "Friends, your chariot awaits."

It was like a field of wildflowers, but instead of flowers, it was cars. They were all different sizes and colors—though nearly all slashed with rust. They weren't lined up in any real order, zigzagging and jagged. Still, the lot was ringed by plastic triangle flags that swung in the sky like it was a carnival.

"What is this place?" I asked as we stepped through the fence. There were ribbons on this one, too, flapping in the breeze. Ilana touched one as she walked by. "Is it a car graveyard?" I asked. In Old Harmonie, when the KritaCars broke, they were taken apart, usable parts salvaged, and the rest recycled. But maybe that didn't happen out here. Maybe they just piled them up and waited for the centuries or millennia it would take for them to break down.

"Not exactly," Tommy said. "It's a used car lot."

"I don't understand," I said. So the cars were used and then deposited here?

Theo, though, rubbed his hand in his hair and said, "You

want us to steal a car?" He was sweating enough that I could see round marks under his arms. I fanned my own face. What I wouldn't give to sink down into Julia's pool, or flop on the couch in my air-cooled home.

"It's not stealing. It's borrowing," Tommy said with a half smile.

Theo looked at the cars a long time. I knew what he was thinking. A car would certainly save us a lot of time. But that was stealing and we weren't thieves. "We can walk from here," I said. "It's really not so far."

"Not so far?" Tommy laughed. "You have no idea what you're getting into, do you? First you gotta walk through the wastelands. On top of that, you want to go around unnoticed, but you stick out like sore thumbs. How you gonna walk through a town like Lexington? Or Somerville? You think you would last one minute in the 'Ville?"

Somerville. The gardeners who'd come to fix up Ilana's house before she'd moved in had been from Somerville. I had thought it sounded like the most beautiful place on earth, but the way Tommy said it, I wasn't so sure.

"We aren't thieves," Theo said. "We can't take a car."

Amnah out-and-out laughed at that. Theo turned and glared at her, but didn't say anything.

"Listen, buddy, I'm trying to help you here."

"I'm not your buddy," Theo said. "You've been real helpful and gotten us this far, but I'll take it from here. Thanks."

Tommy stepped past Theo and up to Ilana. "You need to get to Cambridge, right? Well, I can get you there. I know you are friends and that's great and all, but he's never been out here. He doesn't know. I do. I can get you there. I promise."

Ilana twisted the strap of her backpack around her finger.

"Ilana," Theo said.

"He knows what it's really like out here. He knows the way," Ilana said.

She was right. I didn't want to admit it, but she was. Tommy, Amnah, and Mouse were our best bet.

"They don't know *you*, though," Theo said, his voice cracking. "They're *outsiders*."

"So am I," Ilana said.

But only I heard her, because Amnah kicked her foot into the ground hard, sending pebbles scattering like shattered glass. "And that's all we will ever be to you, right?" she asked.

"That's not what he meant," I said.

"We have to go," Theo said to me. "Now. We're wasting time."

I started to walk, and so Ilana came, too. But Tommy stepped in our path. "I can't let you do this. Listen, I know you hardly know me, but walking, that's like suicide. Sincerely. You need to listen to me."

Theo strode over. His breath came in sharp puffs. "We're

going," he said to Ilana and me. "We had a plan, and we need to stick to it."

"How well has that plan gone so far?" Tommy asked. His voice was soft and he continued to hold up both hands like Theo was some sort of wild animal and he wanted to show that he meant no harm. Maybe that's how Theo seemed to Tommy and the others.

"Out of our way," Theo said.

"I'm really not trying to be a jerk here, but I think you guys are over your head. I can get you a car. I can drive you there. We'll be there in a couple of hours. No big deal. Okay?"

"We can't steal," I said.

Mouse put her hand on my arm. "It's his uncle's car lot."

"What?" I asked.

"Yeah," Tommy said.

"Why didn't you just say so?" Ilana asked.

Tommy shrugged a little sheepishly.

"And his uncle can be a little lenient," Amnah explained. She was sweating, too: little beads of it that gathered on her face like the red dots.

"Meaning?" Theo asked.

"Meaning we're allowed to drive the cars from time to time," Tommy said. "I mean, I'm supposed to stay on the lot, and I am supposed to ask first, but I think this is a special dispensation type of situation. Right? I mean, honestly, he's already at the pub telling the story of the time these kids broke out of Old Harmonie and took a joy ride in one of his cars. *And our Tommy helped them! Ain't that the salt of it?"* He spoke the last bit in a deep voice that I supposed was meant to be his uncle.

"I still don't like it," Theo said.

I turned so I was facing right at him. He was almost a head taller than me now, and I had to lean way back to see him. "We need to get there as soon as we can. We're already so far away."

"Taking without permission is still stealing." He glanced past me to Tommy, Mouse, and Amnah. "We don't know them, Mori. Not really."

"They helped us. They helped Julia."

Theo rubbed his head. His eyes had dark circles under them.

"We're all exhausted, Theo. How are we going to make it all the way there on foot?"

I could see him giving in. He rubbed his head again, then looked over toward the cars. "All right. Fine."

Tommy clapped his hands together. "All right! I knew you'd come around." He grinned at Theo, but Theo didn't smile back.

"Over here, Mouse!" Amnah called. "I think I found one."

We had all spread out to look for possible cars. Tommy

told us to look in the back part of the lot because these were the beaters—*beat-ahs* was how he said it—the cars that his uncle sometimes scavenged for parts. He'd be less likely to notice one was missing. I didn't know what made a good candidate, so mostly I had trotted along behind Ilana, who peered into windows and under the hoods and eventually said, "I thought Theo was really going to lose it."

"Maybe," I said.

"He does have a temper," she said.

"He wanted his mom to dampen it, but I guess it would've messed with his puzzle latency, so they wouldn't do it."

"Really?" she asked.

I didn't get a chance to answer because that was when Amnah called and Ilana started jogging over to the car Amnah had found. I hurried to keep up.

"It needs a new camshaft, and that timing belt doesn't look so hot, either," Mouse said into the hood of a red car whose back was covered in stickers.

"You can tell all that just by looking?" I asked Mouse.

Mouse shoved her hands into her pockets. Her curls were matted down a little by sweat. "It's a classic. They're easier to fix."

It didn't matter how new or old the car was, I would not have been able to tell what was supposed to be there and what wasn't.

"We're gonna need gas. Probably," Tommy said. "I can

sneak up and nab some of that from my uncle's tank out back."

"Gas?" Theo asked. "These cars run on gas?"

"What do you expect them to run on? Rainbows and sunshine?" Amnah asked.

"Well, sunshine, yes," Theo replied.

"Didn't you hear her say these were classic cars?" Amnah asked. When she got angry, the red dots on her face flashed even brighter and angrier.

"Gasoline-powered vehicles were outlawed seventeen years ago," Ilana said.

"For good reason, too. Do you know what that exhaust does to the atmosphere?" I asked. "I don't think we can travel in a fossil fuel–powered vehicle." As far as I was concerned, that was as bad as smoking or throwing an apple core into the garbage instead of the compost.

"No stealing, no fossil fuels, it's like the Goody Two-Shoes Brigade around here," Amnah said. "But whatever, suit yourself. Now Mouse and I can get going. We'll be home in time for *River Loves Zane*."

"Mori's just exaggerating," Theo said. He ran his hand across the top of the car and then looked down at his palm. I half expected the car to fall to dust. "Right, Mori?"

I stayed silent.

Ilana pulled open the front door of the car and slipped onto the front seat. The dashboard was full of measurement devices, and most of the left-hand side was covered by a big wheel. "What is all that stuff?" I asked.

Amnah looked at me across the hood of the car. "For real?"

"It's a steering wheel," Ilana said. "Steering wheel, odometer, speedometer." She pointed at each as she named them.

"Wait," I said. "Is one of us actually going to have to drive this car? Like operate it?"

"I cannot tripping believe this," Amnah said, shaking her head.

"She's never seen an old car before, give her a break," Theo said. "None of us have, actually."

Tommy put his hand on my shoulder. "Things are a little different out here, I guess. But, seriously, you won't believe it—the power, the freedom of the open road. Killer."

Theo said, "But Ilana is right. If we're driving an illegal vehicle, won't we be stopped immediately?"

"The regulations are a little softer than you might expect," Tommy said. He tightened the pack he wore around his waist. "Anyway, I'm off to get some gas while you all salvage some parts and Mouse gets this wrecker rolling. You wanna come with me, Ilana?"

"No," I answered for her at the same time that Theo stepped between Tommy and Ilana.

"I'll be fine, Mori," Ilana said. She looked Tommy up and down. "How's he even going to try anything on me?"

Tommy held up his hands. "Not trying anything. Just thought you'd be able to help carry a can or two."

"I'll go," Theo said.

"I'll search for parts," Amnah said. "Since I'm guessing you won't be much help in that regard."

That left Ilana, me, and Mouse back at the car. Mouse opened up her backpack and pulled out a wrench. She stood by the open hood of the car. It cast a shadow across her face and pulled her features into stark relief—the gentle slant of her nose and her high cheekbones. It also made the scar across her cheek shine an eerie white. She looked down into the engine before she spoke. "I know Amnah can be a little rude."

I leaned in closer to hear her soft voice.

"She's just looking out for me. She has to speak for me a lot of the time. I get nervous and . . ." Mouse stopped talking and just shrugged.

"You talk to us okay," I told her.

"You're not too scary, Mori," she said. "And it's easier if I don't have to look at you." She bit her lip. "Sorry. Sometimes when I get going, I say too much. It's like a seesaw, up to full tilt or down to nothing." Her brown cheeks glowed redder and redder as she spoke, and finally she bit her lower lip as if to keep the words inside of her.

"I'm sorry we got you into this. If you want, you can go back. I mean, if you could get the car going first, that would be great, but after that we can make it on our own," I told her.

She started tightening the bolts on the engine. Ilana watched over her shoulder. Her gaze flicked from part to part and I could tell that she was taking it all in. Her mind was putting the pieces together and in moments she would understand it as well as Mouse did—or almost, anyway. But not me. I sighed and looked down at the sandy ground. There was a small patch of clover and even a wilted dandelion.

"Dandelions grow up in the arctic," I said. "When the ice is down. That's how sturdy they are. Which is good, because they are the bee's best friend."

Mouse looked down at the dandelion. "A camshaft opens and closes the intake and outtake valves. Without it, you wouldn't get the fuel where it needs to be in the right amount, and then the pistons won't go and then the crankshaft won't turn and your car won't go anywhere." As Mouse spoke she pointed at each part of the car. "It's like any machine. All the parts have to work together. It's kind of like a three-dimensional puzzle."

"Theo would get it, then," I said. "He's good at puzzles."

Mouse reached into the engine and pulled out two multi-toothed gears that were caked with rust and grime. Then she sat right down on the ground and picked up a flat rock and began chipping away at the crust.

"Need help?" Ilana asked.

"Sure," Mouse said. She handed a gear over to Ilana, who began cleaning it. All I could do was stand there uncertain what to do with my hands.

"Where'd you learn to do all this?" Ilana asked as she chipped reddish black dust off the gear.

Mouse shrugged. She shrugged a lot. I guess it was easier than talking.

"That whole engine just looks like a mess of metal to me," I said.

"It really isn't so hard," Mouse told us. "It's like anything else: once you understand the general principles, you can apply them across disciplines."

Mouse chewed on her lip and looked back down at the engine piece. She kept chipping away at the gunk on it. Ilana started cleaning hers again, too. I went back to feeling useless.

"I'm guessing Mouse isn't your given name," Ilana said.

Mouse shook her head. "Mercy Isabella."

"That's a big name for a small girl," Ilana said.

"Yes."

"Mercy is a pretty name, though," Ilana went on.

"It is," I agreed, because I didn't want to sit there mute.

Mouse said, "My mom named me before she left."

"Left?" I asked. "Where'd she go?"

Mouse looked past us, out over the field of cars.

"Did she get sick?" Ilana asked, her voice softer now.

Mouse shook her head. "She had to take a job down south after our dad passed."

Ilana stared intently at Mouse. Maybe she was thinking about how they were both orphans of a sort. Mouse might have family she could live with, but they weren't her real parents. Just like Ilana. And me, maybe I couldn't forgive my parents or understand the choices they'd made, but at least I had them with me every night. Or I did until I left.

13

"LADIES, YOUR GAS IS SERVED," Tommy said. And then he let out a huge, loud, impossibly long fart. This set him laughing so hard that he doubled over and held his stomach for a full minute before he said, "Good one, right? I was holding that in for hours, I think."

"Hilarious," Amnah said, her voice flat. She looked over at Mouse. "You okay?"

I didn't have a sister, of course, but I suppose if I did, and if my parents weren't around, I'd be protective of her the way Amnah was of Mouse. Ilana finished cleaning her gear and stood up. The palms of her hands had turned red from the effort, like she had been sorting wet berries.

"We also found a camshaft," Theo said, holding out a slab of metal to Mouse.

This made her grin, ear to ear. Her teeth were crooked and not such a bright white as I was used to. She would get braces if she lived in Old Harmonie. "You like puzzles, I hear," she said. "You think you know where this goes?"

"Mouse, come on, it's not like we have all day," Amnah told her.

But Theo leaned under the hood of the car. His face tightened and then he closed his eyes for a minute. I remembered what he had told me about it feeling like his brain was being pulled in a direction he couldn't control. Was that happening now? "There," he said, extending his long arm and pointing at the engine.

"Yes!" Mouse said. Then she turned to Amnah and stuck out her tongue.

Theo stood up and put his hands on his hips, but he didn't say anything. Mouse leaned over. There was some clanging and banging, and then she said, "That'll have to hold, I guess."

"Then I'll fill her up and we'll let her rip. If you'll pardon my reference to the previous gas attack."

The sun had passed over its zenith. Amnah was right: we didn't have all day. "Come on, then," I said. "Let's get this vehicle on the road."

"Seriously, Mori. You have no idea what a joy you are in for," Tommy said.

He was right. I had no idea.

Gasoline-powered cars are louder than the fans that

power the wind generators at KritaCorp headquarters and louder than the sound of all the treadmills going during the fitness test. The rumble as the car started up shocked me. We were sitting in the back, four of us wedged into the back seat. I was half on Ilana's lap and leaning against the window. Amnah and Mouse had the other half of the seat, but the sound didn't seem to bother them at all.

The inside of the car was reddish brown. I think maybe it had been fully red at one time, but no longer. The front seats were deep burgundy and the back of the passenger one had a deep slice through it out of which gray foam padding sprouted. The roof of the car was fabric of that same burgundy color. It sagged in places and was covered with pills. If fabric could be sad, then this fabric certainly was.

I thought: I will be deaf when I get home and they won't fix me because I don't have enough of my percentage left.

Ilana put her arm around me.

And then we started moving. Which was even worse. We bounced and jerked and all I could see was the blue sky and the occasional cloud, so it felt like we were rocketing through the air.

I felt it in my bones from my toes to my skull. My jaw bore the brunt of it, vibrating at such a rate I wondered if I could knock my own tooth out.

I thought: *this must be what it is like inside the old rock tumbler in the science lab at school.*

Theo, who was sitting in the front passenger seat, turned around. "You okay?" he asked.

It seemed a wonder that I could hear him. "No," I replied. I leaned my head against Ilana's shoulder and pressed my molars together.

A drone flew through the field of blue that I could see, and even though I knew they were normal out here, my heart still beat hard and fast against my chest.

But then we hit the smooth road. We didn't bounce so much. Ilana pressed a button that made the window go down and fresh air pressed against my face. This felt like going on the merry-go-round back at the playground. The wind whipped my face and tangled my hair.

"We're flying," I whispered. All the KritaCars were sealed up with tinted windows to keep the inside environment pristine, the temperature consistent. Driving with the wind swirling through the car was a totally different experience. It made my stomach drop and soar at the same time. Terrifying and exhilarating.

I squeezed Ilana's hand like that would let me hold on to the feeling. She squeezed my hand back and tucked her chin on my shoulder so she could feel the wind on her face, too.

"Pretty different from your wimpy KritaCars, huh?" Tommy asked. He tapped the dashboard. All I could see were his chubby fingers.

I tried to sit up a little higher so I could get a better view out the window. I saw a lot of trees at first. And poles with wires hanging between them. There were big signs, with pictures of people eating huge sandwiches or talking on their phones or riding strange-looking bicycles inside of bubbles. The pictures went by so quickly it was like watching a broken movie.

Faster, I wanted to tell Tommy. *Go even faster.* It felt like if we sped up we could spin right off the globe, like jumping off the merry-go-round or off the swings and flying, flying, flying before tumbling to the ground. Only in the car, we didn't have to land. We could just keep soaring.

Then the trees and the signs gave way to nothing. Empty parking lots, an old baseball field, boarded-up businesses.

"The wasteland. Twenty years ago there was a big chemical spill," Tommy explained from the driver's seat.

"A Krita chemical spill," Amnah added.

My soaring heart plummeted. I winced. First the reservoir and now this. How much land was Krita taking? Destroying?

"My uncle still owns property there," Tommy said. "He says the ground will be clean in another fifty years. It's my inheritance."

"Land baron of the wasteland," Amnah muttered.

Ilana shifted in the seat below me.

"Sorry," I said.

"You've got a bony butt is all."

My mom always said that on those few occasions when I

still tried to climb into her lap. Usually when I was really tired or really sad. *Bony butt girl.* She wasn't saying it to be mean. It always came with a snuggle. I wonder why they hadn't changed that about me? Made me a little bit stronger. That could have protected me, too. But then, that was a physical change, and most of my 30 percent was already used up, gone into fixing my eyes.

The trees and the signs started popping back up. Then the signs gave way to houses. Pointy houses and flat-topped ones. Some made of brick and some of stucco and some of what looked like wood.

"We're coming into Lincoln now. Posh posh."

"Your town isn't posh?" I asked.

Amnah laughed, but it wasn't a happy laugh. It was wiry and angry. "You knew it wasn't posh. You kept looking around like you were lost in a horror movie. Just wait until you get into the actual city," she scoffed. "Cambridge is going to blow your little mind."

"But, so, what's it really like in Old Harmonie? I mean, really?" Tommy asked.

"It's just—" I began. But how do you describe a place that's so familiar that you've never even had to think about the way it was before? It wasn't something to describe. It just was.

"All the streets are cul-de-sacs," Ilana said.

"Cul-de-whats?" Tommy asked. He slowed the car down

a little and swerved around something. It gave me time to see a big oak tree that was covered in the same ribbons we had seen back on the fence. All different colors.

"Cul-de-sacs. Little loops. All the houses are the same design. It's efficient. People are nice. People are smart."

"People are smart out here, too," Amnah interjected.

"She didn't say people weren't smart out here," Mouse said with a sigh. "Tommy asked. She's answering."

"But, like, everything's really nice, right?" Tommy asked.

"I guess, but—" I began.

"Yes," Ilana interrupted. "Everything's really nice."

"I knew it!" Tommy said. "Just you wait until I move to town. Bananas."

A pickup truck passed by our car. A big red one with flames on the side that glittered and morphed, taking on the shape of a dragon, a centaur, a Pegasus, one after the other. It made me dizzy to watch and I closed my eyes.

"Why are you so sure you're going to move there?" Theo asked.

"Simple: StepUp Charter School. You have to apply to get in and they only accept the very brightest—the best of the best. And the kids who go there go on to the top universities and, eventually, get recruited by Krita and go to live in Old Harmonie or one of the other Kritopias."

"Keep smoke blowing," Amnah told him.

"Do you go to that school?" I asked Mouse.

She just shook her head.

"I'd sooner cut my own ear off," Amnah said.

"Amnah has a chip on her shoulder, in case you hadn't noticed," Tommy said.

"It's just another way that Krita messed with us," Amnah said. "Anyway, our school is just fine."

"Exactly. It's just fine. My school is great. We are doing the exact same curriculum that is taught in the Kritopia schools. Plus added mathematics drilling. Plus—"

"Yeah, yeah. Sounds like great balls of fun."

I guess it was something about Amnah's tone, but Tommy stopped talking. Mouse examined the palm of her hand.

We shot over a bump and I rocketed forward. An arm slapped across my waist. When I opened my eyes, I was looking right into Mouse's. They were honey brown, like Theo's, but with tiny golden flecks in each iris.

"Thanks," I whispered.

Mouse smiled and moved her arm off my stomach.

"Do you, um, drive a lot?" Theo asked.

"On my uncle's lot, mostly. He taught me when I was nine so I could help him move cars around. I had to sit on books and he had these flip-flops for me that he glued blocks to so I could reach the pedals." We bounced again. Hard. "The potholes out here are wicked bad. My uncle complains about them all the time. Taxes, taxes, axles, axles. Hey, do you have—"

“You’d better not be asking them if they have potholes in Old Harmonie,” Amnah said.

We didn’t, but I decided not to say so. I peered up at the blue sky, hoping that at least it would seem familiar, but as my eyes focused I noticed drone after drone after drone. Some of them dragged signs behind them. Eat at Moe’s! Ride the Dreamline! Shop the Star Sale! Then a huge truck passed us and cut off my line of sight to the sky. Everywhere there were colors and words and objects darting about.

Tommy hit a lever and something started clicking. He turned off the main road we were on and onto a smaller, tree-lined one.

“What are you doing?” Amnah asked.

“We need to show them the forest,” Tommy said. “We’re driving right by Lincoln.”

“This isn’t a sightseeing tour,” Amnah told him. “They’re on a *mission*, remember?” She said “mission” so snidely I thought the word might break.

“But they have to see the sculptures, right? I mean, it’s a one-in-a-million shot for them, and the park is right up there.”

“Amnah’s right,” Theo said.

But Ilana looked back through the rear window, back toward Old Harmonie. The sooner we got to Cambridge, I knew, the sooner I would lose her. “How long will it take?”

“Twenty minutes, I swear,” Tommy said. “It’s like one of my all-time favorite places in the world. Sincerely.” He slid into a parking spot far away from any other spot.

"We have time now that we're driving," I said. "It's just a little break."

Ilana nodded. "Yeah, sculptures sound nice." She opened the door and climbed out. I got out after her.

Theo hesitated, then he opened the front passenger door and got out. "We can't—" Theo started.

"Yes, we can," I said. I put my hand on his arm. He looked at me and at Ilana and I guess he understood that I wasn't about to let her go.

Tommy was already skipping down the street. The town looked like a museum. There were huge churches with tall steeples. The bells in one rang out a single, clear chime just as we walked into the main part of town. Each store displayed beautiful wares in their windows, like gauzy sundresses that changed color as the sun hit their threads and a toy store full of old-fashioned, clunky but cute-looking robotics and games.

"It's kind of like Fruitlands," I said. That's where everyone went when they wanted a day away—shopping and restaurants and an amazing ice cream stand that served flavors like basil strawberry, goat cheese fig, and gooey caramel cream. This town had its own ice cream shop: Lincoln Licks. The window was painted to look like the world's biggest sundae.

The village green was mostly empty except for the geese, who paid no mind to the swan swimming in the small pond.

"Must have lost its mate," Ilana said. "They mate for life."

"That's sad that it's all alone," I said.

"Not really," she replied. "Swans are actually pretty mean."

We trotted after Tommy as he left the main street and went across the village green. It looked like there were rows of trees ahead of us, skinny ones neatly planted just like back home. When we got closer, though, I realized that they weren't live trees. They were sculptures, made of bronze, of thin pine trees. They were small. Most were just about our heights.

"Stay still," Tommy whispered. "Look closely."

So I did. I looked at the trees. Ilana stood with her back against mine staring at her own tree. I could feel her breath go in and out, could smell her sweet, familiar smell like sunscreen and sunflowers. "Oh!" she said. Just as she said it, a face appeared on the bark of the tree. It had been there all along, but I hadn't noticed it until I had relaxed. The face was wrinkled, of course, with deep-set eyes, heavy brows, and a wide, toothy smile. It wasn't just a face, either; it was a whole body. A whole person! He wore a suit, or maybe it was a uniform. It had large buttons that caught the sun and glinted at me. How had I missed them at first? Now that I saw the man sculpted in the tree trunk, it was impossible not to see him.

I started to feel raindrops on me, though there was still bright sun.

Tommy clapped his hands together. Mouse had a huge grin on her face. Even Amnah seemed a little calmer. "Wait," Tommy whispered. "Man, I wish you could see your own faces! It's almost better watching you than watching the trees."

The rain was warm and fell in big but slow drops. It dripped down my skin and sloughed off some of the salt and dirt. As the rain fell, the trees grew. The ground under us vibrated softly. Up and up and up they went. Real, live birds that had been resting in their branches flew into the sky, swooped around, then gathered in the center of the bronze forest. The trees towered over us now, the people in their trunks turned to giants. I spun around and stared up at the faces. A woman whose hair grew out into the branches, her grin like a boomerang. A man whose chest spread out wide as an ox. His mouth was open and almost-audible laughter spilled down.

"How?" I asked.

Next to me, Ilana shook her head. "It's amazing."

I put a hand on the trunk of a tree and felt it moving under my fingers. The trees were twelve feet tall now and still growing. The faces grew more distinct. And they smiled. All of them smiled down at us, inviting us to smile, too. My dry lips cracked as they spread into a grin.

"See!" Tommy cried with glee. "Totally, sincerely amazing right?"

"Yes," I said. "Thank you."

"Don't mention it," he said. He tilted his head back. The raindrops fell on his face and he stuck his tongue out to catch them.

Theo coughed. I knew what he was going to say. *It's time to go.* We'd all said it, a million times. Still, this time the words fell with added weight. We were getting closer to good-bye.

14

A SMILE STAYED ON MY own lips as we got back into the car. "What was that all about?" I asked.

"You feel better, right?" Tommy asked.

"Yes, but I still don't understand it."

"Human psychology," Tommy said. "When we see a smile, we smile, too. And the more we smile, the happier we feel."

"So that whole big thing—all those sculptures and the way they grow—it's just to make you happy?" I asked.

"You say that like it's no big thing," Amnah said.

"It's the only thing," Mouse whispered. She smiled, too.

"Thanks for showing us," Ilana said.

"Yeah," I agreed. "Thanks."

"Back on the road now," Tommy said as he started the

car. The rumble didn't seem so loud now, more like a cat purring.

Theo turned around from the front seat. "We'll be there soon," he said. "It's all going to work out." He looked at Ilana, but I got the feeling he was really talking to me.

We drove out of the town in friendly silence. All because of a sculpture garden. Maybe they were right. Maybe that's what art was supposed to be for—to bring us together, to fill us with hope.

Tommy turned the car onto the main road we'd been driving on before. The billboards came back, promising the best food, the best cars, the best experiences. After the sculptures, the signs felt cruder. They pushed their way into my head and pushed out the nice feeling the trees had given me. What a strange world that would hold those two things so closely together.

Tommy rearranged the rearview mirror. "Did you know that your body creates more than six cups of saliva every day? I was thinking there's got to be a better use for all that saliva than just swallowing it."

"Swallowing spit? That's a little gross," Ilana said.

"What? You *do* swallow it. I mean, it's only natural. And what a waste, right?"

I thought back to the statues. They must have been on hydraulics or something, but they appeared magical. They *felt* magical. It was like real, live giants were growing up next to us.

"Irrigation is the most obvious choice," Ilana said.

"Right, I thought of that. Of course."

"Of course," Theo said.

The way I felt after being with those sculptures was the way I felt in Oakedge. Like anything was possible. I settled back in against Ilana. She didn't mention my bony butt this time, but instead tucked her chin onto my shoulder.

"The problem is there's bacteria in saliva. And what if those bacteria are dangerous to the plants?"

"Filtration?" Theo said. He had turned his head so he was looking more at Tommy, and I could see circles under his eyes, but also that he was looking a little more relaxed.

"That's one option," Tommy said. He waved one hand as he spoke. "But really, then we're starting to lose efficiency."

"Shouldn't you have both hands on the wheel?" Theo asked.

"So I'm thinking gray water. I mean, not gray water exactly. But, you know how you can reuse water for like toilet flushing and stuff like that. We could add our excess saliva to the gray water, thereby using even less clean water. Pretty brilliant, huh?"

Tommy swerved the car when he slapped the steering wheel.

"Okay, that's a plausible option," Theo said.

"I really think you should concentrate on having your hands on the steering wheel," I said.

"But there is one problem," Theo went on.

"What?" Tommy asked.

"Collection," Ilana said.

"You really shouldn't encourage him," Amnah said. I wondered if she'd heard Tommy's thoughts on saliva before.

"Au contraire, my friends. I have thought this through. You know how you go to the dentist and they have that thing that sucks the saliva out of your mouth?" He turned over his shoulder to look at us in the backseat.

I didn't know much about driving cars, but I knew you were supposed to look where you were going. "Tommy!" I cried out.

"Seriously," Theo said to him.

Tommy spun his head around and looked in front of us, but he still waved his right hand around as he spoke. He tucked his finger into his mouth. "Mr. Thirsty, that's what my dental hygienist calls it. Anyway, we'd use those."

"When?" Ilana asked.

"All the time, of course. Constant collection into a little bag. Like what your friend Benji had in his pack, only in the opposite direction."

"You want people to wear those things all the time?" Amnah asked. "By the way, let me remind you that this is the kid whose plan we're all following. The kid who wants us all to go around with straws in our mouths that suck out our saliva, we're letting him lead us on this foolish errand."

“It will only seem weird at first, but then it will seem normal.”

“He’s right about that part,” Mouse said. “As for the rest of—”

But she didn’t get to finish her thought because Tommy, who had peeked over his shoulder to see Mouse as she spoke in his defense, did not see the large pothole.

Theo saw it. He yelled, “Tommy, look out!”

Tommy swerved, but it was too late. The front tire slammed into the pothole. I slid hard against Ilana, who slid against the driver’s seat, knocking Tommy forward so his foot pressed down on the gas, shooting us back out of the pothole with another *thud* as the back tire hit.

Then there was a *thud, thud, thud*. And then the car stopped.

“To be fair, we were all way into the conversation,” Tommy said. “I mean, on balance, it wasn’t just me.” He stood next to the flat front wheel of the car. The sun glinted off the windshield and into his eyes, so he held up a hand to shield them.

“Whenever you know you’re wrong, you add in all those extra words. ‘To be fair.’ ‘On balance.’” Amnah kicked the ground as she spoke.

The trunk was still open after our futile search for a spare tire. There was a jack and a lug wrench, but just air where the spare tire should have been.

The car was parked under a huge billboard that kept changing its picture. I had watched them cycle around as the others talked. An advertisement for a hearing specialist that showed a tiny man standing inside a giant ear. A picture of a bowl of fruit next to a can of juice and the words "An orchard in every glass." A pair of glasses that shimmered and shined in the late-day sun and made me touch my own glasses.

"I'm just making sure we all understand that blame can be spread around," Tommy said. He still had a hint of smile, like he was holding out hope that maybe somewhere deep, deep down he would be able to find the humor in this situation.

"Can we get another tire somewhere?" I asked.

"Not tonight," Tommy said. "All the stores will be closing soon, and there is the whole not having any more money issue."

"There's also the sun," Mouse said.

"Yeah, it's going down. I know, I know," Tommy replied.

"It's going down over there. It's setting in the direction we were driving."

"West," Ilana said.

"West," Mouse agreed.

"West?" Tommy asked. "No way."

But there was no denying the setting sun.

"Really, it was more that way," Tommy said, pointing southwest. "It wasn't strictly west. If we looked at our whole route, I bet we weren't even heading directly west fifty percent of the time."

Theo leaned back against the car. "So how far out of the way do you think we went?"

"Ten, fifteen miles," Amnah calculated.

Theo's shoulders slumped.

"It wasn't all out of the way. We needed to go south, too. It wasn't all out of the way," Tommy insisted. His cheeks turned red and he started to chew on his lower lip.

Off in the distance I could see a drone heading our way. I nodded toward it, and Theo looked up. He just shrugged. He was right. What could we do now if a drone from Krita saw us?

"What are we near?" Theo asked. "Are there any towns close by?"

"I'm not one hundred percent sure where we are. Precisely," Tommy admitted.

Ilana stretched her arms above her head, her fingers laced together. "We can't just stand here on the side of the road. Six kids and a car, that's bound to draw attention."

"So what do you suggest we do?" Amnah asked her.

"Step one, push this car onto the shoulder. Step two, head into the woods and start walking east." She looked right at Amnah as she spoke. Amnah didn't respond, but she was able to hold Ilana's stare. Ilana turned away first and shut the trunk. She probably could have pushed the car all by herself, but I didn't want the outsiders to know that, so I stood beside her, and Theo came and stood on the other side of me, and together we pushed against the rear bumper of the car.

It was actually pretty satisfying when it gained momentum and slipped onto the soft shoulder. It came to an easy stop, like a paper airplane landing on a rug.

"My uncle is going to flip!" Tommy said, but the merriment was back in his eyes. "May the road rise up to meet us," he said. "And the wind be at our back."

"It is getting pretty late," I said. "What if we go into the woods and find a place to sleep, and then go at it in the morning?"

"We've been gone all day. Everyone will be out looking for us," Theo said.

"Maybe. But I'm just so tired, Theo."

"Me too," Ilana said. "To the bone."

Theo agreed. "Let's find a good place to sit down, eat something, and then sleep for at least a few hours. Maybe we'll think of a way to fix the car or to find another vehicle. If not, we'll have to walk, and for that we'll need to rest."

I turned to Tommy, Mouse, and Amnah. "If you want to call someone to come get you or something, we'd understand."

"Yeah, about that calling. Mouse and Amnah aren't allowed to have phones and mine has been, well, let's just say its integrity has been compromised."

"He dropped it in the toilet," Amnah said.

"And flushed," Mouse added.

"To be fair, it was a particularly powerful flush. Anyway, in for a penny, in for a pound, my uncle always says."

Amnah looked over at Mouse. "We could probably hitch a ride home."

Mouse just shook her head.

"I figured as much," Amnah replied.

"Great!" Tommy said. "So we will be camping out in the woods with you tonight. You're actually lucky because I brought some beef jerky and I'm thinking I could make some soup out of it."

Ilana went into the woods first, her back disappearing between the branches of two trees. Tommy followed, still talking about the beef jerky soup. Mouse and Amnah followed, so it was just me and Theo.

"We'll get there," he said.

"I know," I agreed. "We have to."

The clearing we found was a lot like Oakedge. There was even a big, split oak, and Ilana and I climbed up into it. We turned our backs away from the others and looked out into the woods. The quiet helped me to forget about the chaos of the day, but I still felt a little unsteady, like the world was rushing by while I stood still.

"I'm glad we have a little more time," I said.

She ran her hand against the rough bark. "What do you think's going to happen once I'm with Dr. Varden? I mean, assuming she'll even have me."

"She will," I told her. "She'll keep you safe."

Ilana leaned against the trunk. "Safe out here."

"Yeah, I think so," I said.

"And you'll be back in Old Harmonie."

I tilted my head back. Farther up in the tree, a bird perched on a branch and looked down at us. It was a magnolia warbler, but it didn't trill out a warning. It just watched us with interest.

"You will, won't you?" Ilana prompted.

"If they let us back in," I said.

"Of course they will."

"How can you be so sure? We've been out here, exposed to who knows what—"

"That's your fear clouding your judgment," she said.

I turned to look at her. Her face was soft in the fading light. "What do you mean?"

"Out here, it isn't so bad as we thought. They'll disinfect you, of course, and run some tests, but you'll be fine. And you'll go back to your house on Firefly Lane. All of you will—you and Benji and Theo and Julia, all fixed up. And at first you'll talk about this all the time. About how you went outside the fences." The wind blew through the tree and tousled Ilana's hair. She kept talking. "But after a while, you'll talk about it less. And then maybe you won't talk about it at all. Once you stop talking about it, you won't think about it so much. And all of it will start to fade."

My chest tightened as she spoke. "It won't be like that," I told her.

"It will," she said. "And that's okay. Everything fades."

"Ilana."

"Really. Tell me one thing you remember from being two."

"I don't—" I began. I tried to remember something, anything. All I could pull up was the feeling of a doll's cool plastic skin against my own. "There's nothing really substantial, but I was still pretty much a baby then."

"It's not that you couldn't remember things then, though. Memories just get squeezed out of the way to make new ones."

"Unless that's your latency. Then you remember everything."

"No one really wants to remember everything."

"I do," I said.

The warbler finally decided to make a sound then, letting out a low, sorrowful trill of notes.

"No, you don't," Ilana said with such certainty, it felt like she was sucking all the air out of me.

"I want to remember you," I told her.

The bird sang some more. The notes fell on top of us. Ilana held herself so still, I wasn't sure she was even breathing. But then her hand reached out and held on to mine. Her palm was warm and her fingers laced between my own. My breathing stilled and fell in time with hers.

"I will remember you," I promised. "Always."

15

TOMMY SAT ON A ROCK and unpacked the pack he wore around his waist. He pulled out a super bounce ball, a deck of cards, and the promised beef jerky. He dug around a little more, muttering to himself. Theo and Ilana gathered sticks and dry leaves. Theo had brought a laser flick, and he got the fire going. I was glad for that—the sun was already starting to set. Tommy kept pulling things out of his bag: a spool of clear string, a flat rock, and then something black and small but heavy-looking. Tommy pushed a button and a blade swung open. I rocked back. "Is that a knife?"

"Utility knife, yeah." He used the blade to cut open the bag of beef jerky. "Well, it's not just a knife. It's a multi-tool. See?" He started pushing and pulling and revealed a second, smaller blade as well as a screwdriver, a file, a pair of tweezers, and a corkscrew. "I've never used the corkscrew," he admitted as he held the tool out to me.

Theo eyed him, and it, warily. Theo would never let me hold his knife, I felt certain of that. I let Tommy's fall into my hand. It was lighter than it looked.

"Cool, right? It's made with super-light, super-strong metal. Can't break it, but barely feel it."

I touched the tip of the smaller blade. It pressed into my skin, but didn't break it.

"Mori," Theo whispered.

Tommy reached over, put his hand on top of mine. He carefully closed the two blades. "The edges are wicked sharp. I once cut through a tin can."

Snap!

I turned my head sharply. Amnah snapped a branch over her knee.

"Oh!" I cried out.

Something warm and wet oozed on my palm. Blood.

Ilana was beside me in a second. "What happened?" she asked.

"What did you do to her?" Theo demanded of Tommy.

Tommy stood up. "I didn't do anything!"

I uncurled my hand. There was a small hole in the center of my palm. Hot blood trickled out. "I did it myself," I told them. "I was startled. I squeezed my hand."

Snap! I jumped again.

Theo turned his anger toward Amnah now. "Do you have to do that there?"

"It's okay, Theo," I said. "I'm fine. I just need a bandage. You got one of those in your bag, Tommy?" I forced a smile.

Tommy smiled back. "I think so. Hold on." After a moment of digging, he held out a wrapped bandage. Theo snatched it from his hand.

"We should clean the wound first," Ilana said. She opened a water bottle and dumped it over my hand. I bit the inside of my cheek. "Okay?" she asked.

"Uh-huh." I didn't want to tell her how much it stung.

Theo stuck the bandage onto my palm, pressing the tape against my skin with firm but gentle pressure.

"Take this, too," Tommy said. He handed Theo a roll of gauze.

"I don't need that," I said.

"It's to keep it clean and keep the bandage on." Theo wrapped it around my hand three times, then used his knife to cut the end—the same knife he'd used to cut our watchus off. Had that only been the night before? He tied it with a square knot. "Good as new."

I closed my hand into a fist and then opened it again.

"You're a warrior, Mori," Ilana told me.

"Wicked tough," Tommy agreed.

"Yeah, the kind of warrior who stabs herself with a corkscrew," I said. "Wicked stupid is more like it."

"We're gonna need more wood," Amnah said. "I don't

want to frighten you little baby bears anymore, so I'll go out into the forest and get some."

Mouse pursed her lips and poked at the small fire.

Little baby bears. Mouse was Mouse, but that was a term of endearment. Mice could be clever. Mice got things done. But baby bears? They bumbled around and made a mess of things and hid from things that shouldn't make them cower. That was me. Weak and needy and foolish enough to let my best friend get bitten by a wild dog, to not know the first thing about running away, to stab myself because I get startled by every small noise.

It was that last one that stung the most. It was like Amnah had found my sorest spot and pressed it. There was a time when a loud noise would not have made me jump like that. I might not have even noticed. Or maybe I would have liked it. I couldn't remember what it felt like before my parents dampened my bravery and made me scared and skittish. Hot anger pulsed through my veins and right to my wound. I half expected the blood to come spurting out like some sort of geyser.

"I'll go," I said.

"What?" Theo and Tommy said at the same time.

Even Tommy knew I was a wimp.

"I said I'll go. I know more about the woods than any of us. Right, Ilana?"

Ilana nodded, but her brow was furrowed.

"Okay, then," Theo said. He stood up and wiped his hands on his jeans.

"Amnah and I will be fine on our own," I said.

"Mori, I don't think—"

"Are we going or what?" Amnah asked. "I don't care who all comes, but we need to get this done before it gets any darker."

"Let's go," I told her. Then, to Theo, "We'll be back soon."

Amnah's steps were heavy and I followed her clomping while my eyes adjusted to the darkness away from the fire. My glasses gave a comforting whirr and I could see easily. Then Amnah's pace slowed and her footfalls came more quietly. I stayed a couple of steps behind and didn't say anything. Mostly, I watched her feet, which she placed carefully to avoid snapping sticks or scattering pinecones. She seemed like she spent a lot of time in the woods, though I wondered how in that paved-over neighborhood. Maybe she was one for slipping outside of fences, something I had never been brave enough to do.

"I'm surprised he let you go," she said as she came up along an old birch. The white bark peeled off its trunk in wide swirls that would burn easily. But peeling the bark off would kill the tree, something I'd never be willing to do.

"He doesn't decide for me."

Amnah just raised her eyebrows.

We kept walking up the incline, away from our friends. "It's not like Tommy makes all the decisions for you," I added.

At that, she harrumphed. "Tommy's not in charge."

The path split in two. Amnah didn't even hesitate: she bore right and I followed her. The ground up here was more thickly covered with pine needles. I thought we should go in search of oaks, which might be a little drier.

"What about Mouse?" I asked.

"What about her?" Amnah said, her voice icy again.

"You look out for her. I mean, I can't even ask about her without you getting all agitated."

"She's my sister," Amnah said. "Come on, there's nothing up here. Let's cut down this way." I followed her back toward our original trail. Our feet crunched over the ground. "The thing about Mouse is, she's got all sorts of strength, it's just not the kind you see easily."

I wondered if I had that kind of strength. The hidden kind, deep in me, like a latency ready to be set free. "So why do you need to protect her?"

"There's all kinds of strength. She might not stand up for herself, but she'll fight for the people she loves and what she believes in. She's not raising her hand and calling out all the answers, but she understands better than anyone. I just step in when someone tries to take advantage of her. When she needs me."

"We're like that, too. We're all different and we all look out for one another in our own ways." I didn't tell her why, that once we knew the truth about Ilana and Krita and what they wanted to do to her, we had to rely on each other.

"But it just seems like he's extra protective of you. Like he values your life more than his."

"That's what friends do, isn't it?" I asked. "That's why we're out here in the first place."

"That's why *you're* out here."

"And you're out here for Mouse. And probably Tommy, though you won't ever admit it."

She pushed on a dead-looking tree, but it didn't move. "Yeah. Maybe. That kid needs looking after. You haven't even known him six hours and look at the problems he's caused."

"Does she like it?"

"What do you mean?"

"Like when you talk for her. Does she ever tell you not to do it? Or do you ever think that maybe if you didn't step up, she would?"

"I'm not babying her."

"I didn't say that." I wasn't sure whether I was talking about Mouse and Amnah or my friends and me. Maybe my parents weren't the only ones to blame for my lack of bravery. Whenever something risky came up, one of my friends was there to try to stop me. I rubbed my arm.

"What is it now?"

"Nothing." The truth was I felt ill thinking of the day that

Ilana had grabbed my arm and squeezed so hard to keep me from going into number 9. I could still see that look in her eyes, cold and scared and determined. But it wasn't just Ilana. Theo hadn't wanted me to look at Tommy's multi-tool, let alone touch it. All of them had kept me out of number 9 for years.

"What does it feel like? When you're worried about her, how does that feel?" I tugged on the gauze around my bandage to tighten it.

"You don't know what it feels like to worry about someone?"

"No, of course I do. That's why we're out here, after all. I just want to know how it feels to you."

Amnah looked annoyed by the question, but then she said, "It makes me queasy. And angry at whoever might hurt her. Rage, actually. And I just want to lift her up and put her somewhere safer."

"I get that," I said. "When I found out what they wanted to do with Ilana—I mean, when I found out the trouble she was in, I started to sweat. But I was cold, too, you know?"

"Exactly," she said.

"You think that's how Theo feels about me?" Theo never looked queasy when he was stepping up to help me, he looked angry or tired or sad. Was that the same thing?

"Listen, I was just making an observation. I didn't expect the third degree." She pointed into the underbrush. "There's something there." She bent over and tugged out first one, then another long beech tree limb. It looked like a storm had come through and ripped them from the tree. The ends were jagged like a quiver of arrows with the points sticking out.

"We could carry them together," she said.

I knew they would burn easily if we could figure out a way to chop them into smaller pieces. I thought I should ask her if there was an ax in the car, or if there was something else we could use, but her face was as closed as the shutters on the common house at night. So all I said was, "Okay."

We each squatted down and took one limb in each hand. We walked like we were carrying a stretcher, which of course made me think of Julia. By now they should have brought her to the hospital. They might even have her back at Old Harmonie, safe in one of our clinics. I looked left, then right, but realized I wasn't sure where I was in relationship to Old Harmonie. I didn't know where home was. It was an unsettling feeling, like walking on the deck of a ship in a storm, and I wondered if it would ever feel steady again.

I told myself that Julia was just fine. That they had patched up her leg and shot her full of antibiotics. She was probably sleeping or, if she was really lucky, watching a Zane and River show on television. She could milk this injury for all it was worth.

I did not let myself imagine them interrogating her and

Benji about where the rest of us were. I didn't let myself imagine the angry, scared faces of our parents.

Or, at least, I tried not to.

My toe stubbed against a rock and I cursed under my breath. The limbs hadn't seemed so heavy when we started, but now I said, "I need a break."

She didn't answer, but she stopped walking and put down her ends of the tree limbs. I wished I'd brought a water bottle. Instead I rubbed my sore hand on my jeans and tried to imagine that my mouth wasn't dry.

"It's not too much farther, right?" I asked. "I can probably go again."

"Right down there."

"I thought it was to the left," I replied. My chest tightened. I was certain that we had come up the path from that direction—I remembered the way the skinny trees bent over the path—but this was Amnah's world.

"You spend a lot of time out in the woods?"

"Yeah, actually, I do." My sharp voice cut through any progress we had made. "Ilana and I were out in the woods all the time. We have our own place and know what we can eat and what we can't. Plus, we all took this wilderness course and went night camping and stuff. So, yeah, I know my way around the woods." But even as I spoke more and more, I wasn't sure if I believed myself. Maybe I was wrong. I bit my lip and told my heart to slow down.

"A wilderness course? Whoop-de-doo. Did they tell you how to destroy the forest on the first day or the second day? That's how you manage things, isn't it?"

My face turned as hot as fire embers. She didn't know what she was talking about. But then, even worse, maybe she was right? They wanted to manage Ilana by destroying her, didn't they? "That's not what it was like," I said. "That's not what *we're* like. Not all of us."

"Enough of you," she said. "Come on. This way."

"No," I said.

"What?"

"We're lost. When you're lost the best thing is to stay where you are and let other people find you. That's one of the things they taught us." My voice caught an edge. I wanted to hide it, but it was no use. My whole body tensed and shook like the leaves on the trees before a rain.

"I'm not waiting around to be rescued. No way." She started walking, dragging the branches behind her.

"We could be walking farther away from them," I called. She didn't stop. I hurried to keep up. "You're being foolish. And stubborn. We just need to stop and at least get our bearings."

Her foot hit some small loose rocks and sent them tumbling forward, cracking together in the quiet night. Their call was answered by a deep hoot.

We both froze.

My heart thudded as I raised my eyes and saw the biggest creature I had ever seen in real life. It was in an oak tree not ten feet away, but maybe twenty feet up in the air. Still, its size was undeniable. The barrel chest covered over with tawny feathers, the regal head with the thoughtful, hooded eyes.

"Great horned owl," Amnah whispered.

All I could do was nod. The feathers that looked like ears were the giveaway. My grandmother had told me they used to be called cat owls because those little tufts reminded people of a cat's pointed ears.

The breeze lifted up its feathers and it shifted its head from side to side before giving the low hoot again. Its yellow eyes never stopped watching us.

I leaned forward and my shoulder brushed against Amnah's. I heard her breathing, and maybe her heart rat-a-tatting in her chest as quickly as my own. She leaned forward, too, as if we could both push toward the owl and the owl would somehow know we were friendly, know we just wanted a closer look.

Instead the owl spread its wings wide and lifted off from the tree. I never realized how loud wings could be until they beat the air above me. For a moment it felt like the owl was going to swoop down, talons out, and snatch us up like we were a couple of field mice. Instead, it soared above us in a flap of wings that bristled the air around us. One single feather fell.

Neither of us moved.

Then we both let out our breath at the same time. "I've never seen—" I began to whisper.

At the same time, Amnah said, "That was the closest I've ever been—"

"I've read and seen pictures, but—"

"I never expected it to be so big—"

"So strong—"

"So wonderful."

Amnah took two steps forward, then bent over and picked up the feather. It looked fairly plain at first, and if we showed it to our friends they would have no way of knowing—of understanding—the feeling of having that owl look right at us, to contemplate us, and to fly away.

"I wish Mouse had seen that," Amnah said.

"Me too," I said. "All of them."

"She doesn't like animals as much as I do, but still." She shrugged, and I knew what she meant. No one could be anything but awed.

"I felt the wind from its wings," I said.

"It was warm," she agreed.

I wiped at my forehead and willed my heart to slow down. "I know it won't come back, but I still kind of want to wait for it. Like if we hold real still, maybe it will come back. Like a butterfly."

"It won't, though," Amnah said. "You're right about that.

It probably doesn't get to see too many people around these parts."

"It did look curious," I said. "Like it didn't quite believe we were real either."

Amnah smiled at that, and spun the feather in her fingers. "I guess I figured none of you folks up the hill cared very much about the creatures out here. I didn't expect to find another naturalist."

"I didn't fully expect to find nature," I confessed.

"You have forests in there?"

"You saw them on your maps, right?" But I knew that wasn't the whole truth, so I said, "Some of them are like this, all wild. But most of them are newly planted, so it's straight rows of trees all the same size."

"They clear cut for the developments?"

"I guess so. They had to do it fast once the city started flooding all the time and the measles outbreak and—"

Amnah grew still, so I stopped, too, and closed my mouth. Her face was pinched again, but I didn't know why. "Is everything okay?"

She just shook her head.

"I thought you wanted to hear about it, is all."

"Who cares about Old Harmonie?"

"Tommy sure seems to," I replied.

Amnah sighed.

Little green plants shot up between the dead leaves and

pine needles. "I'm not so sure what you're so angry about with Old Harmonie, and why you don't like any of us that are from there—"

"It's not that I don't like you," she said. "I just don't trust you."

"Why?" No one had ever said they mistrusted me before.

"You take what you want and think that paying a so-called decent price makes it okay."

"Are you talking about the trees? They did replant them. Some people think it was actually the more environmentally sustainable thing to do because then you're building all the homes at once and there's less construction waste and—"

"We didn't always live in South Concord," she interrupted. "We used to live in this town called Acton. I was two when we left, so I only remember a little bit of it. But it was a great town."

"Okay," I said.

"Tommy's family, they came from South Boston maybe twenty-five years ago. It got to be too much with the flooding all the time and people cramped so close together that illnesses hopped around from person to person and back again. A lot of families in Concord came from South Boston or Chelsea—the lower parts of the city. They've been here more than a generation, but it's like they're still there, still back in their old neighborhoods."

"They're holding on to it?" I asked.

"They're re-creating it," she said. "The same street names, the same parks, even the same pubs. One guy brought each stool over from the old place."

"I guess that makes sense. So it feels familiar."

"We don't have anything to bring over," Amnah said to me. "It's all gone. We moved out and they burned it to the ground."

"Who?" I demanded.

Amnah looked up at the moon, her jaw set.

But I knew. The reservoir. Amnah had lived in that underwater town. "I saw it," I whispered. "I saw that. Underwater, there were buildings and statues, right?"

"There was a statue garden," she said. "One of them was this giant man, he reached right up to the sky. Looking up to the future. That's what they said when it was built. It wasn't even there five years before the whole town was gone. Some future."

I sat down hard on the ground. "Now it's the reservoir."

Amnah looked down at the owl feather that she still had between her fingers. As it spun, it looked like it was ready to take flight after the owl that had left it behind. "It was supposed to be for everyone, that's what they said. It's been done before. They said that, too. For the good of many." She shook her head. "Now we don't get any of that water and we don't have our house and I have to live in the middle floor of a triple decker and never have any quiet unless I slip out into the woods."

I put my head in my hands. “We’re not all like that,” I said, shaking my head. “My great-grandmother was one of the founders and she—she never would’ve wanted it to be like that. Taking things . . .” My voice trailed off. How could I apologize for something so big with the small words we had?

The forest grew noisier and noisier around us as we grew more still. Night creatures rustled and the wind picked up, shaking the leaves even more. But none of it could drown out the truth.

16

WE SAT IN SILENCE. AFTER the owl and the truth about the reservoir, we'd both stopped moving or talking. Neither one of us said out loud that we were lost. Hopelessly lost. Somehow it was all so strange that the terror ebbed and there was weird peace like that moment just before the sun rises and nothing seems to move. I don't know how long we waited. Long enough for the moon to move. Amnah crouched on the ground next to a boulder that I leaned against. Its roughness felt good against my back.

I pictured Theo pacing by the fire. I'd been stupid, that was true. I'd taken that wilderness class. I knew we should have left blazes, maybe some little piles of rocks to mark the way we had come so we could find our way back. I could've taken Theo's compass, not that I really remembered how to use it. Amnah probably did, though. If I had taken a minute to think instead of stomping off after Amnah, we wouldn't be lost, and I wouldn't have to hear about it from Theo once he found me and got me out of trouble yet again.

Maybe Tommy would try to calm him down. And Ilana. She'd be worried, too. Amnah was right about that: they did worry about me. I scratched at a bug bite on my leg the way I wished I could scratch at the idea that bubbled in my brain. *What if . . . ?* My head would try to form the idea and then I would squash it down. Finally, it bubbled out of me: "Can I ask you something?" I braced myself for her response. Even if she said yes, it wouldn't be a nice yes.

"Shoot," she replied. Not so bad.

I rearranged the guaze on my hand and took a deep breath. "Is it really obvious that Ilana and Theo look out for me? Like on a scale of one to ten?"

"Nine," she said. "To me. I'm pretty observant. Maybe a seven and a half to other people. Why?"

"They're probably real worried back at the fire."

Amnah wiped her chin on her shoulder. "Unless you're right about Mouse thinking I baby her. Maybe she's happy to have me gone."

"I didn't mean that. I was actually thinking about Theo and what you said about him worrying about me. It's just that, sometimes I wonder if it was something they did to him. To make him watch out for me and Benji."

"The boy who stayed back in South Concord?"

I nodded.

"Because you're smaller?"

I nodded again. "In Old Harmonie, some kids are natural, and some are designed." I picked up a dried oak leaf and held it in the palm of my hands. "It's not supposed to matter. They tell us all the time that it doesn't matter."

"Of course it matters," she said.

She was right. "We don't even find out for sure until we're thirteen. That's when we get our genetic code. I always thought I was designed. I thought it was human error that made me so small and gave me this rotten retina." I pointed to my glasses.

"That kind of makes sense," she said.

"Theo got his code. He's a mix. He's designed from some DNA that he would have gotten from his mom anyway, and genetically engineered DNA, and maybe some cloned stuff, too."

"Wait, we're not just talking genetic therapy here? We're talking pick and choose?"

"Yeah. And so I've pretty much come to terms with the fact that I'm a natural. Benji, too. And I noticed how Julia and Theo were always looking out for us. After his—after his birthday, Theo even had dreams about having to save me and Benji. And I guess I've been wondering if somewhere in that mix, they put it into him that he should look out for those of us who are natural." I hadn't put all these thoughts together before. I hadn't let myself. I'd noticed things, sure, but it wasn't until we were sitting in those woods and I had nothing to do but talk to Amnah that I let myself connect the ideas and say them out loud. They made a frightening kind of sense.

"You keep talking about Theo and Julia, but what about Ilana? I mean, honestly—"

"She's different," was all I could say.

Amnah tilted her head back and looked at the sky, searching for the owl, I guessed. "We will get back to them," she said. "If they don't find us tonight, we will find them in the morning."

"Or maybe we'll all circle around and around the woods forever."

She tilted her head back down toward me. "We can't stay out here forever."

It was the truest thing anyone had ever said to me.

We heard them before we saw them: crashing, snapping, fumbling their way through the woods. We heard their footsteps and then their voices. Amnah stood up. "It's them," she whispered.

"I know," I whispered back.

"There you are!" Tommy's voice rang up the hollow, and the animals we'd been hearing fell into silence. Tommy clomped up the hill. "This one thought that you'd gone and kidnapped her, Amnah." Tommy hooked his thumb back toward Theo. "Cooler heads prevailed, though. Mouse and Ilana and I told him he was crazy. And see, look, here she is, right as salt."

"She wouldn't kidnap me," I said. "I don't have anything she wants."

Mouse frowned, confused, and Tommy shook his head.

Far in the distance, the owl hooted.

Theo said, "I didn't say she kidnapped you. I said she'd gotten you lost. Which she did."

"Maybe I got *her* lost," I replied. "I'm perfectly capable of doing that."

Tommy laughed and said, "Sure you are. Though it's not something I'd brag about."

What I'd meant was that Amnah hadn't necessarily been in charge. I'd been as much of the leader as she had. And maybe I had gotten us lost or maybe she had, but at least Amnah hadn't treated me like a child. At least she'd been honest.

"Anyway, we found some wood," I said. "We're going to have to find a way to break it into smaller pieces."

"No problem," Ilana told me. She smiled her warm smile. She was probably programmed to look out for me, too. I guess I'd known that already. They'd turned up that protective instinct too high and that's when she'd grabbed my arm to keep me from going into number 9. Was there even one part of our lives that wasn't planned and programmed for us? Maybe my parents dampening my bravery was just the tip of the iceberg of what they had done to me.

Ilana bent over and picked up both of the limbs. "Tommy's beef jerky soup is almost finished stewing." She started walking down the hill dragging the limbs behind her. Tommy followed, then Mouse.

Amnah hesitated. She glanced over at me and I thought she was going to say something, but she just shrugged before heading off after her sister.

She disappeared into the dark, leaving me alone with Theo. "You okay?" he asked.

"What if I said no?"

"What?"

I tugged the hood of Julia's sweatshirt more tightly around my face. "I mean, what if I said no. That I'd fallen and hurt myself."

"I'd get you help. What kind of a question is that?"

I shook my head. "What if I started running down this hill. Backward? With my eyes closed?"

"If you're running backward, what does it matter if your eyes are closed?" he said. But I noticed he was squeezing his hands so tightly that the muscles in his forearms were rigid.

"You'd be scared, right?"

"Confused, mostly."

I started marching down the hill—forward, with my eyes open.

Theo was right beside me. Ready to catch me, probably. I quickened my pace.

"What's this all about?" he asked. "Did something happen out here?"

I stepped around a protruding root. The last thing I wanted was for Theo to have to save me. Again. "I'm not a baby. You all treat me like I am, but I'm not. Just because I'm smaller and a natural, it doesn't mean I'm going to break."

"Did she tell you that? Did she tell you that you were weak?"

"No," I said. My foot fell hard on a pinecone, crushing it. "I'm starting to see things for what they are."

"What do you mean?" he asked.

"About you and me."

He pushed his bangs out of his face. He did have nice eyes. But would I ever be able to trust them?

"You didn't have a choice," I told him. "As soon as I said I was going, you had to come. That's what it felt like, right? Like you were being pulled?"

"I guess."

"Like when you were solving puzzles after your latency and your brain got pulled?"

Theo frowned and it was like I could see his brain

working out the puzzle of me: putting together the pieces of what I was saying, trying to make sense of it.

"Remember when Ilana hurt me?"

"How could I forget?"

"And it was because of her programming. She was trying to protect me and—"

"That's one theory."

"That's what happened. And it happens with you, too. And Julia. They put it in you. I don't know why. Maybe part of the whole community thing. Like we all need to look out for one another and they wanted to make sure it happened. And naturals are more fragile. But it's not really you thinking it. It's what they did to you—amping up your concern for the meek. Amping up your concern for *me*."

Theo was silent. I thought he was figuring out how to tell me I was wrong. But he didn't. Instead he put both hands on his head and tilted his head back to the moonlight. "When you said you were leaving Old Harmonie, my first instinct was to grab you and drag you back to your parents. Like, I had to stop myself. And then that's when I decided I'd go with you."

"To keep me safe. Not because of Ilana."

"I felt worried for Ilana, too."

"But that could be from them. I mean, of course they'd want us to look out for her, so long as that meant keeping her inside Old Harmonie. She's valuable to them." I stopped myself. "So why am I valuable to them? Me and Benji? If we're the weak and imperfect ones, why are we valuable?"

"We're all valuable. It doesn't matter if you're a natural or designed."

But that didn't sound right to me anymore. "No, there has to be something more. I don't feel that way about you guys. I mean, I don't think I do."

"When Julia was hurt, you ran to her even though the dogs were still there."

"That was different. When you guys said you would come, I didn't feel like I needed to stop you. I felt safer. I think it only goes one way."

"Well, maybe that's because we are stronger. If we're going to be stronger, then that comes with the responsibility of taking care of people who are—people who aren't as strong." He chewed on his lower lip, still processing.

"That's not the whole of it," I said. "What if—what if everyone was designed? What if everyone started from that same few sets of cloned genes, recombined and manipulated and copied over and over again?"

"There'd be no natural evolution. It would be accelerated."

"And there could be mistakes," I said. "We're the safety measure. Naturals. We're what you all can go back to if something goes wrong. If you have our genes, you can get a clean slate. That's why we're valuable."

"Mori, that's a big leap, don't you think?" He tilted his

head back down away from the sky and looked right at me, and it was like he was looking at me for the first time and wasn't quite sure how I'd gotten in front of him. "I mean, I know I like you, Mori. That's me, right?"

I shook my head. "I can't trust you, Theo," I told him. "I can't trust you because I don't know what's you and what's them."

"What do you think I'm going to do?"

"Leave," I said. "Bring us back to Old Harmonie."

"Why would I do that?" he asked. But something flickered on his face, a little twitch that told me I was hitting close to the truth.

"To protect me," I told him. "Not because you want to, but because you have to. I can see it in your face. I bet you've thought of going back a hundred times."

"We've all thought of going back a hundred times," he said. The wind picked up and shook pinecones loose from the trees. They fell around us like tiny bombs.

I pivoted to go down the hill. "I'm sorry, Theo. Maybe tomorrow morning you should go back."

Theo grabbed my shoulder, his fingers tight over my bones. "You're losing it!" he cried. We both looked down at his hand on my body. He yanked back like I was on fire. Then he rubbed his eyes hard. "I would never do anything like that. I would never betray you."

"Maybe it's not even your choice," I said.

"It is my choice! It is!" Tears sprang into his eyes. "It doesn't matter what they do to us, I still get to make choices. I get to choose who I care for, and you get to choose to be brave, and Ilana gets to choose what she really is."

"But if we can't control our own thoughts and emotions, then it isn't really a choice."

"Even if they put it into us, it doesn't make it any less real," Theo said. "So maybe they did put some little program in me—some feeling or memory or notion that I needed to watch out for you and for Benji. So what? It doesn't mean it isn't true."

"But it does!" I yelled. "If the only reason you like someone is because of a program in your brain—"

"That's the only reason anyone does anything, Mori! Our brains are programmed by genes and experience and our communities. This is just one more thing. You can't separate it from the other parts of who we are."

"But they can manipulate it. And that's what they've done to you. To all of us! It isn't real and it isn't fair!" My voice grew louder and faster as I spoke, and by the end I almost couldn't breathe. Theo's face was red and he kept blinking away tears. I suppose mine looked the same.

"Mori?" Ilana's voice came up the hill. "You guys okay?"

"Coming," I replied. My feet crunched the leaves as I trotted down to her. I almost stumbled at the bottom of the hill, but righted myself before she had to catch me.

"I heard yelling," she said.

I rubbed my eyes. "I'm really tired, Ilana. Can we go to sleep?"

She led me back to the campfire and scooped out some beef jerky soup. It tasted salty and the jerky was tough and slimy, but I ate it all.

They'd found some blankets in the car. "There's one for us to share," Ilana said. It was made of itchy wool and had a musty smell, but curled up next to Ilana, it didn't seem to matter so much. The fire was down to embers that burned red and sparked yellow. Next to mine, Ilana's body stilled as she fell asleep.

Theo's silhouette appeared on the other side of the fire. He grabbed a blanket and wrapped it over his shoulders, then sat down. He picked up a long stick and poked at the fire, sending sparks up into the night sky to join the stars.

17

IN THE MORNING, THEO WAS gone. Where he, Amnah, and Mouse had slept, there were rumpled blankets. His pack was gone and the fire was dead. I stared at the charred remains and felt the blackness come over me.

Ilana was next to me with her back against mine, still sleeping. Her breath came even and sure as a metronome. I should wake her, I thought, but I didn't.

In the brush behind us, something scampered. Some forest creature that was baffled by this sudden apparition of three children lying on the ground it had considered its own. It made a screeching, scratching noise, but then moved along to find some better, safer place.

The trees spread out over us, but in between the leaves

the morning sky was visible. Satellites spun up above us, collecting information, beaming it back down to earth. I couldn't see them, but perhaps they could see us. Anyway, so many drones had flown overhead, surely one of them had sent some imagery back to Old Harmonie.

This thought made my stomach turn even more. Maybe they knew we were out here, lost, and they weren't coming for us. I had thought being found was the worst possible outcome, but as I lay there in the cold under a scratchy blanket, I realized there could be something even worse: they weren't going to save us. They weren't going to save us because they didn't want us anymore. Theo could get out, find a town, make a call home, and it wouldn't do any good. We were stuck out here.

"Ilana!" I whispered. "Ilana, wake up!"

She kind of moaned, then blinked her eyes three times. Her face was still and cold, but then she blinked once more and there was the Ilana I knew so well. "What time is it?" she grumbled. "Are we really still in the woods? I thought maybe that was a dream or a—an experiment, I guess, something they ran through me."

"Ilana, Theo's gone! Theo and Amnah and Mouse, they're all gone!"

Tommy sat up and stretched his arms above his head. When he did, his shirt went up and revealed his pale paunch, like a deepwater fish's belly. "Gone?" he asked.

"Gone! All of them. You don't think they went together, do you?" But maybe that made sense. Amnah was done with our escapades. And Theo was done with me. So they'd left together while we slept.

"No worries," Tommy said. "They'll be back any minute, I bet. They wouldn't leave without telling me."

I wanted to believe him, but I still had a cold pit in my stomach. Ilana stood up and put her arm over my shoulder. "Theo would never leave you here."

"I told him to go last night," I said.

"You told him to go before, too, and he stayed," Ilana replied as she zipped her sweatshirt up closer to her chin. Her breath made small puffs.

"Exactly. I keep telling him I don't need him, and now he's finally listened to me." With Amnah and Mouse. That was the strangest part. Was it just a matter of convenience, or was something else going on?

"What are you thinking?" she asked.

"I think Theo and the others are going back to Old Harmonie. Or they're contacting Old Harmonie somehow."

"What are you talking about?"

"It's like number nine all over again! When you wouldn't let me in. They programmed you for that—to watch out for me and to keep us out of there. Right? Right? And it's been coded in Theo all this time, too. Amnah even noticed it, the way he watches out for me."

"It's not exactly hidden," Tommy interjected.

"And he slept and that was like a reset maybe."

"He's not like that," Ilana said, and I knew she meant *not like her.*

"I told him! I told him I couldn't trust him because I didn't know if he really cared about me or if the stupid Krita people made him care about me. And he said no, but he had time to think on it and his brain, it pulled him and told him he had to protect us, he had to get us home."

Ilana rubbed her nose. "I guess all of that is possible," she said.

"It is?" Tommy asked. "What do you mean it's coded in him?"

I shook my head. "It's really, really complicated."

"It's not all that complicated," Ilana said. "The adults in Old Harmonie, they have a certain degree of control over the kids."

"Their emotions?" Tommy asked, eyes wide.

"Their behaviors, and I guess, sure, their emotions."

Tommy wrapped his arms around himself. "Like with a remote control?"

Ilana smiled. "Not exactly. It starts with genetics. Then there's some targeted brain stimulation techniques to get some behaviors in line."

"Whoa," he replied.

Above us, a chickadee called out and another answered. *Chickadee-dee-dee. Chickadee-dee-dee.*

Tommy took out a laser flick and held it to some dry

leaves. I could practically see his brain working as he built the small fire. The flames cast an orange glow over his skin. "It's all about synapses and connections and hormones and memory—" he said.

"That's part of it," Ilana said.

"But what do they *do*?" he asked.

"I don't know," I said. "Maybe nothing." Or, I thought, maybe something that makes your friends abandon you in the middle of the night because they think they're helping you. "We should get going."

"Going? To Cambridge?" Tommy asked.

"We can't sit around waiting for them," I replied, a little sharply.

"I just got this fire going," Tommy said. "Don't you want to warm up? Have some breakfast?"

"Do we have any breakfast? Theo had the protein bars. I have half a sandwich left. That's it."

"I have an apple," Ilana said.

We used Tommy's knife to slice the apple and we tore the sandwich into three equal parts. That was breakfast.

"I really thought they'd be back," Tommy said as he stomped out the fire with his heavy boots. "Well, at least you're left with me." He put on a smile as he re-strapped his pack around his waist. "And traveling with three is easier. We might even be able to get on some public transit. Save time that way."

"You don't have to be fake-jolly for us," I told him,

scratching at my palm through the bandage. The wound itched now as it started to heal.

"Fake-jolly? My jolliness is one-hundred-percent grade-A-certified real and true, I'll have you know." His smile grew a little warmer. "Come on. Miles to go and all that."

He set off through the woods, and Ilana and I followed him. We'd just gone up a slight rise and were headed over the top when we heard the yelling.

"Hey! Hey! Where are you going?"

Amnah. It was Amnah!

I turned around and when I saw Theo rolling a tire—a tire!—through the woods, it was all I could do not to run and hug him.

"Mouse had an idea in the middle of the night," Amnah explained.

"A dump," Theo said. "It's where they keep all the stuff they throw away. And they throw away a lot. Perfectly good things just piled up."

"Most of it comes from you guys," Amnah told him. "You send us your castoffs and then we have to deal with them."

"Anyway, Mouse says it's the right type of tire for the car."

"Hot dang!" Tommy exclaimed. "I knew I loved you, Mouse. We'll be rolling again in no time!"

I looked at Theo, but he looked away. The night hadn't smoothed things over. If anything, something in him had hardened. I stayed by Ilana's side as we walked back toward where we'd left the car. It was still there, dull as chalk in the morning sun. Tommy took a seat in the shade while Amnah opened up the trunk. She handed what looked like a folded metal arm to Theo. He held it for a second, confused, but then he squatted down next to the car.

"Quick learner," Tommy said.

"You're not helping with the tire?" I asked.

"Division of labor," he replied. "In other words, not my department."

Mouse walked in front of him and sniffed the air, but didn't say anything.

"You should sit down, too, Mori," he said. "I get the feeling you aren't exactly a tire expert either."

I held up my good hand to shield my eyes so I could see him in the glare. His skinny legs poked out of his shorts, and his bright blond hair stuck up in all directions.

"Not exactly," I said.

"So take a load off. Save your energy for later. That's the smart thing to do." As if he could sense me looking at his hair, he pulled out a ball cap, one with a red *B* on it, and put it on his head. "I know exactly where we are now. Let it never be said that Tommy McPhee is a man without a plan."

"I didn't see you at the dump getting a tire," Amnah said. "Anyway, we never said you didn't have a plan. We said that you didn't have a good plan."

Amnah situated the tire jack under the car and Theo started cranking a handle. His forearm tensed with each turn, but it was nothing compared to the harsh set of his jawline.

"But what is a plan really?" Tommy went on as if nothing was going on around him and we were all rapt with attention. I liked that about him. "If it goes off course a bit, but works out in the end, that's not a problem with the plan itself. I mean, it's still a good plan, just one made better by improvisation."

"Clearly no dampening ego out here," I joked.

Theo looked at me, finally, but only for a second, and his eyes were dark.

"Dampen?" Mouse asked. Her back was to me and she watched as the car was lifted up.

I glanced at Ilana. "It's just a thing we do," I said.

Mouse turned so she was in profile, not looking at me, but not looking away, either. "Does it hurt?" she asked. Her voice was so small, I felt myself leaning in to hear her.

Ilana shoved her hands into her pockets. "I'm not sure," she replied.

"I've only had it done once, I think. And I was already sick. But I don't think it hurt much."

"What did they change?" Mouse asked.

A *clang* came from over by the car. Theo rubbed his knee. "Sorry," he mumbled as he restarted the crank. His hair was all mussed but, for once, was out of his eyes. He stared right past Mouse and at me, but I wasn't sure what message he was trying to send, whether he wanted me to tell her or not. Maybe he wanted to hear for himself.

Amnah and Tommy were still now, too. Tommy had lifted himself up so he was sitting on a log. He pushed his ball cap back from his face.

I said, "I used to be braver. Maybe a little too brave. My parents worried I might do something foolish and hurt myself, so . . ." I took a deep breath. Even the birds listened to me. "So they dampened my bravery a little bit and made me more cautious."

Amnah blew the air out between her teeth, but she didn't say anything. Theo kept looking at me.

"It was to keep me safe," I said. I believed that. I was still angry, but I really did believe that my parents had made the choice to keep me safe, and it felt important that these people from outside of Old Harmonie knew that. Our parents were making all these choices because they thought it was what was best for us.

"Well," Tommy said with a laugh. "I guess that procedure didn't work very well."

"What do you mean?" I asked.

"Here you are, aren't you?"

Ilana threw her arm around my shoulder. "You're right about that. Mori's the bravest person I know."

18

MOUSE AND AMNAH TOOK THE front passenger seat. Mouse spread the map out over her lap.

"We figured we'd better have a navigator, and Mouse is the best," Amnah explained. Ilana climbed in back first, then Theo, which meant I had to sit next to him. I tried to scooch so our bodies didn't touch. There wasn't quite enough room to avoid touching, though, so I turned away from him and looked out the window as Tommy started driving.

Almost immediately, we entered a town. White clapboard houses with black shutters lined the streets. They reminded me of number 9, and I was glad when we passed through the downtown area. We passed a huge store with pictures of bread and fruit and fish in the windows, blown up to ten or twenty times their actual size.

"This is Lexington. Like as in the Battle of, way back in the Revolutionary War. It's real posh. You've got to have clams galore to live here. They say their school is even better than StepUp, maybe even better than the Kritopia schools, but I don't believe it."

It was a little strange to be driving through this town that reminded me of home. It was like we were on a Möbius strip going round and round and upside down and never quite getting anywhere, but never leaving anywhere either. And all the things we'd been taught about the outside world—dirty, scary, dangerous—those things were wrong and they were right. It's like everything contained its opposite, and that made me dizzier than anything else. And all the while, Theo kept his stony face tipped up and away from me.

"You know where we're going once we get to MIT?" Amnah asked.

Theo said, "The Gehry building, we think. Over near Massachusetts Avenue." At least I knew he could still talk.

"Call it Mass Ave unless you really want to draw attention to yourselves," Tommy said. "Mass Ave in C-Town."

"Cambridge is not C-Town," Amnah told him.

"Says you," Tommy replied.

"Maybe we could just be quiet for the ride," Theo told them. "I'm sure you all are tired, and we've got some thinking to do. At least, I do."

He still wouldn't look at me. I pressed my forehead to the

window. Each time we bounced, it jostled me and my head hit against the glass, but I didn't say anything. I didn't even groan.

They said it wouldn't be much farther now. That was good. Soon we'd be with Dr. Varden and she'd be able to take care of things. I wouldn't have to worry anymore.

I must have fallen asleep, because then Theo was nudging me, and Tommy announced, "Welcome to the People's Republic of Cambridge, home to Harvard, MIT, and almost a million people."

"Really?" Theo asked.

I sat up and looked out the window.

Cambridge was busy. And dirty. And confusing. People crowded the sidewalks in front of brick and cement buildings of various sizes. Bright shop signs flashed and streetlights flashed and even people's clothes flashed with tiny lights. I rubbed my eyes.

"This isn't what I expected," Theo whispered beside me.

When I looked up at just the tops of the buildings, I could see that many of them were quite old, with interesting details like bricks stacked in curved arches or windows as tall as a room. But when my gaze drifted down, all I saw was chaos.

Our car was barely moving through the traffic of old cars

and newer electro-solar ones, of motorcycles and scooters and bicycles. The sidewalks, too, were jammed. I had never seen so many people in my life. Theo was wide-eyed, but Ilana sat still looking straight ahead.

"We need to get off this main road," Amnah said. "We're starting to get some looks."

Tommy nodded and then, without warning, dragged the steering wheel to the right. I don't know how we didn't hit anyone. Maybe they were used to these sudden turns from drivers. The pedestrian traffic shifted to allow us through.

I put my hand over my mouth.

"Can you take it a little easier?" Theo asked. "Please."

"Sorry, folks. Turbulent conditions, you see. But it'll be smoother from here on out."

Smooth sailing. My stomach lurched again. "Maybe we should pull over here and walk."

"According to the map, we're only a couple of blocks away," Amnah said. "It's not a terrible idea." Which, I supposed, was about as close to a compliment as I was ever likely to get from her.

"It's all parallel parking," Tommy said. "I don't know how to parallel park. Not yet. Actually, I'm not much good at regular parking, either. Unless there are no cars around. And then I'm okay. Excellent, actually. Do you think we could find a big lot somewhere? Is there anything showing on that map?"

"Anywhere we go, there will be lots of cars," Amnah said with a sigh.

So Tommy kept driving. Occasionally he would hit the brakes and then say, "No, no, no."

"I can't!" I finally called out. "I'm going to throw up!"

"Vomit!" Tommy yelled. "We have a vomiter. Repeat! We have a vomiter!" And he jerked the car to the side.

I grasped at the door handle and pushed it open just in time to lean my head out and empty my stomach of its apple, sandwich, and beef jerky soup.

I felt two hands on my back and a soft voice said, "It's okay, Mori. It's okay." That's what my mom had said to me when I'd first gotten sick as a little kid. I'd thrown up and she'd rubbed my back and said, "It's okay. It's okay." But then I'd kept throwing up and it hadn't been okay. This felt so much like that, I retched again. Nothing came out this time but a thin stream of watery bile. I used the back of my wrist to rub my lips and sank back into the car.

It was both Theo and Ilana with a hand on my back. They didn't even look disgusted. I stared at my lap.

"We good?" Tommy asked. "You okay back there, Mori?"

"Are you?" Theo asked me.

I nodded.

"She's okay."

"There's a spot up ahead that's pretty big. I'm just gonna try to nose in as best as I can. I mean, what's the worst that can happen to this beater? It gets hit? I mean, car, you've been a real lifesaver, but you aren't exactly beautiful. Don't hold that against me or anything. We still need to get home."

The car inched forward and he eased into the spot, pulling forward, then sliding back. He turned off the engine, then put both hands on the steering wheel. "So," he said. "What next?"

19

WE PARKED ON A CORNER near a small playground. Kids were running around on the snatch of green grass that was smaller than any backyard on Firefly Lane. Their laughter flew out toward us. My stomach was still unsettled and the ground felt unsteady beneath my feet. Maybe *I* was glitching now.

Theo said, “It’s number thirty-two Vassar Street. I had the city map pretty well in my head, but I’m turned around now. Give me a minute.”

Tommy, though, stopped the next person walking by. “Excuse me, sir, which direction is Vassar Street?” he asked.

“Right up there, then go two blocks, then you’ll intersect it,” the man answered without even stopping.

Ilana took my hand and helped me up onto the sidewalk. "Drink some water," she said.

"I don't know if I'm still feeling sick because of the car or because, well, because of her. Of finally meeting her."

"Me too," Ilana said. Then, again, "Drink some water."

I took a long sip while Tommy set off with Mouse right behind him. Amnah said, "It's not far now." She hesitated a moment, like she might say something else, but then she shrugged and followed her sister and Tommy.

There were throngs of people on the sidewalk. I held tight to Ilana's hand, not wanting to lose her, or, really, not wanting her to lose me. Some of the people wore masks over their faces, and they all had clothes that covered the skin on their arms and legs. The fabric appeared very lightweight and came in bright colors that swirled together so it was like we were walking through a maze of gauzy clouds. Tommy would disappear and then reappear. I had only his baseball cap with the green shamrock on the back to guide me. Amnah stayed close to Mouse, but kept looking back at us, and Theo stayed behind. I wondered if anyone even realized we were all together, this strange procession.

When we turned onto Vassar Street, the crowd thinned out. Most of the people here were younger. Their clothes were a little more subdued. They wore headphones and when they spoke, it was into the little mouthpieces that curved around their heads. I didn't know if they were speaking to one another or to people miles and miles away. But it was quieter here, and I took a deep breath. My feet moved more slowly, too, and Ilana tugged me a little to keep up.

"I don't know why you're so nervous," she said with a smile. "It's my life that's in her hands."

"That's why I'm so nervous," I told her.

I stopped and she looked right at my face. Her eyes were that remarkable color, and I knew I would never know anyone with eyes like that. Sure, maybe someone else would be designed with that color, but there would never be anyone else who I could look at their eyes and they would look at mine and we'd just know.

A man cut between us. He didn't even look at us, just walked right on through while he tapped at a screen that was part of his sleeve and laughed under his breath.

"You're my best friend."

"Forever sisters."

"No matter what happens in there."

"No matter what happens," she said, and squeezed my hand.

My cheeks were hot and my eyes burned with tears that I fought to keep inside. Of all the times I needed to stay brave, this was it. This was the last step. We had gotten Ilana this far, and now she was going to be safe. We had done it. I just needed to walk through that door.

Theo came up beside us. "You ready?" he asked.

We nodded and the three of us walked side by side down the sidewalk.

I knew which building it was without even seeing the number. In between the regular brick facades were silver sides that bent at odd angles. I put my hand over my stomach, afraid I might be sick again.

"Come on," Tommy called. "The door's wide open!"

The floor was marble, or some sort of swirly rock: gray and silver and even flecks of gold. There were tall columns of rock, too, like the whole building had been carved out of an ancient cave. But my eyes kept being drawn to the splash of red against the wall. Paint? Fabric? It was too hard to tell.

Students and researchers and professors sat at small tables, but none of them noticed us. The noise of their conversation echoed around the room and burst into my ears. I closed my eyes and took a deep breath.

"There should be a directory somewhere," Tommy said.

"See sale," Ilana said. Or maybe it was "Sea sail."

"Like a boat?" I asked. My eyes went back to the red. I supposed it did look a bit like the sail of a boat.

"What?" Theo asked.

Ilana spelled it out: "C-S-A-I-L. Computer Science Artificial Intelligence Lab. My parents used to work there. That's where . . ." Her voice trailed off and she shook her head. "It's all so fuzzy."

"CSAIL is like every floor here. Do you have any more details?" Tommy asked.

"Artificial intelligence?" Amnah asked. And I watched the realization come over her face. She didn't get all the details, of course, but it came to her what Ilana was, or at least part of what she was.

"It's not what you think," I told her. "Not wholly."

She stepped away from us.

Across the room, someone laughed: loud and throaty.

"Varden," Theo said. "Is that name anywhere?"

Tommy used his finger to scan through the names on a directory screen. "Nothing is showing up."

"Really?" Theo asked. He stepped closer to the screen.

Mouse cleared her throat. "You'll be okay," she said to Ilana.

Amnah said, "A whole person? They made a whole person?"

"You'll be okay," Mouse said again.

"Wait," Theo said. "Here. Lab number nine. That has to be it, right, Mori?"

Be brave! I told myself. *You can do this. You can do this for Ilana.* I didn't even know what I was afraid of, and perhaps that was the most frightening thing of all.

"That's it," Ilana said. She rubbed her temples.

"It must be, right, Mori?" Theo asked.

All I could do was nod. I squeezed my fists and forced myself to talk: "Yes, that's it."

"All right, then. Second floor. Stairs right there," Tommy said. "What are we waiting for?"

But none of us moved.

The people around us stilled. Or maybe it was my eyes and my ears that stopped working. What I saw and what I heard was no longer crisp. I pulled off my glasses and cleaned them. The camera whirred when I put them back on my face. It didn't help.

"Come on," Ilana said. "All we can do is face this."

She led the way to a set of stairs at the back of the room. The stairs were normal size, but they seemed enormous, and like they stretched out for miles and miles. Really only about a minute passed until we were on the second floor and following Tommy and Theo down the hall. Mouse walked next to Ilana and me, while Amnah held back. I wondered if she would run off. She didn't owe us anything, so I wouldn't blame her.

The doors were painted bright colors and had windows like portholes on a ship. I peered inside but all I could see were people working at desks and the occasional robot.

Number 9 was at the end of the hall.

Without even hesitating, Tommy grabbed the handle, turned it, and pulled the door open.

20

THE WOMAN STANDING IN THE center of the lab seemed impossibly small. She wore wide-legged pants and a button-down shirt with a painter's apron over it. The lab had a metal table at the center, slate countertops all around. Above the counters were high glass cabinets filled with beakers, scales, tablets, and more. All these things dwarfed the woman, who was both one-hundred percent familiar and one-hundred percent strange. Maybe I swayed a little bit. Ilana held on to my elbow.

"Little Mori," the woman said. "How long I've waited to meet you."

My body pressed against Ilana's.

"Dr. Varden?" Theo asked.

"Yes, I am Agatha Varden. And you must be the Staarsgard

boy," she said. She shrugged off her lab coat and hung it on a red hook beside a door on the far side of the lab. "Here is not the place for a reunion. Come with me."

None of us moved. Ilana held me up.

"We really must be going," Dr. Varden said.

"Where?" Theo asked.

"Someplace safer." She glanced toward the window. The sun beat off the metal sides of the building.

She had the same features as in all the pictures I had seen of her, of course, but wrinkled. It was as if someone had drawn a sketch of her in pencil, then smudged it over.

"But where?" Theo pressed.

Dr. Varden turned to me. "Lucy and I had a deal. The kind that doesn't need to be spoken. We looked out for each other. And that means I'm looking out for you."

Ilana squeezed my arm gently. I blinked hard. I was still having trouble making the world come into focus. But there was Theo, his hands clenching and unclenching. And Tommy, his gaze taking in every last detail of the lab, a slight smile on his lips. Amnah, her jaw tight, standing right behind Mouse, who looked as confused as I felt. I realized they were all waiting for me to make a choice. But how could I make a decision when Ilana was the one at risk? My breath came in shallow gasps. "Ilana?" I whispered.

"We should go," Ilana said.

"Are you sure?" I asked.

Ilana nodded. "I think she means it about your baba. It's how I feel about you."

"Okay," I said, quietly at first. "Okay. Let's go."

"Good."

Dr. Varden strode out of the lab and we all scurried after her.

Theo fell into stride with me. "We're going to be okay. She's going to help us," he said. "But if something goes wrong, I want to have a way out."

"Okay," I said. But I didn't know what he meant, where we would go, or what he was planning.

Agatha pushed the button on the elevator and the doors opened immediately. We stepped inside. She didn't push the button for the first floor, but instead one marked "G."

"What's that floor?" Theo demanded.

"Garage. We'll go out the back door. It's closer to my street."

"You're taking us to your house?" I asked.

"Yes. We can talk more freely there." She tucked a stray lock of gray hair behind her ear. "Not everyone at the university is on board with the work that Krita does. And some are very much involved. Either way, it's better that we stay out of their line of sight, if you will."

"What do you mean?" Tommy asked. "I thought this place was like a pipeline to Krita."

"It has been in the past. And it still can be. There's always been a tension between the academic and the corporate worlds. It's grown stronger as Krita keeps pushing the outer limits with little regard to . . . repercussions. But really, we should wait until we get to my house. You all look hungry and tired. We'll get you freshened up and then we can talk more."

"What street?" Theo asked. "What street is your house on?"

I knew Theo had memorized the map of the city. Now he was planning all possible escape routes, thinking of all possible emergencies. If-thens, the ultimate logic puzzle.

"Athenaeum Street," she said as the elevator doors slid open to reveal a flat gray expanse dotted with cars both new and old. Cool, metallic-smelling air rushed to meet our faces.

"All these people drive here?" I asked.

"We encourage public transportation, of course, but many of our researchers are coming from quite a distance, and occasional public health issues make the subway system a less than ideal mode of transportation."

"Is there a public health situation right now?" Theo asked.

"Code level yellow—just the normal pathogens. Nothing out of the ordinary."

"Normal pathogens?" I repeated, and swallowed.

"It's fine," Tommy told me. "You've got all your vaccines and your antibodies. No worries, okay?"

But as Agatha led us out onto the busy streets of Cambridge, I could feel my chest grow tight. The streets were teeming with people. They brushed up against us as we made our way northeast. Someone coughed beside me, loud and phlegmy. I put my hand over my mouth and nose.

This was what we'd been warned about all our lives—the people, the lack of control. There could be a public health outbreak and they didn't even keep people at home, just told them to avoid public transportation. Tears stung in my eyes.

Agatha turned and suddenly there was quiet all around us. "Not much farther," she said. She turned over her shoulder to look at Theo. "You've got it all locked away in there?"

He looked surprised, but he said, "Yes. I do."

"I'm glad she has friends like you."

We passed a park with red bushes and hedges cut into a circle. No one played inside.

"Right here," Agatha said. She led us up the walkway and brushed her hand over a silver box next to the door. The door swung inward. "Come on in. Make yourselves at home. I'll get us some lemonade."

The hallway was cool and dark. It was painted a pale blue and lined with pictures. Pictures of bees, of scientists in lab coats, of Old Harmonie in the old days. Then there was Baba, looking right back at me. Smiling. I wanted to believe that she was telling me I was safe here. That we all were.

Mouse, Amnah, and Tommy were already in the kitchen.

I could hear their voices coming down the hall. Tommy told her that they were from South Concord, and Amnah said that yes, lemonade would be great. With Theo and Ilana in front of me, though, I couldn't see the kitchen until I stepped into it. When I did, my vision swirled.

Yellow walls. White cabinets. Tile floor.

It was exactly the same as the kitchen in number 9. Exactly. Right down to the bright curtains on the window above the deep, white porcelain sink. My legs tingled and then gave way as the lights went out around me.

Ilana's and Theo's faces were inches from my own. My retina camera whirred as it tried to bring them into focus.

"Too close," I mumbled.

They sat back a little bit. "Are you okay? What happened?"

"It's this room—" I began, then shook my head. I still felt groggy.

Ilana looped her arm around me and pulled me up to a sitting position.

Dr. Varden squatted down next to me, gently pushing Theo out of the way. She put her hands on my cheeks and stared right into my eyes. "I'm afraid this is all a little too much." She turned to Ilana. "Help her into a chair."

Ilana carefully tugged me to my feet and guided me over to a chair.

Off to the side, Amnah, Mouse, and Tommy stood silently. Of course I'd gone and embarrassed myself in front of them. And Dr. Varden. She opened a bottle of water and placed it down in front of me. "Sip slowly," she instructed.

I did as she said.

"So you've been in my house on Firefly Lane?" she asked.

I nodded. I was sweating all over. Cold sweat from head to toe.

"She always wanted to go in," Theo explained. "We told her not to, but then—"

"And what did you find in there?" Dr. Varden asked.

Theo and I exchanged a look. "Mori found a robobee," Ilana told her.

"Prince Philip, yes," Dr. Varden said.

Theo drummed his fingers on the table.

"Did you go onto the computer?" she asked.

I sighed. Theo said, "Yes, we did."

"I know we aren't supposed to use other people's technology, but Julia booted it up and we started looking and—" I glanced over at Ilana. I couldn't say out loud what we had found on the computer.

"Official files rarely tell the whole story," Dr. Varden said.

"So what is the whole story?" Ilana asked.

Dr. Varden, though, shook her head. "In time. Look at you all. You're filthy and tired. We already had a slump from little Mori. Plus, my goodness, is that a bandage on your hand? Have you been hurt?"

I squeezed my hands shut. "It's fine."

"Well, it ought to be cleaned. I think I can find some clothes for you all." She looked at Ilana and Theo. "Even, perhaps, for the giants amongst you. There are bathrooms on the second and third floors—a shower in each of them."

"We don't have time for this," I told her, my voice sounding far stronger than I felt. "We need to make sure Ilana is safe."

Dr. Varden rose to her feet. "I'll gather those clothes and you get cleaned up and then we can talk about our plans, okay? There's no sense making a plan when your brain isn't at full capacity."

I shook my head. This didn't seem right. But Ilana said, "She's taking care of us. We need to do this her way, all right?"

Since Ilana was the one in real danger, I agreed.

The shower felt like summer rainstorms, cool and warm and strong and soft all at once. It stung my open blisters and the cut on my hand at first, but that gave way to a low ache, and the clean wound really wasn't so bad. I let the water rush over me and watched as brown pooled at my feet. I had been covered in sand and silt and even old charred coal from the train tracks. With my skin clean, I could see the insect bites that dotted my skin like red, raised freckles.

When I got out, I wrapped myself in a warm, thick towel, then put on the oatmeal-colored linen sundress that Dr. Varden had left for me. I did feel much better, more like myself, but also like I was in a play. My skin smelled odd to me, like the lemon soap I had used to wash myself. The dress was a strange costume, made all the more strange because my friends were clad in similar flowing, washed-out-colored clothing. Theo looked the most out of place in his sleeveless shirt with mother-of-pearl buttons and pants that fell just below his knees, all in a pale avocado color.

Ilana, of course, looked like the clothes were made for her: a simple sundress like my own, but in a pale blue-green that matched her eyes and made them flash.

They were all in Dr. Varden's living room: Mouse and Amnah on the couch in matching short-sleeved shirts, Tommy on a chair that reminded me of Theo's furniture back home. Theo himself stood by the window, his gaze trained outside. Ilana sat on the floor next to Agatha. Together, they looked at a photo album.

"There she is," Agatha said. "I worried you drowned."

"It's a nice shower," I said. Then, because no matter the situation, I knew to be polite, I said, "Thank you for letting me use it. And for the dress."

"Your great-grandmother always loved dresses. She always had a new dress or skirt. Pretty ones with big, bold patterns."

"Flowers made her happy." Baba had always loved fresh flowers. She kept her small apartment full of them, and every time we came to visit, Dad and I would make a bouquet for her. I remembered sitting in a KritaCar, holding the vase carefully so the water didn't spill. And I remembered the smile that came over her face when she opened the door and I peeked through the flowers at her.

Dr. Varden turned the page, then activated a holopic of Baba. She stood right in a field of wildflowers. Beside her, a small child—my grandmother, I realized—blew the seeds of a dandelion. Behind them was a chain-link fence woven through with ribbons whose tails fluttered in the breeze. On the other side of the fence were tall trees, oaks and pines. "Wait," I said. "That's our fence. Out in the woods past Firefly Lane."

"More or less," Agatha replied.

"She's standing in Oakedge," I said to Ilana. "But where are all the trees?"

"Beneath her feet," Agatha said.

I shook my head. The topsy-turvy feeling was coming over me. "No way," I said. "Those are old-growth trees. And that picture was taken, when? Sixty, seventy years ago, max."

Amnah stood up and started walking along the edge of the room. She pulled back the gauzy curtain and peered out the window.

"Sixty-seven, to be precise," Dr. Varden said. "And you're right. They are old-growth. Cut them down and you'll count a hundred fifty rings, maybe more. It was a side project of your great-grandmother's. Reforestation. Trees would grow more quickly at first, then level off. She made it work, too."

"Like the sculptures," I said, thinking of the smiling trees.

"I've never heard of that," Theo challenged.

"You've probably never heard of a lot of what we did."

"But that's major," Theo said. I stared at my baba, young and happy in the field of wildflowers, the trees ready to push their way through the soil below her. As always, it filled me with a mix of awe and insignificance. She'd done so much. Theo kept talking: "Rapid reforestation could be global. Even right here in Boston. If we planted more trees down by the flooded areas, they'd absorb the excess water. And in the rainforests—everywhere. The trees could've slowed down climate change."

"That's exactly what Lucy thought," Agatha said.

"So what happened?" Tommy asked. "Did something go wrong? Did the trees grow so mammoth that they swallowed whole cities?"

"Nothing like that. It worked very well. I'm sure Mori can attest to that if she's been out in that forest. If anything, it worked too well."

"How can something work too well?" Tommy asked. "Let me tell you, when my spit solution takes off, there will never be enough spit."

"It worked and so Krita tried to take advantage of it, right?" Amnah asked from the window. "What? Did they set up whole forests of it just to cut it down?"

"Precisely," Dr. Varden said.

"How'd you know that?" Tommy asked.

"Because that's how Krita operates."

"You're not wrong about Krita, Amnah," Agatha said. "But cast your net a little wider. Greed goes beyond one corporation, however large it may be."

Ilana sat curled up with her knees to her chest. She stared at the holopic of my great-grandmother, too. All of us sat so still in our simple clothing, sipping lemonade like this was a weekly visit to our relatives. It was so easy to fall into complacency, but the little twitch-tap of Ilana's foot on the floor reminded me that this was not the truth. "This isn't why we're here," I said. "I can learn about my great-grandmother at home."

"Why are you here, little Mori?"

"You know! We need your help."

"Ilana needs my help," Agatha said.

"Yes," Ilana said. "I do."

I stepped closer to Agatha. "They want to scuttle her. She didn't work out the way they wanted and so they want to get rid of her. But that's not how science works, right? That's what Baba always said. That when it doesn't work, it's a chance to make it better. It's a responsibility. And anyway, that's not what people do to each other. You don't get rid of people because they're inconvenient to you."

Theo stepped away from the window. He came up next to me and put his hand on my arm. "We need someone to convince them that they're making a mistake. Or someone to take care of her," he said. "We need someone to help her." His voice cracked. His hand slipped down, and I clasped it in my own. With my other hand, I reached toward Ilana. She stood, and took it.

"Just look at you three," Agatha said, and shook her head.

We must have looked odd, standing there in her living room holding hands, but I wasn't letting go until I was sure Ilana was safe.

"It's best, I think, to go back to the beginning in cases like this," Agatha said. She stood up herself and went to the bookshelf, where she removed another album. "I'm not sure you even understand what you are, child. I'm not sure any of you do." She put the album down without opening it. "Lucy always said that scientists needed open minds to dream big, but common sense to hold themselves to the ground. It's actually a hard combination to find. I didn't always have it, but she kept me in check. If you don't have someone to keep you in check, then you muck about and make messes you can't clean up. Even when you think you've cleaned them up, they come back."

Ilana stiffened, but she didn't look away from Agatha.

"She's not a mess to be cleaned up," I said.

Dr. Varden turned to look at me. Her eyes were bright and flashing. "Isn't that why you came to me? To clean it up again?"

"She's not going to help," Amnah said. Her voice was low and quiet. Beside her, Mouse shook her head. She knew, too.

"Of course she's going to help," I said. "She has to. She owes Ilana and she owes me."

"Owe you?" Dr. Varden asks.

"Yes. Because of Baba. You broke her heart when you left. So I think you owe me this much."

"Perhaps," Dr. Varden agreed. "But that doesn't mean I can do whatever you need me to. You might as well have shown up here and asked me for a unicorn."

"You could make a unicorn if you wanted, I bet," I said.

This made Dr. Varden smile, and I saw the woman I had studied in history books and in the museums. "Would you like a unicorn, then?"

"No," I said. "I want you to help Ilana."

"I already have," she said with a sigh. "I've been trying to help all along, for what it's worth. They never listen." She spun the ice cubes around in her glass and watched as they clinked together.

"What are you talking about?" I asked.

"My parents," Ilana said. "My so-called parents."

Dr. Varden shook her head. "Your parents actually did

listen to most of my advice. They were the most reasonable. That's the first way I helped you. I chose them. Other people on the project were less reasonable."

"If she's a Krita project, why were you involved?" I asked.

"Not everyone who works for Krita lives in Old Harmonie. There are contractors. Special projects. A back-and-forth. Things that need to be out of sight."

"A pipeline," Amnah said, glancing at Tommy.

"People at MIT?" I asked.

She shook her head. "No, the university, wisely, was not involved in this project. It was just me," she said. "I went to Krita's lab in Boston."

Mouse tugged on one of her curls. Tommy said, "Hold up. Start from the beginning. Who are we talking about? *What* are we talking about?"

There was a buzzing noise and Dr. Varden pulled a round disk out of the pocket of her apron. Her face darkened. "Bah," she said, dropping the disk back into her pocket.

"What was that?" Theo asked.

"One of the students at the lab," she replied. "Wanted to know if she should go ahead and sequence the DNA on a flower we're developing. She couched it all in concern about how tired I must be and how surely I needed rest." She shook her head. "They can't comprehend how someone as old as me can function."

Amnah leaned in. "So that was a work message?"

"Yes."

Amnah and Theo exchanged a look.

Dr. Varden sipped her lemonade and said, "I think I made this a little too sweet. My honey was a little richer, a little less sugary. You've tasted it?"

I glanced over at Ilana. "The Firefly Five in the Honey Hangout," Ilana said.

"I figured you'd find my stash."

"It's all gone now," Theo said, his voice icy. "They burned your house down."

Dr. Varden hesitated, but then she put her glass down on top of a marble coaster on a small table. It was next to a dish full of sea glass. Condensation dripped down and pooled on the coaster. Silence filled the room.

Finally, she sat down on a high-backed chair. She folded her hands in her lap and looked at each of us in turn.

"Here's the story. Listen closely."

21

"ALANA STARTED AS A LARK. I suppose you don't want to hear that, but it's true." Dr. Varden sat back in her seat and spoke more to the ceiling than to us. Ilana and I took seats on the sofa, still holding hands. Theo stood behind us.

"I had been working on AI for so long, focused on the animals. I kept dancing around human intelligence. People used to joke that if the computers could think for themselves, they would take over, and I wondered if that was true. I wondered if the computers could ever think for themselves or if our programming would always show through. I considered what we had: the AI that could have conversations, those that could diagnose health problems, those that could do basic things for you by voice commands. I started to build the brain. And once you have a brain, you need a vessel. It was just supposed to be a doll. No more than the chat machines. But the thing is, when you're in the project, when you're in the middle of it, it becomes all about solving the problem in front of you, or figuring out the next thing you can do.

"Well, what if, I thought, what if she could do more than just respond? What if she could start a topic? And then came memory. Computers have always stored memories, but it became about accessing them, all the connections that people have so that one memory leads to another, not like a chain of dominoes or a series of commands, but like a web that she could access at any point. Could I do that? And it turns out I could. I did. I got the memories from the daughter of one of my colleagues. First it was something simple. I got her to tie her shoes. And then from there, other memories. A birthday party. Jumping waves at the beach."

Ilana nodded. Were those memories that she had?

Dr. Varden took another sip of her lemonade. "What else? What else could I do? What else could she do? Could I fool someone into thinking she was a real girl? That would be a feat, wouldn't it? Maybe even prize-worthy. So I worked on and on.

"Lucy told me I was in too deep. And I told her she was being small-minded, and of course I'd considered all the negative consequences. So I brought Alana to a real birthday party. With real kids. And she didn't last ten minutes before those kids knew something was up. They wouldn't talk to her. And I tried one-on-one groups. And I tried her with adults. No one could get past the uncanny valley."

I remembered the file on the computer, the other projects that had been abandoned because they were almost perfectly realistically human—but still a tiny gap, and that gap was creepy.

"I was thinking I was a failure. That my project had sunk. All that time. All that money. But then I was sitting in the lab with Alana and she says to me, 'Aggie, I'm lonely.'"

Next to me, Ilana shuddered.

Dr. Varden glanced at her, then kept telling her story. "The worst of it was, my first thought was, *I did it! She feels*. But then almost immediately, my heart sank because I realized what I had done. And I had to shut the project down. That's when I moved out to Old Harmonie full-time.

"I was happy there for a while. I worked with animals again, and the food supply, and my bees. Those bees, they confounded me. Where were they all going? Were they really all dying? And if so, how? I dug right in. Deeper and deeper. I tried to keep perspective. Lucy had the idea of the robobees teaching the natural bees what to do. I didn't even think about what the problems might be. I was in too deep again.

"And all the while the Krita scientists, they were in deep, too. Successes were rewarded and failures were punished.

That's not the way science should work. It's the process, not the outcome. The failures should be celebrated because that's what we learn from. But we weren't learning anything. Krita kept us from learning with incentives and quotas."

She stopped talking and looked down at the ice cubes in her glass.

"So then what?" Amnah demanded.

"So I left. I left and came back here. MIT let me build my lab again and I got back to work. And I paid attention this time. No more animals. No more humans. I invented a way to get drinking water out of saliva."

Tommy gasped. "No way!"

"No one was much interested in that." She smiled at Tommy. "Then about two years ago, some Krita people showed up. They were going to revive the ALANA project. I told them no. Flat-out no. But when you sell your soul to a corporation, the way I did to get Old Harmonie up and running, you sell them everything. They owned ALANA. They didn't have to come to me, but they wanted me to consult. I thought if I did, maybe I could influence it. Maybe I could keep it contained. That's what I told myself. But maybe I wanted to see it through. Maybe I wanted to see my failure become a success. If I'm being honest, maybe that's what I was thinking."

She sighed. Outside, a siren blared by.

"They sent some scientists out to me. A dozen, maybe.

Your parents were two of them, Ilana. They were the most concerned with the ethics. They had studies and research. They asked the questions. And so when they said the project was ready for the next phase, for in-house testing, I said she would need parents. I said it should be Meryl and Greg. At least they listened to me about that.

"You weren't supposed to leave the lab. They were supposed to bring kids to you. I wrote out a strict protocol for the testing. The kids would need to be blind to the situation at first, but they would be fully debriefed after each session.

"That didn't happen. Clearly.

"And here you are. Looking for my help. Well, I've helped you the best I can. I did what I could. And you won't believe me, but what I did, it really was to help you. It's the best thing I could do."

Mouse opened her mouth. We could all see her stuck on that first word, that first syllable. Amnah touched her shoulder, and that seemed to let Mouse speak. "But you could've stopped it if you wanted to," she whispered. She said what we all were thinking.

"You're right," Dr. Varden admitted. "I also knew that they would have done it with me or without me, and I really did think I could control it somehow."

"What was the endgame?" Amnah asked.

"The endgame? I'm not sure what you mean."

"Krita isn't making buddies for their kids. I mean, I get that they think their kids are super-duper special and all, but I don't think there would be a project this big just so the kids could have the latest and greatest toy."

Agatha wrapped her hands around her glass. "True. It's something we've been chasing for a long time. Since people first realized they would die, I suppose."

"Immortality," I said.

"Yes. We've been chasing immortality as long as we've been mortal."

"We've always been mortal," I said.

"Smart girl," she replied. But it didn't sound like a compliment. "Are you familiar with the singularity?" she asked.

"The ultimate merging of humans and technology," Tommy said.

"That's, like, the most basic level," Amnah said.

"Good enough for our purposes. We've gotten so we can collect the memories. The consciousness. That's what I was working on way back then. Now we need the vessel."

Like that hard drive that ALANA had been sitting on all those years before it found a home in Ilana.

"I want you to know that right from the start of this second project, I really was thinking of where it was headed. I did my best. And I hope you'll forgive me." She didn't give us a chance to answer. "I do think it would help if I could show you something. Let's go for a walk. We could all use some fresh air."

Nothing about this city seemed fresh to me, but we all stood up and followed Dr. Varden out the door. Her street was quiet, and none of us spoke to break the silence. I still held on to Ilana's hand. I wasn't sure what was going to happen next. I wasn't sure what Dr. Varden's plan was, if she even had one, or what the rest of us would do if she couldn't or wouldn't help her. I kept holding on to Ilana's hand because I felt that, no matter how things played out, there was only so much more time that I would be able to hold it.

22

"THERE'S SO MUCH I NEED to show you," Dr. Varden said. "And not a lot of time. The key will be to find the pieces with the most impact." She stopped at the end of her walkway and bit her lip. Bright tulips bloomed in planters. They were out of season, but still full and heavy. "Have any of you ever been on a boat?"

"A boat?" Tommy said. "Like in the water?"

"No, the other kind of boat," Amnah replied.

"Well, there are other types of ships," Tommy said. "Airships, for example. Spaceships."

"But no space boats."

"Not yet," he replied.

"Your next great invention, I'm sure."

"Children!" Dr. Varden's voice rang sharply. We all fell into silence. "Follow me. We'll take a water taxi."

Dr. Varden started walking. Her strides were small but quick. She wore little black sneakers that bounced her along the sidewalk.

"Are we going?" Tommy whispered to us. "Because I would really like to go on a boat, but if this isn't looking cool to you, I'll hang back with you all."

"We're going," Ilana answered. She tugged my hand and we quickly caught up with Dr. Varden. I walked awkwardly in the sandals Dr. Varden had given me to wear instead of sneakers because of my blisters.

Theo hung back behind the others like a bodyguard. I could practically feel him swiveling his head from side to side as he took it all in. I wondered if his latency made it overwhelming for him: all these new possibilities coming at him, his brain trying to compute them all, work out all the possible solutions for problems that hadn't even presented themselves yet.

"Is this where you lived before Old Harmonie?" Ilana asked.

"Does it look familiar to you?" Dr. Varden replied.

"No, not really. I was just making conversation."

"I lived closer to Inman Square before—a good healthy walk to work. Plus, there was the most amazing Portuguese place for breakfast. Closed ages ago. The owners got forced out when rents went up." She stopped at an intersection, then turned left, back into the sea of people. I held on more tightly to Ilana's hand. It was all too easy to imagine the vast swath of people separating us, her fingers slipping from mine, and then she'd be gone forever.

"Where do you think we're going?" I whispered to Ilana.

"I'm not sure. It seems important to her, though."

"But how is this helping you? We need to get you somewhere safe." Each person passing by was a threat. Any one of them could be from Krita, ready to snatch her and bring her back to—to what? Dr. Varden's story was heavy on my mind. They'd scuttle Ilana or change her or something else—whatever it was, she wasn't going back to Firefly Lane, I was pretty sure of that.

Theo whistled. I turned around just as we were passed by a man flanked by two huge dogs. Their heads were up to my shoulders. One sniffed us. It stopped. Sniffed again. Sniffed Ilana. Then curled its lips.

The clock of my heart ticked so fast, it stopped. It exploded.

The dog snarled.

"Control your dog, sir!" Dr. Varden snapped at the man.

The man tugged on the dog's leash and muttered a low, "Sorry."

"Dogs!" Dr. Varden said, shaking her head. "I don't know why everyone loves them so much. They smell, they drool, they leave their droppings everywhere. They are foul and stupid beasts that can barely be trained. That's man's best friend? I think not."

"About what you think of dogs, I'll bet, huh, Mori?" Tommy said with a laugh.

"What?" I asked.

"This crew was attacked by dogs. Took one of their gang right out. She was a tough one, though, and my people patched her up. I bet she's sitting pretty now."

"Julia Sloane," Dr. Varden said.

"How'd you know that?" Theo asked.

"I know all about your neighborhood, your friendships. I expected to meet both her and Benji. I'm sorry to hear she's been injured. Right this way, please. And let me do the talking." She steered us down an alleyway that smelled of mildew and urine.

Theo jogged up next to me and Ilana. "Did that seem suspicious to you?"

"Not as suspect as this alley," I said, and sidestepped a puddle with a green-yellow sheen.

"I don't like this," Theo said, looking over his shoulder. "Something's up."

"I trust her," Ilana said.

"If you want my opinion, I'm with him," Amnah said. "She's a weird bird."

"Come along, come along. There's a taxi waiting at the pier!"

We crossed over a strip of land that couldn't decide if it wanted to be a burned-out lawn or a gravel pit. Broken bottles sparkled in the sun. In front of us, a brown river. Beyond that, a city. I stopped short. "Boston."

I recognized the city from our schoolwork, but seeing it in front of me was something entirely different. The buildings loomed, bigger than anything in Center Harmonie by a factor of ten, and my brain spun thinking of all the people each building could hold.

"Yes, dear. Boston. The Athens of America."

"Maybe a million years ago," Theo muttered.

An old shopping cart, twisted and rusted, poked out of the water. The river's edge was dotted with cans and candy wrappers and overstuffed trash bags. Right up next to a bridge was a pile of stained blankets. It didn't seem to me that flooding could be blamed for all the mess.

"Why did you want to show us this?" I asked. "What does it have to do with Ilana?"

"It's important for you to see the problems we face. So you can see what we're up against. Your world up there is so pretty. Even that little city they've made outside of Old Harmonie." She turned to me. "You Old Harmonie kids think that everyone outside lives in poverty, but you have no idea. None of you do. You're kept in your safe little bubbles, and never see that much of the world looks like this. Or worse. Unusable. We were supposed to fix it. We tackled little parts and did what we could. We congratulated ourselves. All the while, the layers below the surface eroded."

"I still don't understand how this will help Ilana," I said.

"It won't," Amnah said.

"Part of me hoped that ALANA would help with this," Agatha said.

"What, like a cleanup crew?" Tommy asked.

"No." Agatha laughed. "No, our problems were escalating faster than our intelligence. We needed greater intelligence, but also compassion. That's what I was going for. At least, that's what I told myself when I questioned what I was doing. I still think we can save this world. I do. And I'd do anything to save it for you."

I tried to understand what Agatha was telling us. Something by the blankets stirred.

"It's the 'do anything' that causes all the trouble," Amnah said.

"True," Agatha agreed. She looked down at the ground. Broken glass glinted beneath her feet. "If you had seen this place before. This street, they closed it down and people would walk and bike and skate. They'd row and sail on the river. It was beautiful. And we let it slip away. The pieces we fought for—" She shook her head. "The demise of the Cambridge side of the Charles River was not actually the point of our journey, interesting though it may be. We are going across the river. To Boston."

"No," Theo said. "Absolutely not. No way."

Dr. Varden shook her head. "Have you ever been to Boston, Theo?"

"No, of course not."

"It's dirty," I said. "It's unsafe. Everyone there is sick. There are so many people that they live practically on top of one another."

"Ah, so you've been to the city, then, Mori?"

"No," I said. "But I know all about it."

"You've *learned* all about it. Which is to say you've been *taught* all about it. Anything that is taught can be a lie. I'd say a vast majority of it is, intentional or otherwise. Boston was, is, and shall be a grand city and I am taking you to one of its marvels, so please go down the pier and get into the waiting boat."

Ilana made the first move. Right down the pier and into the boat. She helped me in. It shifted back and forth beneath my feet, but she steadied me. I sat down on a little green chair that folded down from the side of the old, rickety boat. It was maybe ten feet long, with a wooden bottom and a green prow. "Tessie" was printed along the side. The others got in and took their seats.

"The Mass Ave pier," Dr. Varden said as she took her seat.

"Welcome to the Charles River Water Taxi." The voice was computerized, but still had the telltale dropped *r*'s of the city: *Welcome to the Charles Riv-ah Wat-ah Taxi*. "Please remain seated at all times. You may love that dirty water, but do not touch it. Hands must remain inside the vessel. Do not dispose of any rubbish in the river or in the taxi. Enjoy your trip."

"Why would we love the dirty water?" Mouse asked. I could barely hear her above the chop of the boat through the water, but Dr. Varden smiled.

"It's an old song about Boston and the river." She sang a little of it, off-tune. "They cleaned the river up—oh, it was beautiful—but clean things have a tendency to get dirty again."

We bounced along the river, westward, if I was reading the sun correctly. On the far side of the river were shells of buildings, some of them seeming to come out of the water itself. "What happened there?" I asked.

"Flooding," she said. "Right up from the ocean and up the river. The Rejuvenation crew hasn't been through yet. The plan is to take all the buildings down, use the pieces to build levies. It won't be as beautiful, but the city will be safer."

There were other boats on the river. Small ones, mostly, like ours, that traveled up and down.

"It used to be full of sailboats," Dr. Varden said. "And crew shells. I can still see them sometimes. Or I expect to. My brain folds in on itself sometimes."

"Everyone's brain folds in on itself," Ilana replied. The sun lit her from behind and made her newly washed hair glow and her clothing almost translucent. I half expected her to lift right off the ground, to fly above us as we floated down the river.

"Not yours," Dr. Varden replied.

The boat veered to the left and docked itself at a sturdier-looking pier than the one from which we'd embarked.

"You have reached your stop: Mass Ave Pier. Please remember to take all of your belongings. And thank you for riding the Charles River Water Taxi."

Theo got out first. He offered his hand to Amnah, but she refused. Mouse took it, though, and so did I. He looked away from me while he pulled me up.

When we were on the pier, Dr. Varden counted us all. "I can't lose any of my ducklings," she explained. "It's not much farther now. Right this way!"

Another boat pulled up and docked at the pier. It was full of people wearing face masks and skintight outfits made of neoprene.

"Well," Tommy said. "If we're going to die of exposure to the city, at least we'll have a story to tell."

"Dead people don't tell stories," Amnah told him.

"But the stories people will tell about us!" His grin spread from ear to ear as he trotted to catch Dr. Varden. I was less certain, but we had no choice, really. We fell in line and trailed after her through the city I had heard so much about and had been raised to fear.

The air on this side of the river smelled the same. The people looked the same. The sounds were the same. It was hard to trust my senses, though, in the face of all I had been taught. The washed-out buildings, those were real—real life and real to what we had learned. But this street we were walking down was not. The buildings were grand, with high, leaded windows. Small gardens were planted with flowers and tomato vines. One building had a stoop, and a group of children sat on it playing a clapping game. Julia and I had loved those when we were younger. I could still sing all the songs. My head swirled.

The farther we got from the river, the nicer it got. We passed a street full of stores with big glass windows and holograms that danced outside and invited us in. We passed restaurants that tempted us with their smells.

Where were the sick and hungry children? Where was all the pain?

Dr. Varden kept walking. "It's not all like this," she said, as if she had read my mind. Maybe it was clear on my face. "This is one of the nicest parts of the city. Always has been. I thought you should see it."

"It is nice," I said. "But we didn't come here for a tour, Dr. Varden. We need your help."

"I am helping you. You'll thank me someday."

"That sounds like a threat," Theo muttered next to me.

"I'm not talking about someday help. I'm talking about right now. I'm talking about Ilana."

Ilana herself walked close beside me, but said nothing.

"You aren't patient. Your great-grandmother was always patient. With everyone, but with me especially. I suppose that happens when you know someone well. She knew that eventually I would come around to the point."

I felt my cheeks flare. But this wasn't the usual embarrassment at failing to live up to Baba's legacy. This was something different. "We don't have time for this!"

"My dear, if you want to help Ilana, then you will make time." She turned on her heel down a side street. Looming in front of us was a huge, domed building. "Anyway," she said. "We're here."

But we didn't go into the large building. We went into a plainer, but still very big, building on the left. "Mary Baker Eddy Library" read the sign. Maybe there was more for us to learn? Something we could only read in books or see in old files?

Inside, the air was cool. The walls and the floor were a sort of stone, and quotes were printed on the walls. There was a photograph of a woman with her hair parted right down the middle, tight curls close to her head, and a pleased, pleasing smile on her lips.

"Holy cheesecakes, this is the biggest library I've ever seen!" Tommy exclaimed. His voice echoed around the hushed hall.

"You haven't seen anything yet," Dr. Varden said. And she opened the doors to a world of color. We stood on a bridge.

The walls around us were all glass and seemingly lit from within. They curved up and around so it was as if we were in a ball. We were in a ball! I peered down from the bridge. The whole room was a sphere!

"It's the earth," Mouse whispered.

She was right. We were inside a stained-glass globe.

"It's beautiful," Ilana said.

"It's the Mapparium," Dr. Varden said. "My favorite place in all of Boston."

Amnah's eyes were wide as she took it all in. She and Mouse leaned close together, studying the walls, the lines of each country. Dr. Varden explained that when it was built, it was meant to be changeable as borders and politics changed, but eventually they decided to keep it as is, a monument to history.

Theo tugged on my shoulder and nodded his head to the far side of the globe. He wanted Ilana and me to follow him. We tucked together on the far side of where we'd come in. "I don't like this," Theo whispered. "What are we doing here?"

"She wanted to show us the city," Ilana said.

But Theo was right. This wasn't helping Ilana, no matter what Dr. Varden said. "It is weird that she seemed to know that Julia was hurt before we even talked about it. I mean, maybe it was just making an educated guess—but still."

"The showers and the lemonade and now this. It feels like stalling to me."

"Me too," I said.

"And that message she got," Theo said. "I didn't buy her explanation for a minute."

"But if she's not going to help us, why not just send us away?" I asked.

Theo glanced back in Dr. Varden's direction. "Because she let them know we're here."

"Krita? You don't really think so, do you?"

"I do. I've been through all the options. I laid them all out. It's the only one that makes any sense." He took a few steps farther until he was at the edge of the walkway, by the door. He tried to turn the doorknob, but shook his head. "It's locked," he said. And we all looked back across the bridge to where Dr. Varden blocked our path to the exit.

"Just take it slowly," Theo said. "We'll walk back in that direction. I'll talk with Dr. Varden—distract her. And then you two get out of here."

"And then what?" I asked. "We don't know where we are or what will happen to you."

"You'll figure out where to go. And I'll be fine. My mom won't let them do anything too terrible to me." He tried to force a smile. "Worst thing that happens, she gets me two nannies and they never leave my side. Benji will think I'm the luckiest kid ever."

"Theo," I said, but at the same time I reached down and grabbed Ilana's hand. He was right. We needed to make a break for it, and I had to make sure she came with me. "We can't leave you here."

"Perhaps I should have told you . . ." Dr. Varden's voice was soft, but right next to us. We all turned. She was still on the far side, by herself. Tommy, Amnah, and Mouse had moved to the middle. "The acoustics in here are such that sound travels around the edges. We can hear one another perfectly, but those in the center can't hear us at all."

"So you've been listening to us?" Theo demanded. The blue of the map's ocean colored his face.

"Not intentionally, but yes. I suppose you have reason to doubt me. The Krita Corporation, in the person of your mother, actually, called me and let me know you had left and that they thought you might come this way. And I did promise to let them know as soon as you arrived."

My knees felt wobbly. I leaned against the railing of the bridge.

"I didn't," she said. "Though I don't know how I can convince you of that."

It was odd to have her voice beside us, her body far away. It made her seem even more powerful.

"As for how I can help, in case you haven't noticed, I'm a very old lady. My help is limited and dubious."

"Then let us go!" I said, loud enough so that some sound traveled to Amnah, Mouse, and Tommy, though each of them looked in a different direction. Amnah watched me.

Theo stepped closer to me. He pushed on my back, urging me and Ilana forward. He still wanted us to try to escape.

"You're free to go at any time, of course," Dr. Varden said. "But be certain that's the best choice. And remember, I didn't say that I couldn't or wouldn't help. I was expecting this. I have pieces put in place, and I've toppled over the first domino. Now I just need to make sure the rest of them will fall the way I want them to."

"Just say what you mean," I begged. "Please."

"There are people ready to help us. It's a big risk for all of us. We're stealing in the eyes of the law. So forgive us if we have our ways and means, our little quirks."

"Is being here part of the plan?" Ilana asked.

"It is," Dr. Varden answered. They faced each other over the long expanse of the bridge. LED lights shifted and highlighted a different part of the map, casting Dr. Varden in shadow.

"Go," Theo whispered.

Dr. Varden reached out her hand as if beckoning us toward her. Ilana took a step.

Behind Dr. Varden, the door burst open.

23

THEY WORE JUMPSUITS. GRAY ONES with reflective visors. They swarmed the bridge and grabbed us all. Dr. Varden first. They sucked her right back through the entrance. Then Tommy, Amnah, and Mouse. Amnah swung at them and tried to break Mouse free. It took two of the jumpsuits to hold her.

Screams and footsteps echoed around us. They came from every direction. Above, below, all sides.

Ilana and Mouse huffed behind me. Theo scrambled against the glass, looking for another door. There was none.

As the jumpsuits got closer, I turned. There was a door, but it was locked, so I pounded against the glass with my fists. It was more than a century old and just as strong. Not a movement. Not a crack. And then the arms were around me, too. Strong arms. Heavy breathing that I could hear but not feel. My arms were pinned at my sides, so I kicked out my legs. I tried to grab on to rails of the bridge with my feet. It was no use. The jumpsuits could grab Theo easily. They could take Ilana. How could I expect to fight them?

I didn't stop, though.

I kept fighting.

I kept fighting as they dragged me through the door I didn't even know was there and as they pulled us into a building with no windows.

I kept fighting until I realized I was the only one still trying.

In this new room, the lights were dim. We sat on the floor.

Dr. Varden.

Theo.

Tommy.

Amnah.

Mouse.

Me.

Ilana was gone.

"Tell us where she is!" I begged the jumpsuit. She wasn't in a jumpsuit anymore. She wore the uniform of Krita security: a dark green suit and mirrored sunglasses. The fluorescent lights hanging from the ceiling in this prison of a room cast a strange glow over her skin.

"Information will be given in a time and manner deemed appropriate."

She had a gun crossed against her chest. I wasn't sure if it was a stun gun or something more serious. She held it tightly in both hands.

"My mother will be furious when she finds out how we're being treated!" Theo said. "I demand to talk to someone in charge right now!"

The jumpsuit smirked at him.

He shook his head at me. We sat back down with the others. Mouse lay with her head in Amnah's lap. The gray floor was hard and cold. Our neutral clothing from Dr. Varden made us look like a faded landscape.

"I'm sorry," I said to them. "I had no idea it would end up like this. I'm so, so sorry."

"It's okay," Mouse whispered.

"Yeah," Tommy said. "Totally."

Amnah didn't say anything.

"I wish they would tell us something. Anything," Theo said. He tugged at his hair. "It's infuriating being in here."

Dr. Varden stood up and walked to the far corner of the room. Then she started pacing the perimeter. The room wasn't very big, maybe ten feet by twelve feet. Around and around she went.

"You don't think she told them, do you?" I asked Theo.

"I don't know. Maybe."

"She's in here with us," Tommy said.

"That could be a cover," Theo said.

"What does it matter?" Amnah asked. "We're in here, and Ilana's somewhere else. It doesn't matter how it happened."

Dr. Varden's pace slowed.

"All this way," I moaned. "All this way and this is how it ends?"

Mouse put her hand on top of mine. Her hands were tiny and warm and it was such a kind gesture that I couldn't hold in my tears anymore. I started to sob. Big, messy, gross sobs. Theo put his arms around me and hugged me. I got snot on his shirt, but I didn't care. I felt another arm around me. And then another. And another.

24

"YOU'RE LEAVING," THE JUMPSUIT TOLD us. Maybe it was a new one. They seemed to rotate through. It was hard to tell with them all dressed in their uniforms, their eyes hidden.

"Where are we going?" Theo asked.

The guard didn't answer.

We were gathered up, brought outside, and stuffed into waiting KritaVans. We were split up. Amnah and Mouse climbed into one van, Theo and Tommy into another. Dr. Varden was ushered into mine. The lights at the front were on, but we didn't move.

"Do you think . . . ," I began, but I didn't know how to finish the sentence. Dr. Varden didn't know any more than I did.

She sat against the tinted window of the van. Her feet barely touched the floor. The creases around her eyes had grown deeper in the day I'd known her. She was an old, old woman. I had known that. But still, I had thought she could help. I thought she had some power she could use to save Ilana.

She couldn't even save herself.

"Lucy would be very proud of you," she told me.

"Why?" I asked. My eyes still burned from all the crying.

"You tried."

I laughed. A bitter, painful laugh. "What good did it do her?"

"It's not over yet," she replied.

"What do you mean?"

Before she could answer, the doors of the van slid open. My parents pressed in. "You're okay, you're okay, you're okay," Mom said, over and over.

"Are you hurt?" Dad asked. "Did anyone hurt you?"

"We're bringing you home," Mom said.

A nurse got in behind them, wearing a white jumpsuit with a red cross. At least I could see his white freckled face and red hair. He slid the door shut. We began moving almost immediately.

The nurse shined a light in my eyes, took all my vitals. "Good, good," he said. He had kind green eyes. "Tough kiddo," he said to me. "But you'll be okay." He cut my hair. A snippet from the back.

"Just cut it all," my mother said. So he did. Right to chin length. The extra pieces fell to the floor of the KritaVan.

Dr. Varden watched me as we drove back toward Old Harmonie. My parents ignored her. We took a different road back than the one Tommy had driven. This one was bigger, and the cars all moved in rapid, silent synchronicity.

When we came up to the main gate, I started to cry. There were two stone pillars, one with an owl and one with a lion: the symbols of knowledge and wisdom. I'd never seen the gates from the outside before, but in drawings they'd always seemed so serene. Now they felt ominous.

"Nothing bad will happen to you here," Mom said.

"I'd always thought it was beautiful here. I always thought it was perfect."

"It is perfect," Dr. Varden said. "It's just not for everyone. It never was."

"Enough," my mom told her.

A jumpsuit opened the door. "Mori Bloom, you need to come with me."

My mom tried to hold on to my hand. She said, "We'll see you as soon as we can."

"Be good, Mori," Dad said.

The decontamination showers were as bad as I had expected. Stripped down. Hot water. Cold blasts of air. Bright flashes of light. A mist that smelled of lemons but something dark and fake underneath.

I looked for my friends but didn't see them.

Then I was dressed in a pale pink jumpsuit like the kind they put new babies in. It was soft, at least.

My glasses were taken, scrubbed clean, but my body kept moving, passed from station to station. I couldn't have seen any of my friends if they were there, but I was pretty sure they were not, that we were being kept apart.

And then my glasses were back on my face and I was in bed, back in the white, stagnant world of the hospital. Back in my bubble where the fear had all begun. Alone.

Every detail was the same as I remembered. The way the overhead lights both shined through and reflected off the plastic. The way it made a sticking-squelching noise when I moved. The room around the bubble, all white and static. There was a window on my left, but the blinds were never up. There was a television, but it was never turned on. And so I drifted in and out of sleep.

My parents arrived and stood outside the bubble and cried. "Am I sick?" I demanded.

Dad said nothing, just shifted his eyes—angry eyes?—away from me. Mom shook her head, but I didn't know if she meant that no, I wasn't sick, or that she couldn't talk about it. I didn't feel sick. "Am I sick?" I asked again.

"It's complicated," Dad replied. His voice was thin and so I knew he was angry. Angry at me? Well, of course. I had run away. What a mess that must have made for both of them.

Still, I had thought he would understand. I had thought he would see that I had done it out of friendship.

"If I'm not sick, then why I am in here? Why am I in this bubble?"

"There are other people involved. We need to check everything."

Other people. "Are they okay?"

"We're still assessing," Dad said.

"When will I go home?"

"Soon," Dad said.

"*Soon*'s not a precise answer," I told him.

This, at last, made him smile. "My dear, there aren't exactly protocols for this situation."

My hands looked so small and useless lying on the pink blanket. I had a new watchu strapped around my wrist. This one had a deep red band with gold flecks. Very stylish. Julia would be jealous, and Ilana would say it was . . .

My parents had stopped crying, but their eyes were still damp looking and had dark circles. "I want to go home," I told them.

"We want you home, too," Mom said. "But for now you need to rest."

And like they were turning off a switch, I fell asleep.

Maybe they had.

An orderly pressed her fingers against my IV line and I blinked my eyes open. She came into hazy focus in her pale yellow hospital scrubs.

I asked for paper and pen, and the orderly passed them to me through one of the access holes in my bubble. She stood there for a moment, watching me, so I said, "Am I sick?"

She shook her head, but then she said, "Not for me to say." Her voice sounded like she was speaking through a paper tunnel as it traveled from her outside world into my cocoon.

I wondered why nobody would tell me if I was sick or not. I didn't feel sick. Only tired. So very tired. But maybe that was the boredom of lying inside a plastic bubble inside a white room.

"The others?" I asked.

She looked over her shoulder. She wore a tight cap that went almost down to her white eyebrows. "The girl with the bite, she's fine. She went home. The boy that was with her—"

"Benji?" I gripped my pink blanket tightly.

"They got his lungs working again."

My stomach turned. It had never even occurred to me that something might have happened to Benji.

"Allergic reaction," she said, as if anticipating my question. "Something out there that we don't have in here. A little airborne particulate matter, it would seem."

"But he's okay?"

"He's on the mend. Asking to be let out." She smiled. "You all are tough cookies."

"Theo?"

"Theo Staarsgard? Not much could slow down that boy. He's been asking to see you. They said no visitors, though. Him and those outside kids, they've all been by to see you more than once. Stubborn crowd, every single one of you."

"If they come again, tell them . . ." But I wasn't sure what I wanted to say to them. Certainly nothing that could be passed on from me to this orderly to them like some kind of game of telephone. "Tell them thank you."

"I'll do that," she agreed. She checked over her shoulder again.

I didn't want to get her in trouble, but I had to know. "Ilana?" I asked.

"I'm not allowed to tell you anything about her." I watched her face. Something flickered there, but I didn't know her well enough to read it.

Some stray puff of air moved the bubble and it crinkled around me.

"Do you know when they'll let me out?"

Another shoulder glance. I imagined the hallway behind her as never-ending. There'd be door after door after door that hid another one of Old Harmonie's mistakes. Projects that didn't pan out. Girls who disobeyed.

"You didn't hear it from me, but it looks like tomorrow."

I relaxed as best I could, but then I said, "How long have I been in here?"

"Three days."

"Three days! Did they—" I began. I wanted to ask her if I'd been dampened again, but I got the sense she wouldn't answer that question directly. "Did I undergo any procedures?"

She shook her head. "It's primarily been monitoring. Your white blood cell count was a little elevated and they took care of that. You were exhausted, hon. Mostly, you've been sleeping. A regular Sleeping Beauty."

Sleeping. I couldn't remember any dreams. No nightmares. That had to be a good sign, I thought. When they'd messed with me before, I had nightmares. Terrible ones that bled into my waking life.

"Thanks," I said.

She smiled. "No worries, little one."

My hand was shaking, but I wrote carefully:

Please do not change me.

I handed the paper to the orderly. She read the words and frowned. But she clipped the paper to my chart. I could only hope that the doctors and my parents would read it, too.

25

THE HOSPITAL WAS A RESEARCH and teaching hospital, and it was connected to the main Krita building by a covered walkway and a shared courtyard. My room overlooked the courtyard and so the day I was released I waited for my parents by the window and looked across to the Krita labs. Some of the windows were tinted. Others had brightly colored bars across them—red and yellow and blue. But some I could see into. People worked in little cubicles. Two men adjusted mirrors and then sent a laser ricocheting around the room. *What could that be for?* I wondered. I tried to look in each window that I could, hoping for a glimpse of Ilana. But nothing. Of course, this was just one side of one building. They could have her anywhere.

In the courtyard below, there were small tables where people sat with their tablets and their coffees. None of them looked concerned that a group of us had left Old Harmonie and returned. None of them looked concerned about what might be happening to one of our friends.

The door slid open with a whooshing sound and my parents pressed in together. My mom had a stuffed bear with a bright red heart on its white chest and my dad had three balloons that bounced in the air. They wrapped me tightly in their arms so that my face was smashed against the bear.

"You gave us such a fright!" Mom said, as if she had not ridden in the van or come to see me in the hospital.

"Honey," Dad said, his voice strained.

"I'm sorry! I'm sorry, we weren't going to stress you. We weren't going to talk about—well, but you did scare us, Mori. You did!" It was like she had hit the REDO button and expected us to start over. How far back had she rewound? Back before I had left? Maybe she was just pretending I had been sick again. Maybe that was easier than the truth.

"I'm sorry," I said as I disentangled myself from them. They wouldn't hold my gaze. After that, I wasn't brave enough to ask them about Ilana. I'd have to ask someone else. Someone who would tell the truth.

"You're all clear now," Dad said. "You were exposed to some particulate matter out there, and after the reaction Benji had, we wanted to be sure."

"And it's a good thing, too, because it seems you caught a cold out there. Just a small one."

I rubbed my throat, which was, I realized, a bit sore. "So I was just resting here, right?"

They glanced at each other. "We didn't do any dampening, if that's what you mean," Mom said.

"Though after this stunt—" Dad began, then stopped himself. "There's a KritaCar waiting out front."

On the way out of the room, I passed a mirror. It was the first time I could see my new short haircut. It swung at chin length. It made my face look a little longer, my eyes a little bigger. I looked older. Before, that was all I wanted: to be older, to get my latency, whatever it might be. Now I only wanted to stay the same.

"We'll take you to the salon and get it fixed," Mom said.

"Maybe take you to Sal the barber and go really short," Dad tried to joke. It fell flat as a pancake between us.

"Can we just go home?" I asked.

Mom and Dad exchanged a look. "We need to do one thing first," Mom said.

"Tova Staarsgard has arranged a meeting of the families involved."

"Oh." My voice cracked on the single syllable. "Is Theo okay?" I asked.

"He's fine. Strong kid," Mom said, and smiled. "This is no big deal, really. We just need to get the story, get out ahead of it."

"Get out ahead of the story?" I echoed. I had no idea what she meant.

Dad was still holding the balloons. They bobbed above his head. "What you guys did—taking Ilana out of here—it violates quite a bit of protocol, and we need to make sure we dot our i's and cross our t's so we can get everyone home."

"Everyone?" I asked.

"We should really be going," Mom said. "Tova likes to start on time."

"Mom, Dad," I said. "What about Ilana?"

"I think it's better if we wait until the group's all together," Dad said. "We'll sort it out, I promise."

But that didn't sound like a promise to bring her back. It sounded like a promise to do nothing. Mom put a cardigan over my shoulders and helped me get my arms through the sleeves, then they led me outside.

The KritaCar was a new one: slick black with purple-tinted windows and shaped like a pear on its side. Benji would think it was so dope. "Is Benji okay?" I asked.

"He is now. It's lucky he got out of there when he did. His lungs couldn't handle the stress and the air."

"It wasn't all bad." I thought of the night in the woods with Amnah, the way the pine scent had filled my nose.

"There was a lot of pollution in that first town you found," Mom explained.

"They still drive fossil fuel–powered cars," I told them, and then winced. All we'd ever been told about the outside was the bad. "But they keep them going forever," I said. "They don't just junk them. They fix them over and over. Mouse and Tommy and Amnah, they're really good about that. About finding ways to make use of old things." I wanted to tell them about the tree sculptures, but wasn't sure how I could describe the way the joy had bubbled up inside of me as I watched the trees and smiles grow.

"They seem like nice children," Mom said. Her voice, though, was flat, disinterested.

Our KritaCar pulled out of the complex of buildings and onto the main street of Center Harmonie. The light reflecting off the buildings bent and glared at us as we drove by. They were all so high and oddly shaped. Like the lab building at MIT, I realized, which made sense, since so many of the Krita people had started there. We drove past the green, where people were working. Oblivious. Or not. They all seemed ominous to me now. What dark projects might they be working on? What unintended consequences?

We had barely driven five minutes when the car turned and parked in front of the Biltmore, the nicest hotel in Old Harmonie. A porter opened the door of the car. Mom and Dad got out. The building loomed up behind them, and it made me feel woozy.

"Mori?" Mom asked. "Mori, are you okay?"

"Yes," I said, making my voice sound firm. "Yes, I'm fine."

I got out of the car. I was not fine at all.

Ms. Staarsgard had gathered us all for breakfast in a dining room with a high, glass ceiling. Potted plants with long, thin leaves circled the room. The tables were set with white tablecloths and purple napkins. Fresh flowers were at the center of each table. There was orange juice poured for each of us, coffee for the grown-ups. Waiters brought around blueberry pancakes and fresh fruit cups.

"It's a lovely solarium, isn't it?" Ms. Staarsgard said as she snapped her napkin over her lap. She and Theo shared a table with my family, Mouse, and Amnah. "I love the way the interior and exterior worlds are mixed together so completely."

"It's quite nice," Mom said. "Thanks for arranging this."

"Thanks for arranging this"? Like we were all on a lovely vacation together.

Theo cut his pancakes into square bites and poured maple syrup over them.

There was one empty chair at our table. I peered around. Julia's and Benji's families sat together. Julia saw me and gave a small wave. I think we both knew we were expected to stay in our seats. Tommy was at that table, too, and he and Benji were deep in discussion about something—I'm sure Benji would have all sorts of thoughts on Tommy's saliva plan. The two of them would make quite a team.

"Is this seat taken?" Dr. Varden asked, though she was already settling herself into the chair.

"We're honored to have you with us, Agatha," Ms. Staarsgard told her. "It's been too long since we've seen you."

"I've kept myself busy," she replied.

"I'm sure you have."

Next to me, Mouse sipped her orange juice. She was calm and still, quiet as ever.

"Girls, tell us about yourselves," Ms. Staarsgard instructed. "We know you hail from South Concord, but what else can you tell us?"

"I like owls," Amnah said, her voice flat.

"Any owl in particular?" Ms. Staarsgard replied.

Theo rolled his eyes.

"Barred owls. Snowy owls, too, I guess."

"You have a lot of them up your way?"

"Not as many as we did in Acton," Amnah said, her words a whip.

Ms. Staarsgard barely flinched. "Have you been to the reservoir? There is great birding there, I'm told. And what about you, Mercy? What do you like?"

Mouse gripped her fork tightly in her hand. Her lips moved, but no sound came out.

"She likes fixing things," Amnah said. "Solving problems. Making new things out of old things."

"A tinkerer, you could say. But won't you tell us yourself, Mercy?"

Amnah leaned forward. "It's hard for her to talk to strangers, okay?"

"Acute anxiety disorder, correct?" The smile never left Ms. Staarsgard's face. "We could fix that. It would be the easiest thing. When your parents come, have them talk to me. You can come up to Old Harmonie or we can send a doctor out to you."

"No, thank you," Amnah replied.

She hadn't noticed that Mouse's mouth had opened.

"Not everyone wants our fixes, Mom," Theo told her.

"Actually," Mouse croaked. "Actually, that would be nice."

Amnah snapped her head to look at her. "What are you talking about? You can't let them mess with your brain."

"Mori said it didn't hurt at all."

"That's not the point. You can't—"

"You don't know what it's like," Mouse whispered. "Opening my mouth is like jumping out of the tree house, even around people I know. Strangers make it like skydiving."

I could see what she wanted. I felt the same way. I wanted to be brave again, and, in a way, so did she. Maybe she had never even known what it was like to not have that anxiety in the first place.

"I'll talk to your parents," Ms. Staarsgard said. She smiled in a way that passed for warm, but I could see something cold and calculated underneath. "It's the least we could do to thank you all for looking out for our children. They aren't as savvy as you all."

"Thanks to you," Theo said.

She ignored him. Instead she turned to Dr. Varden. "I'm glad you're all here together, Agatha, Ellen, Sean, and Mori. I have some exciting news about the latency. As the people closest to Lucy Morioka, you'll surely be happy to hear it."

"Really?" Mom asked.

"Do you girls know about the latency? Mori's great-grandmother developed it, and it's been a truly remarkable advance. You see, each of us is blessed with many talents. Clearly, Mercy, you have a mechanical mind. And Amnah, I can see the makings of a leader in you. But we also have talents that remain hidden. Dr. Morioka found a way to release them."

"More surgery," Theo interjected. "More messing with our brains."

Ms. Staarsgard went on as if he hadn't spoken. I guess she was good at ignoring people. "At first it was haphazard. We weren't always sure what the talent would be. Then we started doing some testing that could predict the talent. From there we realized there could be some choice involved—so long as the latent talent was there, we could stimulate a particular part of the brain and bring it out. You see, the latency is emblematic of how we do things at Krita, always building on the advances of the past to move the world forward."

"Good line, Mom. You should've had that in the speech at my Thirteenth."

"Theo," she said, the tone of her voice a warning. "At any rate, the choices were based on testing, which was based on aptitude. But we got to thinking, in Dr. Morioka's original work, she was looking at patients who suffered a brain injury and then developed a talent where none had existed before. And so we asked, 'What if we could look inside and see what was hiding?' Our scientists have been working on this question for years, and we have finally found a way to scan the brain in order to identify—specifically—untapped potential. We'll be entering testing in the next year. Mori, you'd be an excellent candidate for the first round."

"Me? I don't think so," I said.

"Perhaps we could save this discussion for another time," Mom said. "We've all been through an ordeal."

"The spots in the trial will go quickly, Ellen."

"Yes, of course, but—"

The conversation whipped around me. Ms. Staarsgard wanted to scan my brain to see what might be hidden there? Would I have no secrets from the world?

A waiter came and took my plate. My fork clanged against my knife. I had barely eaten anything. I put my hand on the fruit cup so at least I would have that, but I wasn't hungry. What were we even doing here?

"Thank you, but I don't think you need to save a spot for me," I said.

Ms. Staarsgard reached across Theo and put her hand on top of mine. "Your mother is right. It's been a trying time. Take a week or two to think it over. I'll hold a spot in the trial for you. You and Benji both."

Benji. He probably had a million talents hidden in him, and each one would only make him better able to help other people.

"Tova," Mom said. "Is there any sort of agenda for this meeting?"

"We're beginning with breakfast. I thought the children might enjoy a nice meal after their escapade."

"Yes, of course, it's just that we'd like to get Mori home. She's been in the hospital all this time and—"

"I'm well aware of where Mori has been," Ms. Staarsgard said. She rose to her feet and nodded at a man by the door who wore a suit. A podium came up out of the floor at the front of the room. "And so we shall begin."

As she crossed to the podium, the room itself lifted up and up and up. It was like a giant elevator carrying us to the very top of the building. I grabbed on to the edge of my seat. Mouse whispered to Amnah something I couldn't hear.

When the room stopped moving, we could see all of Old Harmonie—and beyond: Nashoba, Firefly Lane, our woods.

The reservoir shined in the morning sun. And beyond all that rose the hazy skyline of Boston.

"It's beautiful, isn't it?" Ms. Staarsgard asked. Her back was to us all, but we could still hear her clearly. "This little world that Agatha Varden built and Krita improved. It's the way of science, isn't it? One person builds it, and another person improves it?"

"Not all projects need to be taken to the end," Dr. Varden said, but I think only the people at our table heard it.

Either way, Ms. Staarsgard didn't respond directly. She turned around and stood at the podium. "It seems we're in a bit of a pickle here." She looked at each table in turn. "Our children, good children one and all, have been caught up in something much bigger than them. Why, they even dragged in some poor waifs from the outside."

I could practically hear Amnah bristle at that. And why shouldn't she?

"We've had a team working on the incident since it began several weeks ago."

Weeks? We hadn't been gone two days. That plus the days we'd spent in the hospital didn't even total a full week.

"I must say I was eager for the project to succeed, of course, but I had my concerns. Concerns I made clear from the outset. I asked explicitly to be notified of any problems."

That was true. I had heard her tell the Naughtons to let her know immediately if something was amiss. Then I had thought she was talking about Ilana not fitting in or something. I'd had no idea.

"I will shoulder some of the blame here. When Ilana first showed signs of going rogue, the day she injured our poor Mori, I should have put a stop to it. But I, like our children, had been won over by the project. I let my emotions get in the way."

Dr. Varden scoffed at that.

"What is she talking about?" I whispered to Theo.

He pressed his lips together. The red slashes had surfaced on his cheeks. He was angry, but he wouldn't tell me anything.

"The asset collapsed completely approximately five days ago. We believe that is the day that she launched a plan to leave for the outside world."

I turned to face Theo. He twisted his napkin in his hands. "I'm sorry," he mumbled.

"Perhaps motivated by misplaced memories, or perhaps because of something more sinister in her design—a possibility we are still investigating, I assure you—she recruited our young people to aid in her escape. She removed their watchus as well as her own tracking device: clear evidence that she herself was the mastermind of this plan. Would our children really know how to remove a tracking device? How to find one?"

"Yes!" Benji answered. "It was me. I made the app and I—"

His mother slapped her hand onto his arm. "You don't know what you're talking about Benji," she said. "Ilana confused you."

"No, that's not—"

"Stop, Benji!"

"It's okay." Ms. Staarsgard held up her hands. "It's natural that the children are confused. They are just children, after all."

Across the table, my parents watched Ms. Staarsgard. Were they really going to go along with this?

"Ilana led the children out of Old Harmonie. They were unwitting accomplices to this theft, but cannot be blamed. It was like the Pied Piper leading the children from Hamelin."

"Because the parents didn't pay him for getting rid of the rats," Amnah said.

I pushed my cup away from me. This could not be happening. They were going to blame Ilana for all of it? She was the one who wanted to go alone. She hadn't even wanted to go at all, not really. I thought of what Julia had said about why she had come along on the rescue mission: to take responsibility. Now here we were back at the start and the grown-ups were trying to avoid responsibility again. They were trying to shift blame, and that wasn't right. That wasn't what scientists did. It wasn't what good people did.

"It wasn't her," I whispered to my parents.

Mom shook her head. "Not now, Mori."

Not now? But when? When would I be allowed to talk? To clear her name?

Beside me, Theo wrapped his napkin around his hand, tighter and tighter. He knew it was wrong. So why wasn't he saying something?

"It's a tragedy that the project failed in such a spectacular way, and that our children were so egregiously harmed by it. But now we must move forward. I will be launching an investigation of the lab and the project directors. We will get to the bottom of what went wrong. As for the children, it's important that we stay on message. Ilana led the escape."

I stood up. "No," I said. Loudly. Clearly.

"Mori," Dad warned.

"No," I said again. "That's not how it happened. Not at all."

"Mori, dear, you're confused."

"I'm not. And I'm not going to participate in your lies. I'm not going to let Ilana save me yet again. You're right, though. There was only one person behind this." I took a deep breath. "It was me."

"Shut up," Theo hissed at me.

"*I* heard what was going to happen to her and *I* had the idea to get her out of here and get her someplace safe. She didn't want to go. None of them wanted to go. But you did whatever you did to make them want to protect me, so that's why they came."

"Sit down," Theo said to me.

"Mori, this isn't possible," Dad said.

"Why not?"

"What you're saying doesn't make any sense," Dad said. "It would be totally out of character and, frankly, outside of your skill set."

The sun cast half of his face in shadow. "Of course you think that. Of course you think I couldn't do something like this. You figured you'd prevented me from ever doing anything like this. Anything brave."

"What are you talking about?" Dad asked.

"I know about the dampening."

"We did that for your own safety," Mom exclaimed. She clasped her hands in front of her like she was praying.

"You were so reckless," Dad said.

"You'd fly off the swings," Mom said.

"Off the merry-go-round," Dad added.

"Off everything," Mom said.

"I loved flying!" And as I said it, I remembered it. The way it felt when my stomach dropped toward my feet, a strange sort of tickle that electrified me.

"And that's why we had to do it, Mori, don't you see?"

I didn't see. I didn't see why they had to change me. "Baba and Dr. Varden and the rest of them, they didn't come up with all these advances so you could mold us like Play-Doh. I don't even understand why you do it, why you mess with us so much."

"It's to keep you safe," Mom said. "Everything we do is to keep you safe."

"Because we're your most valuable resource," I scoffed. That's what Ms. Staarsgard and the rest of the Krita people always said. *The children are precious*. "All the while you were changing us. I guess we were only precious if we behaved exactly the way you wanted us to—and if we didn't, you'd fix that."

"Because we love you," Mom said.

I ignored her. "And I guess I need more protection, right? Because I'm a natural?"

"What?" Dad said. But he only looked a little confused.

"That's what we were thinking. That the designed kids, they look out for the naturals because we hold some of the genetic diversity, and—"

Mom shook her head and Dad said, "Nothing is so simple."

"Then it's because we're weaker and they need to look out for us! Whatever it is, it isn't right." I slapped the table in front of me so hard that my hand stung. "I can't even be sure if my friends really like me or if it's just something a little coding tells them to do."

"They like you," Mom said. She tried to make her voice sound calm, but it sounded like it was teetering on a thin wire.

"I was brave!" I cried. "You *took* that from me!"

"Mori," Mom said in a soft, pleading voice. I was drawing attention to us. The bad kind of attention. That was something else I had never done before.

"I can't stand this, Mom! I can't stand the not knowing what is real and what isn't. This isn't what Baba wanted. This isn't what Old Harmonie is supposed to be. We don't lie to protect ourselves. We don't take from other people to make our lives better. We don't fix or hide or get rid of people when they're a problem. I'm not doing it anymore."

"We told you we won't be dampening you again," Dad said.

"No. I won't be doing any of it. This is me," I told my parents—I told all of the families, really, because, of course, everyone was still listening. All of their eyes were on me. "I'm sick of people deciding who I'm going to be."

"Stop," Dad said.

"You tried to change me, and I changed myself back. You took away my bravery, but I found it. I found it to help Ilana. Isn't that what we're supposed to do? Look out for each other? How can we look out for each other if we aren't brave?"

"Calm down," Mom told me.

"Our four core values of our community are creativity, ingenuity, experimentation, and order. How can I help with any of those if I'm not brave? Why would you do that to me?" My voice cracked. Theo stood up next to me. Side by side.

"I don't want to be changed again. I'm not getting dampened and I'm not having my latency done."

People gasped. Sharp intakes of air. Julia stared at me with eyes agog. She shook her head. Even Theo next to me stared in shock.

"The latency doesn't change you," Ms. Staarsgard said. "It enhances you. It's a customary procedure—every child of Old Harmonie has it done."

"Not me," I said, surprised at the firmness of my own voice. "I was brave. And you took it. You *stole* it. You can't do that to a person."

"We were trying—" Mom began.

"But it didn't work," I interrupted. "Not all the way. I was able to leave and help Ilana and I need to know where she is. I need to know if she's okay!"

"Mori—"

"She's fine." It was Meryl Naughton who spoke.

"But where is she?"

"All of this has been quite overwhelming for her," Greg Naughton said.

I shook my head. "No, that doesn't make sense. She was fine before. She wasn't even glitching or anything."

Meryl smiled that same soft, patronizing smile I had found so warm before. "You're a good friend, Mori. You all are. But there are things going on here that you can't possibly understand."

The light was so bright around us, glinting and glaring like knives.

"I understand that you want to get rid of her," I said.

"Enough!" Ms. Staarsgard said. "Mori, this has clearly been a trying few days for you. I suggest you go home and rest and reconsider what you've said here."

I held still for a moment. I wanted to stand there forever, to stand up for Ilana. But I knew I wasn't going to win this fight, not right away. I slumped down into my seat.

"I think we've covered all we need to cover. If there are any press inquiries, please direct them to me. You should go about your days in a normal fashion, without drawing too much attention to yourselves." I felt certain that last bit was directed at me. "Enjoy the rest of your day."

My parents were up and on me in a second, hurrying me out of the room. But they weren't fast enough to stop me from seeing something I'd never expected: Theo Staarsgard was crying.

26

AMNAH AND MOUSE RODE HOME with us. They were going to stay in our guest room. It was a relief to have them in the car so my parents couldn't tell me how disappointed they were or try to convince me to stick to the story that the whole thing had been Ilana's idea.

Out the window, the landscape rushed by, but no air hit my face. There was no flying in this safe, sanitary KritaCar. And then we were in Nashoba. There was the old common house—our museum. And there was our school, closed for the summer. Then came Firefly Lane—past Julia's house and Ilana's and Theo's, and then the KritaCar stopped in our driveway.

Mom opened the door. I couldn't move.

"Come on in. We have a surprise for you!" she cooed.

I pushed myself off the seat and out into the hot summer air. I hadn't felt the heat of the sun in days.

Mom took me by the hand and pulled me into the house, giddy as I was on Christmas morning. The air inside was still and cold. The gray tile floor gleamed and clicked under Mom's sandals. My own sneakers seemed toxic in all this clean. A picture of me—an old picture—stared right back at me and I almost couldn't recognize the girl.

Amnah and Mouse took it all in, their gaze flitting around the entryway and hallway. They glanced into the kitchen as we passed by.

The lines of the tiles seem to warp and swoop. I put a hand out to steady myself. Mom didn't seem to notice. She said, "Come on, come on," and dragged me into the living room with Dad right behind.

There, curled up on our couch, was a tiny kitten. It was asleep and its little chest went up and down as it breathed.

The air cooler hitched on and I shivered.

Did they really think they could replace my best friend with a kitten?

"We're going to the playground," I told them.

Mom and Dad exchanged a look but they didn't try to stop us, probably thinking of Ms. Staarsgard's instructions that we live our lives as normally as possible. Or maybe they wanted to escape me as much as I wanted to escape them.

"It's just around this way," I said as I led Mouse and Amnah away from my house.

"All the houses are the same," Amnah said.

"Not exactly the same," Mouse said.

"On the inside they are," I told her. "Different colors on the outside, different furniture on the inside."

"All through Old Harmonie?" Amnah asked. She turned and looked up and down the road.

"No, just certain streets. It depends when they were built," I explained. "This is the oldest part of Old Harmonie, but one of the newer neighborhoods."

"It's actually pretty smart," she said. "You could do everything in bulk—saves a lot of resources."

"I guess," I replied. It was a hot day. The sun beat down on us as we walked around the cul-de-sac. "When Benji was younger he used to go into people's houses and pretend he thought he was at home. He just wanted to see what the food delivery had brought for snacks. He said his mom never chose the good stuff."

Mouse smiled at that. She had a wry little smile that I liked. Amnah said, "They deliver food to your house?"

"Every day."

Amnah spun around as she walked. "Where are the woods?"

"You'll see. They're over by the playground."

We rounded the lower half of the circle and saw the big, black space where number 9 had been.

"Whoa," Mouse whispered.

"That's where Dr. Varden's house used to be. She left it behind. They burned it when we found out about Ilana."

"They burned it right to the ground?" Mouse asked.

"That surprises you?" Amnah asked in return. She was right. It wasn't the first time Krita had burned homes to the ground.

We passed Mr. Quist's house. Tiger lilies swayed in the breeze like an invitation.

And then we were at the playground. Theo sat on the dome climber. He looked like he'd been waiting there a long time. Julia sat on the ground with her bad leg propped up by the lowest rung of the climber. She stretched over her leg. Tommy sat beside her, eating an apple. Benji had his skateboard and was rocking the front end up and down, up and down.

Theo jumped down as soon as he saw me. "I'm sorry, Mori. Really, I am."

"For what?" I asked.

"I knew what my mom was going to do, how she wanted to play it. She told me that if we were all willing to put our lives on the line for Ilana, then Ilana would surely be willing to shoulder the blame for this."

That made a certain sense. But only if Ilana's fate was so tightly sealed that there could be no redemption for her, no chance of her coming back to us.

"It's okay," I told him.

"No, it isn't." He shook his head. "She said she was trying to help us. To protect us and to make sure no one else got hurt. But it's not right. None of this is."

Julia pushed herself up with a wince. It was like I felt her pain in my leg. "You were joking, right? I mean, you can't not get a latency, Mori."

"Why not?" Theo asked. "I wish it had occurred to me to say no." He looked down at his feet. "No. It did occur to me. I wish I had been brave enough to say I wouldn't."

"You don't mean that," Julia said. "You're just mad about everything."

"He should be mad," I said. "We all should. The things that Krita has done—that Old Harmonie has done—it's not okay. That town under the reservoir, that was Amnah and Mouse's home." I pointed to the sisters. Mouse looked away, but Amnah looked right back at me. "We took it and what did they get in return?"

"You not getting your latency isn't going to give them their town back," Julia said. She turned to Amnah and Mouse. "I mean, I'm sorry, but it isn't. You can't expect us to throw away good things just because you don't have them."

Amnah held up her hands. "I never asked anyone to give up anything."

Benji chewed on the side of his thumb.

"Anyway," I said. "That's not why I'm doing it. Or not the

whole reason. I'm trying to get Old Harmonie back. Back where it was, what it was supposed to be. It wasn't about shortcuts and quick fixes. It was about the process, the discovery." I took a deep breath. "I want to make myself. I worked so hard to be brave again. And that felt good. That felt really good. Whatever I'm going to become, I want to do it myself. And I want to know that it's really me."

Benji stopped rocking his skateboard. "I see what you're saying," he said. "At least I think I do. But I'm not changing my mind. I want my latency."

"I'm not asking you not to get it."

He continued with a soft voice, "The things I'm going to be able to do with my latency, the people I'm going to be able to help—in here and out there—I can't not do it. That wouldn't be right."

"You can't make a choice like that for other people," Theo said. "It has to be what you want for you."

"Well, I guess I do want to do it for me. I want to know what that's going to feel like. I mean, what does it feel like?"

"Strange," Theo said, while Julia said, "Wonderful."

Mouse, Amnah, and Tommy had been still through the whole conversation, as if they knew this was something between us. Now, though, Tommy tapped his foot against the climber. "You think she's okay?" he asked.

"I hope so, but even if she is, I don't know how long she'll be safe," I said.

"So what are we going to do about it?" Benji asked.

"Are you kidding?" Julia asked.

"She's still around somewhere," Benji said. "We can't just leave her to be—well, you know."

"How do you know they haven't done it already?" Julia asked.

"Geez, Julia, come on," Theo said.

"I'm trying to be realistic."

Amnah leaned against the climber, watching our conversation. She was thinking something, but kept it to herself. Her brown eyes flicked their attention from person to person.

"Seems to me you guys are jumping in at the wrong point in the process," Tommy said.

"Meaning?" Theo prompted.

"Any good plan starts with problem definition."

"We know what the problem is: they took Ilana away."

"Exactly. You guys are jumping to step three, define a plan, when you haven't done step two, gather all relevant information. You need to know where she is—or *if* she is—in order to help her."

"How are we going to find that out?" Julia asked. "Just go up to Theo's mom and ask her?"

"No," I said. "Mr. Quist." Mr. Quist had been more honest with us than any grown-up. He'd even tried to warn me about Ilana. I thought he'd been trying to warn me away from her, but he'd been trying to tell me that she wasn't safe. If he knew anything, he would tell us.

"Who's Mr. Quist?" Amnah asked.

"He's Theo's neighbor. He's a crotchety old man. Sort of. He worked in the Idea Box."

Tommy held up both of his hands. "Wait. The Idea Box? For real?"

"So you know about it?" Julia asked. She tugged her sock up so it covered the lower edge of her bandage.

"Oh yeah, totally. Well, maybe not *totally* totally, but enough to know that is the place for me. No one there will laugh about reusing saliva."

"I think people everywhere laugh about reusing saliva," Amnah told him.

"Fair enough," Tommy said. "But still. Idea Box. Far out."

"He's not like other adults. He'll help us if he can."

"You said that about Dr. Varden, too," Theo reminded me.

"Mr. Quist is different."

Theo tugged on his bangs. "He may not have a choice. He may not be able to tell us and still stay here—"

"We have to ask him," I said.

"Right on," Tommy said. "Let's go see the wonderful Mr. Quist."

Julia picked up her crutches that were leaning against the climber. As she was doing so, someone called her name. "Hey!" he called again. "Hey, Julia!" It was DeShawn. He and his friends rode their bikes across the playground and stopped in front of us. "It's good to see you're back!"

"Thanks," she said. She blushed a little. I couldn't remember if Julia had ever had a real conversation with DeShawn Harris, or if she had just worshipped him from afar. Her whole face went a little smushy as she looked at him.

"Is it true you got attacked by a coyote out there?" he asked.

She ran her hand down her leg. "Just some dogs. I almost outran them."

"I bet." He grinned.

"The dogs took a hunk of my muscle out, but it's regenerating right now. Super-cool process, and once it's done, nothing will be able to catch me."

He leaned back against the dome climber and gave her a half smile. "What about me? Will I be able to catch you, Julia?"

She twisted a strand of hair around her finger.

Theo asked, "What else did you hear?"

DeShawn looked at Julia for a moment longer, then turned toward Theo. "Lots, Staarsgard. Everyone is talking about you. Is it true it's like toxic smog out there?"

"No," I said.

"Then why were you in the hospital so long, Benji?"

"VIP status means I get some extra care," Benji replied breezily.

"Our air is the same as yours," Amnah said. She bristled beside me.

"Not exactly the same, though, right?" DeShawn asked.

Amnah didn't answer.

DeShawn leaned closer to Julia. "That stuff on her face," he whispered. "Is it contagious?"

"Lay off it, DeShawn," I said.

He raised his eyebrows at me.

"You know they're all clear," Theo said. "Or else they wouldn't be allowed in."

"Sure, sure," DeShawn said. But he still backed away from the outside kids.

"Your parents need to dampen your arrogance," I told him.

"It's not arrogance if you can back it up. That's confidence," he said. "Something you actually seem to be developing, for better or for worse." His friends laughed. They all could go in for a dampening, the jerks. "I still can't believe that little Mori Bloom busted out of Old Harmonie. And for what?"

"What's that supposed to mean?" I demanded.

"Haven't you heard about Ilana?" he asked. His face looked innocent, but I knew he was messing with me.

"What are you talking about?"

"All I can tell you is what I've heard." He paused, staring at each of us. "I hate to be the one to break this to you, but word is, they boxed her up and shipped her away. That's what my parents said."

"No." I shook my head hard. "That can't be possible."

But one of DeShawn's friends nodded enthusiastically. "I heard they carried three different versions of her out of the house."

So that was the story going around: half-truths that made Ilana the villain and Krita the ones who took care of the problem. The Krita people were always going to spin the story so they were the heroes.

"I heard four," said another boy. "Creepy little clone robots."

"Stop," I whispered. How could they be joking about this? She was a *person*, and they were going to laugh about destroying her? Was that what this whole town was all about? If you make a mess, you sweep it away. You burn it down and erase it. You laugh about it afterward. "She's my friend, and none of your stupid jokes are going to change that."

For a second, DeShawn actually looked like he felt a little sorry for me. Then he shrugged. "I'm just telling you what I heard. Don't be so broken up over it, Mori. She wasn't ever really real, anyway."

Julia stepped forward. "Enough, DeShawn."

DeShawn held up his hands. "Hey, don't blame me. At least I'm telling you all the truth."

The truth. I'm not sure such a thing even existed. But I

knew my own truth, what I felt in my heart. Ilana was real—a real girl and my real friend. “Come on,” I said. “It’s time to go.” I pivoted and led my friends out of the playground and around the cul-de-sac until we came to Mr. Quist’s house. The fence to his back garden was open, swinging a little bit in the breeze.

27

“ARE YOU SURE ABOUT THIS?” Julia asked.

“He’s our best chance for learning the truth,” I replied.

The sun caught the mica on Mr. Quist’s walkway and made it glint.

“I know,” Julia said. “It’s just that, once we know the truth, we can’t un-know it.”

She was right. How I had wished to un-see the file we had found about ALANA, to un-think what it made us suspect about Ilana. Since going outside, and thinking about what we did in Old Harmonie, whether any of us were real or true or natural or designed—whether those words made any sense at all—*not* knowing, *not* learning, *not* seeing seemed the safer choice.

Theo said, "I think we'll just feel better knowing she's okay."

"What if she's not okay?" Julia asked.

My stomach turned. "Then I want to know that, too."

"But if we find her," Julia said. "Aren't we putting her in danger again?"

I cocked my head to the side. "You aren't siding with DeShawn and them, are you? You don't still think she's a freak?"

"I never thought she was a freak," Julia said, but she couldn't look at us.

"We all did, Julia, at least for a minute," Theo said.

"But she's not," Mouse said quietly.

"Fine. Maybe I did. And maybe I was wrong, but what I know for sure is that all of us are safer with her where she is and us here."

"I spent my whole life being safe, Julia. I'm not going to take the easy way. Not this time. I understand if you don't want to help, but—"

"No," Julia said, rubbing her leg. "No, I'm in. Let's go."

We went through the garden and found Mr. Quist kneeling on one of his little gardening mats and holding a fresh tomato in the palm of his hand. He looked up when we came marching in. His eyes softened and he said, "Well, if it isn't the Firefly Five. And friends."

I introduced Amnah, Mouse, and Tommy and then I said, "We want to know about Ilana."

"What do you want to know?" he asked. His attention had gone back to the tomato. He began twisting the green stem at the top of it.

"Where is she?" I asked.

"That question has a complicated answer," he said as he plucked the green leaves from the fruit and threw them over his shoulder.

"Everything is complicated! That's all people will say, no matter what I ask. *It's complicated*. Even when I asked if I was sick, my parents just said, 'It's complicated.' I'm tired of it!"

Theo put a hand on my shoulder, but Mr. Quist didn't seem bothered by my outburst. Instead he took out a pocketknife and began slicing the tomato while he still held it in his hand. All the juice was spilling out over his fingers like blood. My heart raced.

"We just want to know if she's okay," Theo said.

Mr. Quist popped a slice of tomato into his mouth. After he swallowed, he said, "I believe she is."

"So you know where she is, then?" Tommy asked, pouncing like a cat on a mouse.

"Not precisely."

"You know who has her?" Theo asked.

"I think so."

"Mr. Quist, please!" I begged. "I can't play some stupid game while you eat your tomato! I need to know if she's okay."

"We talked about these plants, didn't we, Mori?" he asked me, holding out his hand that had both a slice of the tomato and his knife in it. "About the way plants had been manipulated?"

I nodded.

"I was trying to tell you—" he began.

"I know," I said. "I know what she is. We all do. I don't care if all this genetic manipulation and whatnot is bad for plants. She's not a tomato."

"Of course she isn't," he said. "Come on inside. I need to wash my hands."

Even though all the houses of Firefly Lane were the same, his felt different somehow. Darker. His kitchen didn't open up into his living room or dining room. Each room was its own separate space. We went in through the kitchen, where he stopped to wash his hands, then into the living room, which he had set up like an office.

"I worked for your great-grandmother," he said. "In her lab when I first got started. She was a wise woman." He sat down in an old leather swivel chair.

"I know," I said as I sat down on a worn couch. The upholstery had faded pink rosebuds on a green background. Mouse sat next to me on the couch, her body warm and still.

He pulled up a photograph on his tablet. "There we are," he said as he turned the picture into a holopic we could all see: Dr. Varden and my baba with a very young Meldrick

Quist beside them. They only looked a few years older than him. "But we didn't agree on everything. And she and Dr. Varden didn't agree on everything either."

"Of course not. No one does," I said.

"What are you getting at?" Theo asked.

"Here's what I can tell you. Lucy said that if Agatha was truly worried about the ethics of the project, then she couldn't just take it down and hide away the pieces. She had to get rid of all of it."

"No," I said, my voice wavering. "That's not the way she thought. She always said that failure was a route to learning."

"But failure wasn't the problem with the ALANA project. Those difficulties they were having—like the uncanny valley—they were solvable challenges. The group didn't have a solution at the time, but knew they would someday."

"Like now," Julia said.

"Yes." Mr. Quist changed the photograph to one of a simple helperbot, a white one with huge, black insect eyes. "They started by making interactive AI lifelike in only the broadest of strokes, like the eyes on this helperbot. Then there was the biomimicry work and we started having helperbots and chatbots that looked like animals, and robots that moved like animals."

"Like my robobee," I said.

"Precisely." He typed something onto his tablet, then

brought up a whole slate of pictures of robotic insects. "Some of the design is simply for fun; for others, it is purposeful. Either way, these were steps forward. At the same time, advances were being made in replication. Three-dimensional copiers could get down to the centimeter, then the millimeter, then immeasurable. Materials work moved forward, too, so it wasn't just a replica in plastic, but any material you could imagine, and now we can print our ice cream."

"Like at Sully's!" Tommy said. "Best ice cream joint around!"

"And in parallel, genetic engineering moved forward. And cloning. And all this progress came together. Scientists would bump into each other in coffee shops or on the way to the restroom and chat about what they were doing. What we were doing. And we'd say, 'Hey, that's cool, have you thought about this?' Or 'What if we tried that?' Or 'We should put our projects together.' It was exciting. It *is* exciting. That's how science works. That's how we advance." He looked at the holopic of the robobees and shook his head.

"That's the whole point of the Idea Box, right?" Julia asked. "Bringing together all these ideas?"

"Yes, but there was no one checking over us. No one putting on the brakes."

"Why would you want to?" Tommy asked from his perch on the edge of Mr. Quist's couch. "Science rushes forward."

"Precisely. And sometimes that means you get where you are going very quickly. You make great advances. But sometimes that means you veer off course, or you crash along the way. If you don't think about what you're doing, if you don't plan for all outcomes, you aren't being responsible. They didn't do that with ALANA. They didn't think through the problems of creating a person," Mr. Quist said. "A whole new person. Back then the lines weren't so blurry. Genetic engineering was new and, frankly, people were scared of it when it came to children. 'Designer Babies,' they called it—and it made everyone squeamish. Now, well, we have our naturals and our designed kids. Everyone knows about it and everyone is fine with it."

"Everyone in here," Amnah said.

"And out there," Tommy added. "I mean, we do genetic engineering out there, too. Fixing problems, making choices."

"Minor choices," Amnah said.

"It's like you said, Mori," Julia interrupted their argument. "That thirty percent is just an arbitrary line."

"Anyway," Amnah mused. "Even if they had scrapped the whole project, someone else would have figured out all the pieces eventually. That's the way science works."

I ran my fingers through my hair. "But all of this is about ALANA. We're talking about *our* Ilana. Where is she?"

"That's what I'm trying to tell you," Mr. Quist said. "Dr. Varden would never completely scrub a project. Even though Lucy told her to get rid of it all, she kept the consciousness on a hard drive."

That made my stomach turn. Next to me, Mouse stiffened, too.

"Ilana is not ALANA," I said.

"I know that," Mr. Quist said. "But Agatha felt responsible for both of them. And as long as she is around, I don't think Ilana will be scuttled. Not completely."

She was safe. I took a deep breath. Dr. Varden had saved her. I *knew* Agatha would do it. Theo and Julia each reached over and grabbed one of my hands. Why were they trying to comfort me? Ilana *was* safe, wasn't she? Wasn't that what Mr. Quist was trying to tell me?

"So Ilana is okay, right?" I asked.

"I didn't say that," Mr. Quist replied, looking down at his lap.

"It means there's still time," Mouse said.

Amnah added, "For now."

Mr. Quist stood up then. "We're finally getting some cherry tomatoes after the storm. Still a little yellow, but quite delicious. Let me send you all home with some. Mori, come with me to get the boxes."

Theo stood up, too, but Mr. Quist said, "No, no. Only Mori needs to come. We'll just be a minute. Meet us out in the garden." He led me into the kitchen. The tomatoes were piled in a blue bowl on the counter, shining and clean, but he said, "Wait here a moment." When he came back, he was holding a slim book. "She left this for you."

"Ilana?" I asked. "When?"

"Before all this. When things started to go bad."

He held out the book to me: it was a guide to edible and nonedible plants of New England. It looked old, with the cover photo faded and the edges of the vinyl cover a little scuffed. When I flipped through, I saw that it had been published in 1997: practically an antique. The cover was thick and even had a pouch for storing specimens or seeds in it.

I flipped through wondering why Ilana had wanted me to have this book. On the title page she had written: "In case of emergency. Love, Ilana."

That was it. In case of emergency? Maybe that meant she really was thinking of us living in Oakedge. But what if it meant something more?

"Your friends are waiting," Mr. Quist said. "Best not to keep them too long."

"Thanks, Mr. Quist." I turned to go.

"Don't forget your tomatoes," he said.

"Right." I stuffed the book into the back pocket of my shorts and pulled out my T-shirt in the hopes that no one would see the book. I didn't want to talk about it until I knew what it meant. Then I picked up the tomatoes and thanked Mr. Quist again.

Just as my hand was on the doorknob, he spoke: "Mori, you can't fix everything yourself."

"I know," I said.

Through the glass, I saw my friends, new and old, out in the garden. Julia tossed a tomato toward Tommy's mouth. He caught it, but it spurt juice and seeds all over his lip. When he laughed, some came dribbling out.

"It's just a matter of who you can trust, isn't it?"

He was quiet for a moment. "You've been right so far. Don't start doubting yourself now."

Theo glanced up. He saw me through the glass and smiled and gave a little wave. Mouse turned and looked over her shoulder and smiled, too. I stepped back out into the sun.

28

I WENT TO BED WITH the book from Ilana stuck under my pillow. It was the only piece of her I had. Everything else had been taken away, erased as cleanly as a hard drive.

I stared up at the ceiling and reached under my pillow and fingered the edges of the pages. Had she read the book, too? I hoped so. Maybe it would be useful to her wherever she was.

I pulled my sheet up and rolled over.

I had told my parents I was tired—I had nearly said I wasn't feeling well, but that would have been a mistake—and gone to bed early.

Mouse and Amnah had gone to bed, too, after they'd spoken to their mother on the phone. She was coming up from wherever she'd been down south. Ms. Staarsgard was working on getting all the paperwork in order for their mother and Tommy's uncle to come and get the kids. I wasn't sure why it was taking so long, but I was glad they were still here. They shared the guest room on the first floor. I'd left them with a stack of my favorite books.

My new kitten was curled up in a ball next to me. She was nothing more than a little puff of fur. I hadn't named her yet. I wasn't sure I even wanted to keep the guilt gift, but I found myself absentmindedly petting her.

On the shelf next to me was the box with Prince Philip, my robobee. I reached over and picked up the wooden box. I held it on my stomach for a moment before creaking the top open. Philip buzzed awake almost immediately. He flew out of the box and landed on my hand, where he purred and flapped his wings contentedly.

"I missed you," I said.

He flapped his wings.

"I don't suppose you know where she is?" I stared into his mirrored eyes. They probably had cameras in them, scanning the world and remembering what they saw. Were they uploaded to some forgotten server somewhere? Could somebody be watching me right now? I doubted that, so I kept talking: "Mr. Quist thinks Dr. Varden is protecting her somehow. Maybe they'll get out of here together. I don't know where they'd go, though. I don't think they can go back to MIT, right?"

His wings went up and down no faster or slower.

The kitten opened her gray eyes and regarded Prince Philip.

"I just want to say good-bye. Good-bye for now. And maybe make a plan, a way to keep in touch? If I could reach her one time and let her know . . ." I sighed. "None of this means anything to you, does it?"

Up down. Up down.

"I used to think the two of you were alike, but you're not. Not at all. She thinks and reacts and has feelings and dreams and hopes and fears and—well, you just record and react and you're kind of cute, so I can think that you have feelings, but you really don't. I could pull a wing right off you and you wouldn't even care. I could do this." I held out my hand so that Prince Philip was resting on my palm, contentedly buzzing the way a real bee might as it returned to the hive. With a sudden motion, I flipped my hand over and Prince Philip fell to the floor.

There was a soft crashing and scraping sound. A bit of scratching and then, not a minute later, Prince Philip flew back up to me.

"You're pretty stupid."

Buzz-buzz. Wings up and down.

"But I guess I am, too. Talking to a robobee and holding on to a book like it's a person."

There was a rustle and then a smack and then the kitten was on top of Philip, batting the robobee around with her paws.

"Stop!" I called out. "Stop it!"

I pushed the kitten off Philip. I barely had time to register his twisted wing before the kitten dug her tiny claws into my hand. "Ow!"

I shook my hand and the kitten fell back off my bed and landed with a small thud just as my parents opened the door.

"Mori, what is going on here!" Mom said.

"She scratched me!"

"So you threw her?" Dad asked.

"I shook my hand to get her off it."

The kitten sat in the center of my carpet and licked her front paw. Mom bent over and scooped her up. "Maybe the kitten was a bad idea."

"You think?" I shot back.

"Mori!" Dad said.

"I didn't ask for a kitten! I've never wanted a kitten!"

"That doesn't mean you can talk to us like that. I don't know what's gotten into you, but—"

"But what?" I demanded. "Are you going to dampen it out of me?"

Mom lowered her head. The kitten stretched out and rubbed Mom's chin with the top of her furry head. Kiss-up. "We understand that you're feeling a lot of anger," Mom told me.

"You took my best friend away and gave me a stupid kitten!"

Dad shook his head, but Mom said, "We didn't take her away from you. If it was up to us, she never would have come."

"Same difference," I said.

"No," Dad said. "Not the same difference. You never would've been hurt and you certainly never would've pulled that foolish stunt."

"Right. It's all her fault. That's the story, right? That's the lie we're telling?"

"Stop," Dad said.

"I just want to make sure I get on the right page, or, what was it you said? Get ahead of the story? Is that what you meant? Make up a more acceptable story before the real one comes out? I guess that's just the way things operate around here. Something is inconvenient, you burn it down. A project isn't justifying its cost, if it goes off course, then you just scuttle it. A kid isn't exactly perfect, just dampen away. Hide it. Fix it. Lie about it. That's what we do here."

"We have a way of life to protect here, Mori," Mom said. "You have to understand that I would do anything to keep you safe. Dad and I both would. If we step out of line here, we risk so much. I don't think you understand that."

"What? Are they going to kick us out?"

"That's a possibility, yes," Dad said. "There's plenty of people who want in to Old Harmonie. People who will follow the rules and people who respect the ideals of this place."

"Which ideals exactly, Dad? I mean, destroying a whole town, which core value is that?"

"What are you talking about?" he asked.

"The reservoir. Mouse and Amnah used to live in that town!"

Mom and Dad looked away from me, and from each other. Part of me had hoped I'd been wrong about the reservoir, or that they hadn't known, but the way they couldn't look at me told me they knew the truth.

"And you'd get rid of Ilana, too. All in the name of keeping me safe. If that's what being safe means—if that's the way of life you're trying to protect—then I'm not interested. I'm not going to lie about Ilana to protect myself."

"This is bigger than you, Mori," Dad said. "It's bigger than all of us."

"And that's a reason to give up?" I asked. "You told me to never give up. Persevere, persevere, persevere."

"But not when persevering is running into a wall again and again and again," Dad tried to explain. "If you had come to us, we would have told you that there was nothing you could do to help her."

"You would've been wrong. I *did* help her," I said.

"For a short time, yes," Mom said.

That stopped me. Either Dr. Varden had her and she was safe or . . . something else. Did my parents know what had happened to her? "Where is she now?" I asked.

Mom and Dad exchanged a look.

"It's possible—" Mom said.

"I'm coming to you now. I want your help. I want to know where she is and if she's okay."

They didn't answer. They were going to keep on protecting Old Harmonie and Krita no matter what.

"That's what I figured." I reached down and pulled up my sheet. "I'm really tired and I just want to go to sleep, okay?"

There was a long moment of silence. The moonlight came in the window and lit the space between us. All they had to do was step through that light over to me. For a moment, I thought they would. But then Mom said, "Okay. Good night, Mori." Still snuggling the kitten, she left the room with my dad right behind.

29

OUTSIDE MY WINDOW, DARKNESS HAD fallen. The clouds were thick, so there wasn't even a moon.

I could make it. I could make it out to the fence.

I just had to wait until my parents went to sleep.

Closing my eyes, I listened hard. Nothing. I went to my door and cracked it open. My father's snores drifted down the hallway, but so did my mom's soft, shuffling feet. I sat down on the floor of my room and waited. And waited.

Eventually, the shuffling stopped. My eyes were heavy by then, but I rubbed them hard and stood up.

Dad had replaced my dirty old sneakers with bright white ones that would carry the evidence of my late-night adventure. I pushed open the hallway closet and found my rain boots. The neoprene tops felt tight against my calves, but they were my best choice.

I opened the front door and felt the cool, fresh night air. Finally, I could breathe.

Firefly Lane at night was just how I remembered it. At least that hadn't changed. The buzz from the solar batteries was the first sound that truly felt like home, and I stepped in each circle of light before I realized that would make me easier to see.

When I went by number 9 I stopped like I'd been punched in the gut. Elma was gone. They must have scooped up my tree when they'd done the cleanup after the fire. I shook my head. No time to mourn a tree. What would Theo think of that? Mourning a tree? Somehow I thought he might understand better now.

The playground was empty. No more DeShawn and his stupid friends. No little kids laughing. This is what it would be like if Old Harmonie ended. Everything would be silent and empty, and slowly, slowly, nature would take it back over.

The forest floor was soft. Without a moon, it was nearly pitch-black, but I knew the way. I couldn't stop myself from running, leaping over the small trickle of water that had swollen into a respectable stream, sidestepping the patch of poison ivy. This was home. This was home.

My breaths came as fast as my skittering heartbeat. *Breathe in*, I told myself. *Breathe out*.

Once my breath was under control, I could listen. Animals rustled on the ground and in the trees. In the distance, coyotes laughed.

But that was all.

An owl hooted and for a moment I actually believed it was the one Amnah and I had seen together. That was impossible, of course.

It hooted again.

I hooted back.

Silence.

Then I whispered, "Ilana!" A little louder, "Ilana!"

Silence.

The owl hooted.

Silence again.

I sat as still as I could.

The forest was big. Really big. It curved all around the neighborhoods of Nashoba.

Next to me was a thick stick covered over with lichen. I picked it up and leaned it against a nearby tree. I found three pinecones and placed them around the stick. A rock shaped like an oversize egg caught my eye. Perfect. I placed it right beneath the stick and then surrounded it with an oval of pebbles. I reminded myself of what we'd learned in that survival class: if you're lost, you should hold still. If you stay in one place, someone will come to find you. Ilana knew I went there at night, and she'd know where to find me. The rock and pebbles, they were a message to her, a promise that I would always come back to look for her. And if she didn't come soon, that was okay. I could wait a long time. I'd stay in Old Harmonie on Firefly Lane so that when things were safer, when we were both grown, she could stroll right down our street, and I'd be there.

I lay down in the soft moss, the kind that could cradle you. Ilana and I always said it would make a good bed. I didn't mean to fall asleep, but I did. And I had the most wonderful-horrible dream. Ilana came back.

In the dream, I opened my eyes. I was back in the hospital. Ilana was there. I told myself, *Stay calm. This is a dream.* I wondered, though, if you could know inside a dream that it wasn't real.

"Mori," she whispered. "I'm not supposed to be here."

"Are you really here?" I asked.

"I'm really here."

But people can tell the truth in a dream and have it still be false.

She reached through the entry tube and put her hand on my arm. The touch was familiar and kind. "Oh," I sighed.

"You're okay?" she asked.

"I think so."

"They wouldn't tell me." She stepped closer to the bed and rustled my plastic bubble. The monitor machines cast a red-green glow over her skin.

"They wouldn't tell me about you, either. My orderly said she wasn't allowed to talk about you."

Ilana turned away. "They're erasing me."

I lifted myself up onto my elbows. "What do you mean?"

She shook her head. Outside, a clock tower chimed eleven. Ilana stilled her body. "Nothing," she finally said. "They're just trying to protect you. So it doesn't hurt as much when I go."

"Where are you going?"

She pressed her lips together and closed her eyes. When she opened them, they were bright again. Even in the darkness, I could see their beautiful color.

"Ilana?"

"It doesn't matter."

We were in the woods now, in the way that people move in dreams sometimes: in one place and then blurring into another. We stood in the tree in Oakedge, side by side.

"But how will I find you?" My voice cracked. I gripped the bark of the tree.

"I'll find you," she said. "I promise."

"I love you, Ilana."

"I love you, too, Mori."

She put her arm around me and we stood like that. Still. Looking out over our windswept kingdom. Until, after minutes or hours or days or lifetimes, she slipped away.

And then I woke up.

I missed her so much, my whole body ached.

But I also thought that maybe the dream was true. That she was someplace safe. That I didn't need to worry so much.

It's a mixed-up feeling, though, to have to wonder if your dreams are your own.

Snap! The sound came from deeper in the forest, followed by a *crash!* I held my body still and tried not to breathe.

The crunching sound of feet came closer.

Could it possibly be?

"Ilana," I whispered. Then, a little louder, "Ilana!"

"No," a voice came back. Theo's voice. "It's me."

"Oh," I said. I couldn't hide my disappointment. Theo stepped into the clearing, then sat down next to me on the moss. I rubbed my eyes. "How'd you know to look for me here?"

He raised his eyebrows. "Come on, Mori. Anyone who knows you would know to look for you here." He rubbed his hand lightly over the moss. "Do you really think Ilana's going to show up here?"

I shrugged. I knew I couldn't lie to him. "Maybe someday."

"Maybe Julia's right. Maybe she's safest if we don't know where she is. And maybe we're safer, too."

"So you want to forget about her?" I asked.

"I didn't say that. I'm just worried about you. This isn't what Ilana wanted for you, I know that much. She didn't want you all twisted and tied up."

The tears came again, hot and fierce. Theo patted me on the shoulder two times, and then, a little awkwardly, he pulled me closer to him for a hug. I kept crying and once again got tears and snot all over his shirt. He held still and let me cry.

"We should go home," he finally said.

I nodded, but neither of us moved for a moment. Then he got to his feet, and I did, too.

We didn't talk as we walked through the forest and the playground. One of the swings was going back and forth, but there was no one around.

He led me around the Kellermans' house and in through the center of the cul-de-sac. The skinny trees shook a little with each gust of wind, which seemed to be getting stronger.

When we got to the very center, Theo stopped. "I looked into it for you. Having a house here, I mean. It would be easy to bring out the water line. Power would be tricky with the trees, but if you had enough batteries, it could work. The main problem would be getting a driveway back in here."

"You really looked into it?" I asked.

"Yeah. I mean, it wasn't that big of a deal. So you could do it. Or you could rebuild where number nine was. Either way."

"Why'd you look into it?" I asked.

"Because I want you to stay," he told me.

"You think I'm going someplace?"

He shrugged. "I think of leaving, so I figured you might, too. Anyway, we should go. If our parents find us out of the house, life as we know it is over."

"Life as we know it already is over."

"Maybe," he said. And started walking.

We popped out behind his house and he walked me around the corner of the cul-de-sac. We stopped at my front door. "Thanks," I said. I wasn't really sure what I was thanking him for. For getting me home, for finding me in the woods, for figuring out how I could have my house. All of it, I guessed.

"Listen," he said. "I've been thinking about what you said, when we were outside. About how I might not really, really like you. How it could just be something programmed into me. And maybe it was. I don't know. But it doesn't feel that way to me."

"My parents said it wasn't programmed, not that I can trust them." I looked up toward their window, which was dark.

"Well, to me it feels real and I think that's all that matters." He held still for a moment. Long enough for us to settle into the noisy silence of our street at night. Then he turned and ran back to his house.

I slipped into my house. The kitten met me with a soft meow, and I picked her up. Her fur was soft under my chin. I placed her in my bed, then crawled in beside her. She fell asleep quickly, and I was about to do the same when there was a gentle knock on the door.

30

MOUSE STEPPED INTO MY ROOM. She carefully shut the door behind her, then she sat down cross-legged on the floor. My parents had bought some clothes for her and Amnah, and she wore a set of pajamas with a moon and a star on the shirt. I waited a moment and then sat down next to her on the braided rug.

"Can't sleep?" I asked.

"I've been thinking," she said. Her voice was as soft as ever, but in the quiet of my room at night, her voice was warm and clear. "In here, they pay a lot of attention to kids. It's like they built the world around you. It's different where we're from."

"I know," I told her.

The kitten mewed in her sleep.

"I think I know how to get to Ilana," Mouse said. "And if we can get to her, we can get her out."

"Did you hear something? Do you know where she is?"

She shook her head. It seems my heart would have learned not to hope so hard by now, but it hadn't, and I felt crushed again. "But I do think we can get to her. I think *you* can get to her."

"How?"

"Apologize."

The word hung there. *Apologize*? To whom? To Krita, who created a person they were willing to kill? To Ms. Staarsgard, who was going to lie about Ilana? To my parents, who wanted me to go along with the lie? "No way."

"You have to. You apologize to your parents and to Theo's mom and to everyone. You go along with their story. And then you ask if you can say good-bye to her."

"They're not going to let me."

"Beg. Plead. Say whatever you need to. If we can get in, we can get her out."

"How?" I asked.

"Opportunity plus distraction. There are eight of us working together now. We can do it."

"So we distract them and then what?"

"We get her out of here."

"Where?"

"Still working on that part. I have some ideas."

"This doesn't sound like much of a plan," I told her.

"Has there ever been much of a plan?"

Fair enough, I thought. My plan had relied on Dr. Varden, who hadn't been able to help us. At least now we were relying on ourselves. "And hey," I said, "we've got master planner Tommy McPhee on our side, so what could possibly go wrong?"

She grinned at that. "Oh, only everything."

We both giggled. On my bed, the kitten stood up and stretched, and looked down at us with a mix of curiosity and annoyance.

"Hey, Mouse, what you said to Ms. Staarsgard, about talking to people? Is it really that hard?"

"Yes," she said.

"But it's not hard to talk to me?" I asked. She had told me that way back in the car lot. "Why not?"

"I don't know. You're just easy. Like Amnah—maybe even easier. But everyone else—it's like I can feel my mouth gluing itself shut. I get all sweaty. My head pounds."

"You should do it, then," I told her. "You should get the dampening."

"Amnah thinks it's crazy. Barbaric, actually."

"What do you think?"

"I think it would be nice to talk to everyone else like this." She smiled at me. "Well, maybe not just like this. It will always be nicer with some people."

The kitten leaped down from my bed. She walked over

my lap, then crawled into Mouse's and curled up. I didn't blame her: I'd choose Mouse over me, too. "If you help us get Ilana out, though, they may not do it for you after all."

"I know," she said. "Some things are more important than yourself, right?"

Exactly.

In the morning, Mom told us that Tommy's and Mouse and Amnah's families were coming that afternoon. Ms. Staarsgard had gotten Mouse and Amnah's mom onto an early morning flight, and they were sending a KritaCar out for Tommy's uncle. We were all going to go to the museum to see them off. Ms. Staarsgard had arranged a special tour.

"We'll have to do it today," Mouse whispered to me as we went upstairs to brush our teeth after breakfast. "I'll get the others ready. You figure out how you're going to convince them to let you see Ilana."

"Easier said than done."

"You can do it," she whispered.

Mouse and Amnah left to go over to Julia's, and I went back upstairs to my room. Convince Ms. Staarsgard to let me see Ilana? Ha! She ran everything in this place. She wasn't going to deviate from her plan.

I looked at myself in the mirror. My haircut made me look older, but I was still just a little girl. That's how Ms. Staarsgard would see me. No more threatening than my new kitten.

But this kitten, I told myself, had snuck out of Old Harmonie. We had done something so impossible that Ms. Staarsgard felt like she had to *lie* about it. I watched a smile twitch on my lips. If I'd done the impossible once, I could do it again, right?

31

THE LOBBY OF THE MUSEUM was empty of employees. There wasn't even anyone at the welcome desk. A new fish tank had been installed, one that took up most of the wall. Theo stood by it with Benji and Tommy. I beelined for them with Amnah and Mouse right behind. The fish in the tank moved sluggishly. They twitched their lazy tails and glided through the water.

"I got caught last night," Theo said.

"I'm sorry."

He shrugged. "No biggie. My mom did tell me I needed to stop this 'highly embarrassing behavior.'"

"Or else what?" Amnah asked. She leaned against the glass, ignoring the fish.

Theo pushed his bangs out of his eyes. "Deportation. Disownment."

"You can come live with me," Tommy said.

"I just may take you up on that," Theo replied.

The door swung open and Julia and her parents came in. Her bandage was purple today, and covered less of her leg. Her long hair swung around her shoulders. Tommy swallowed hard.

"Are you wearing makeup?" I asked when she came over to us.

She didn't answer. Not exactly. "I heard there might be some reporters here."

There were: two of them. They stood over in the corner, chatting and making notes on their tablets.

Mouse looked at her watch.

"They should be here any minute," Amnah said.

"Do you think Ms. Staarsgard will talk to them right away?" Mouse asked. "About the dampening?"

"Why don't *you* ask them about it?" Amnah snapped. "Why don't you explain that you want these doctors to mess up your brain."

"It's not a mess-up—" Julia began.

"Whatever," I interrupted. "Listen, Mouse and I have a plan."

But I didn't get a chance to share it because the door opened and two strangers walked in. Mouse, Amnah, and

Tommy ran to them. Tommy's uncle wore a too-small button-down shirt that slipped out of the waistband of his pants as he wrapped his arms around his nephew. "Tommy, you're a right jammy fool!"

"I know!" Tommy replied. "But look! Look where we are!"

The reporters snapped pictures with their tablets, jostling each other with their elbows to get the best angle.

A small elegant woman folded Amnah and Mouse into her. Tears streamed down her cheeks, but she smiled wide and fierce. It reminded me of the bronze trees, and I couldn't help but smile, too, as she whispered into their hair.

Ms. Staarsgard crossed the floor, her heels click, clicking. Those shoes would fill my nightmares.

"Welcome, welcome," Ms. Staarsgard said.

"What do you mean you have a plan?" Theo whispered to me while his mother went on with general pleasantries.

"We're getting Ilana out," I whispered back.

That's when I noticed Dr. Varden. I hadn't seen her when I'd first come in, but now I saw her perched on a bench to the right of the welcome desk.

"Come now," Ms. Staarsgard said. "Let's have a quick tour. I always love a chance to showcase the wonders of Old Harmonie."

Was she going to take us to the Animal AI exhibit? She couldn't possibly! She pushed open a door next to the fish tank and we entered the botanical exhibit hall. I breathed in deeply. The smell of pine and flowers filled my nose.

"We try to live as sustainably as possible here," Ms. Staarsgard explained. "And we realized long ago that our plant species were our lifeblood. We have this display here, but we also have a secure seed bank."

Tommy's uncle nodded. "Like at the Arnold Arboretum." His accent was even stronger than Tommy's. "Your aunt used to work there."

"Precisely," Ms. Staarsgard said. "There are seed banks all over the world in case of emergency."

The words stung me. I looked up at the flowers of a dogwood tree and tried to blink away tears.

"If you'll just come this way, here is what I was hoping to show you. It's a new exhibit." When she opened the doors, we were in a field of wildflowers. A breeze bent their stems softly. We were still inside. The ceiling and the lights were far above us. But they'd managed to make it seem like we were outdoors.

Dr. Varden held her hand to her chest. She squeezed at a pendant there.

"They did a wonderful job, didn't they, Agatha?" Ms. Staarsgard asked. "The historians mined all the documents and photos to get a perfectly accurate representation."

The field! It was Old Harmonie before all the villages

had been built. It was the photo that Dr. Varden had shown us, out where Oakedge was before the forests grew.

Around us, holograms of trees appeared. The split oak I shared with Ilana grew up from a sapling into the mighty tree it had become. I went to touch it, but of course my fingers went right through.

"This way," Ms. Staarsgard said. We moved around the giant room the same way we would move around our cul-de-sac. There was number 9, restored and new-looking. Outside, two women worked the garden. Dr. Varden and Baba! They laughed and passed each other trowels. Beyond them were Dr. Varden's beehives.

They were all holograms, too, top-of-the-line ones that looked solid.

The real Dr. Varden had tears streaming down her face. "What is this?" she practically moaned. She seemed distraught, but what I wouldn't have given for a memory like this, a world with my best friend that I could step back into.

My mother moved closer to the hologram. "It's just like her," she murmured. "Just the way I remembered."

"Your history is the history of Old Harmonie," Ms. Staarsgard explained. "We've captured it here. It covers the whole development of Old Harmonie."

The holograms shimmered slightly, but otherwise were so real. There was my baba, digging in the dirt, growing a garden and a new, more beautiful world. Just like Ilana and

I had tried to do. Would Baba even recognize Old Harmonie now? Would she want to be here? I didn't think so. And that made me more certain that I had to get Ilana out, and once she was safe, I had to keep working to make Old Harmonie what Baba had meant it to be.

Ms. Staarsgard stepped between me and the holograms. "Right now the scene is set to the Nashoba area, but we can visit any location, any time." She raised her chin. "Simulate Center Harmonie circa 2000."

The field fell away and we were in a parking lot. A strip of stores with strange names was in front of us. One of the car doors opened and a woman got out with her child. Heat radiated up off the tar of the parking lot, and my nose filled with the smell of gasoline. Benji coughed. His parents put an arm over him. "Perfectly healthy," Ms. Staarsgard said. "It's a psychosomatic reaction he's having." She spread her arms. "Suburban sprawl was starting to take over the country-side. Your work out here, with the help of Krita, of course, saved this place."

Amnah sniffed, but Mouse grabbed her hand. We couldn't get Ms. Staarsgard angry. Not today.

"Is there anything else you'd like to see, Agatha?" Ms. Staarsgard asked.

Agatha tilted her own head back. "Simulate Forge Pond, circa 2006."

Ms. Staarsgard smiled.

The tar and buildings fell away and now we stood on the shore of a beautiful lake. People paddled canoes and kayaks. In one of the canoes, people were fishing. Up close, though, two women splashed in the shallows. Baba and Dr. Varden again. The world grew still as we watched them.

"I'm sorry," Dr. Varden whispered. "I'm sorry I left you, Lucy. This wasn't my home anymore. You would always be."

I looked away from her grief. Mouse caught my eye. She was right. This was my moment.

"Ms. Staarsgard," I whispered.

She looked down at me. "Yes, Mori?"

I cleared my throat. "I wanted to apologize for the other day. I was upset and I didn't mean what I said. I know you were trying to help us. I know you are."

Ms. Staarsgard put her hands on my shoulders. "Of course, Mori. We were all very upset by the events of the past weeks. I'm sure many of us said things we didn't mean." She glanced over at Theo. I wondered if that was a confession or an accusation.

"I miss her so much is all." Tears welled in my eyes. I nodded toward Dr. Varden. "They never got to say good-bye. I just want to say good-bye to her." My voice hitched as I started to sob. It wasn't an act.

Mom had crossed over. She leaned in. "Tova, please. Can't the children say good-bye?"

"Friends move away. We've all dealt with it," Benji's mother added. "If the children could have some closure by saying good-bye, I feel this whole transition would go more smoothly."

Ms. Staarsgard hesitated.

"Please, Mom," Theo asked. "Please?"

Ms. Staarsgard closed her eyes. "Yes."

32

THE ELEVATOR WAS MASSIVE, BIG enough for all of us—kids and grown-ups alike. It was made of glass, but as we slid down, the shaft grew dark. We had walked over to the main research headquarters for Krita, the place where the biggest and most profitable work took place.

Mouse worked her way over next to me. "You did your part," she whispered.

"Almost," I said.

Down and down we went. Mom put her hand on my shoulder, soft and reassuring. "Thank you," I said. "Thanks for letting me see her one more time."

She wiped a tear away. "Mori, I don't know what to say."

I wrapped my arms around her, trying to comfort her

while knowing full well I was about to betray her trust again. She'd broken my trust and I'd broken hers. I had to believe that each time we broke it, we could build it back again.

We came to a soft stop and the door slid open.

We were underground, I felt sure of that. The hallway was narrow and the ceiling was lower than on the previous floors.

The clicking of Ms. Staarsgard's shoes echoed as we went down the hall.

Mouse wove around the people. That was the benefit of being small and quiet—of being a mouse. People didn't notice as she slipped pieces of paper into my friends' hands.

Dr. Varden walked next to me. "Do you remember what you said?" I asked. "About playing dominoes?"

"Of course," she said. She had told us she'd been lining up pieces and was waiting to see how they would fall. She had made contacts outside, people who could help her to help Ilana.

"Did you ever get them set up the way you wanted them to?" I asked.

"As best as I could," she replied. "Dominoes are tricky. But they always fall, one way or another." She put a hand on my shoulder and squeezed.

"Okay, then," I told her. "I think it's time to set that chain in motion."

We passed two more doors and then Ms. Staarsgard

stopped. "It will be a brief visit, children. Supervised, of course." All business again. She pushed open the door.

Ilana sat on a cot, a stack of books at her side. Her bright eyes caught mine and she jumped to her feet. We crashed into each other as we held on tightly. Maybe, I thought, maybe I could just never let her go. Maybe that could be our plan.

"Are you okay?" I asked.

"Are you?" she replied.

I laughed. "I'm fine now that I can see you! I've been so worried. No one would tell us where you were or what was happening."

"They won't tell me, either."

"I'm really sorry," Theo said. He stood just inside the doorway of the gray room.

"It's not your fault," she told him. "All you did was help me—all of you."

"Still," Julia said. "We're sorry." And we knew what she was sorry for. Sorry that it had amounted to nothing. Sorry that Ilana was in this tiny room by herself while we were eating blueberry pancakes in the sunshine, hanging out on the playground, visiting the museum.

Out in the hallway, our parents stood in a huddle. It was like we were in a play, and they were the audience. Mouse, Amnah, and Tommy stood in front of them. Ready.

Our plan couldn't possibly work, could it?

Dr. Varden stepped into the room.

"They didn't need to keep you in the dungeon," Benji said. "I mean, geez, this seems over-the-top."

"It's so they don't have to look at me. No one has to," Ilana said.

"No one likes to look at their mistakes," Theo told her.

Ilana cracked a smile. "Gee, thanks, Theo. Now I'm a mistake?"

Theo reddened. He took a step closer to us. It was better when he was by the door, keeping it open. "That's not what I meant—"

Ilana kept smiling but she sat down on the cot. "It sort of is true, though, right? I'm the mistake they need to fix."

Meryl and Greg Naughton looked at the ground. So little to say for themselves. Without the sunlight, the swirling colors of Meryl Naughton's clothes lost their glamour.

"It's not you that's wrong," I said.

"Thanks," she said with a small grin.

"No, I mean, people aren't freaked out by you. They're freaked out by themselves. You just remind them of it."

"Are you freaked out by yourself?" she asked.

"A little," I admitted.

"Mori's not getting her latency," Julia blurted. "Isn't that crazy?"

"Don't be stupid, Mori," Ilana said. "Don't do that for me."

"I'm not doing it for you. I'm doing it for me. I want to

find out who I really am without all this—" I waved my hand around the air. She knew what I meant.

"Okay," she said. "Okay, that makes sense. You're pretty perfect already, if you ask me."

"Hardly."

She looked down at her feet. "Anyway, I don't think there's a latency for what makes you so great. So it would just be a waste."

Tears stung my eyes and I let them fall.

"Is there anything more you children need to say to one another?" Ms. Staarsgard asked. "I know you think I'm being harsh, but drawn-out good-byes can be rather cruel."

"I got the book, Ilana," I said. "In case of emergency."

"I knew I could count on him," she said with a smile.

"I'll study it," I said. "So I'll be ready. I'll know all the plants. I'll keep our garden growing in here."

"And I'll have one out there," she said. "And then someday—" Her voice cracked.

"Someday," I agreed.

I hugged her again. And when I did, I whispered in her ear: "There's going to be a distraction, and when it comes, you run."

She looked at me with her green-blue eyes. A faint shake of the head. "You run," I mouthed to her.

Ms. Staarsgard cleared her throat.

Mouse rubbed her stomach. "Oh!" she said.

Theo turned around. "You okay, kid?"

"Just a stomachache," she whispered.

It was happening.

"I could go with you," I said. Julia tensed next to me. She knew. She was on board and she thought I was blowing it, but I was being careful. The grown-ups would think I was offering to go wherever they took her, like I was so naive to think they were just going to send her to another Kritopia or something. It fit perfectly with their idea of me.

"Not where I'm going," she replied.

"I could," I said. "I would."

"No," she said. "Wherever I'm going, it's not for you. And Old Harmonie, it isn't for me anymore."

"That's a very mature realization, Ilana," Ms. Staarsgard told her. "I'm sure the other children will come to see how right you are in time."

I couldn't help but shake my head.

"Oh!" Mouse said again. And then Amnah, too. "Oh!" Both of them were doubled over.

No! I wanted to cry out. It was too soon, too fast. I needed more time with Ilana.

"Old Harmonie is your home. This is where you belong," Ilana told me.

"I don't want to belong here."

"That's one thing you don't get to choose. Stay here. Grow up. Get smarter. I will, too. And one day, it will all work out."

"How can you be so sure?" I asked.

"Because I have to be."

"Holy cupcakes," Tommy cried. "What did you feed us?"

Mouse fell to the floor, writhing in pain, or so it seemed. The adults crowded around her.

"I love you, Ilana," I told her.

"I love you, too," she said.

Then Amnah fell, too. She moaned.

Dr. Varden stepped into the room.

"What's going on?" Tommy yelled. "Aren't you going to help them?"

"Go," I whispered.

Ilana shook her head.

Tommy yelled again, but this time, he was falling. Then, next to me, Julia coughed. She cried. She gripped her stomach. "Something's wrong," she yelled. She fell forward toward the cot. I pulled Ilana away, closer to the door.

Julia's parents crashed into the room, others behind them. My own parents sprinted toward me.

Julia's wails filled the room, and then she was joined by Benji, who cried out as he dropped to the floor. He crawled toward the cot, too. Deeper into the room.

"Go!" I said. I pushed her away from me. I had to. She wouldn't have gone otherwise. Dr. Varden grabbed her hand.

My parents were nearly on top of me. I closed my eyes and let myself fall into their arms with a long, low moan. It wasn't my body that hurt. It was my heart.

Theo dropped with a thud beside us.

It was the perfect trap. It was the one thing they couldn't ignore: the children of Old Harmonie suffering. The children in pain.

Dr. Varden pushed the door shut behind them, locking us all in the room.

33

IT HADN'T TAKEN LONG FOR our families to realize we had tricked them, but by then we were stuck inside the room. Ms. Staarsgard had to call security to come and get us. Ilana and Dr. Varden were gone.

I had to believe they found that network of people to help. I had to believe they were safe. But it was hard to believe anything after all we'd been through.

Maybe the Krita people had found Ilana and hadn't told us.

Still, at night I went alone and sat in Oakedge and waited. Just waited.

The nights grew cooler. One night I lay down in the moss and stared up at the sky through the leaves. There was a loud rustling and then an owl swooped overhead. I felt the beat of its wings. Tears welled up in my eyes.

Amnah, Mouse, and Tommy were sent home. Tommy promised he'd see us in a decade. Amnah just said good-bye. No one ever suspected that the escape plan had all been Mouse's idea, and Ms. Staarsgard made good on her promise to send a doctor out to dampen Mouse's anxiety. I wondered sometimes if I would even know Mouse anymore. She was brilliant, I knew that, and maybe that was the kind of thing the dampening was meant for: to help someone who couldn't be her full self without it. I hoped Mouse was happier, and I hoped that someday I could find out in person.

Becoming one's full self—I was pretty sure that's what Baba had intended with the latency. I'd been spending more and more time with Mr. Quist, learning about the early days. We'd go to the archives and I was piecing together what Baba and Dr. Varden had wanted, gathering together their early plans. I wasn't sure what I was going to do with it yet, but I wasn't going to let it slip away. I wasn't going to let the people in Old Harmonie forget what we were supposed to be.

Footsteps crashed through the underbrush toward me.

"Ilana?" I whispered. But there were too many footsteps, and too many voices.

"It's us," Theo said. Just like last time. He'd come to check on me again.

"Oh," I said. "Hi." Theo stepped into the clearing, followed by Julia and Benji. They sat down next to me on the moss. I rubbed my eyes.

"You wait for her here?" Julia asked.

"It's like in that wilderness course we took. If you're lost, stay in one place. If I stay here, she'll always know where to find me."

"I think she would find you wherever you are," Julia said. "I know I would."

"I'd find you, too," I said. "All of you."

Julia's leg had healed and, just like they'd promised, it was even better than before. She'd started running with a group of elite athletes, and now they were even talking of sending her to a special school where she could train more intensively. That wasn't for a year, at least.

Benji got a spot in the trial for the new latency program. He said in his initial testing, he showed numerous potential latencies. "Even some they'd never even considered before," he'd told us when he'd come back. I think he was hoping I might change my mind about my own latency, but I didn't.

"You used to come out here a lot?" Theo asked.

"Yeah, me and Ilana. We came here. We were going to make our own perfect world."

"A new Old Harmonie?" Benji asked.

When he said it like that, it seemed sort of silly. We might start with good intentions, just like Dr. Varden and Baba had, but somewhere along the way, trying to make everything good, we'd surely mess up something else. I think that's what Dr. Varden had been trying to show us when she took us to Boston: if you just pull out the beautiful, and leave behind what doesn't work, nothing's beautiful anymore. You need to have the complete picture.

I stood up and stretched my arms above my head. Off in the distance, the owl hooted. "Come on," I said. We tramped through the woods, close to the same path we'd followed the night we left. If anyone was watching our locations via our watchus, they were probably going on high red alert. But we weren't leaving.

The fence had been repaired. It stood taller and was made of shiny new metal laced through with the same wires we had found down near the reservoir. Theo glanced over at me. "To keep others out or to keep us in?" he asked.

"It doesn't really matter in the end," I said.

We all stood along the fence, shoulder to shoulder, watching the colors change and the light fade until we were in that in-between time: not night and not day. The gloaming, my dad had called it. In summer, it seemed to go on forever. So we didn't move.

A breeze came up over the ridge. It tousled Julia's hair and blew it into my face. That's when I noticed the patch of wood sorrel. It grew right along the edge of the fence. And there, a few yards off, something twisted in the wind:

a ribbon, new and bright, tied to the fence about a foot off the ground. I dropped down and felt it between my fingers. It was a gorgeous shade of aqua green: the precise shade of Ilana's eyes. When I looked up, all my friends were looking down at me.

Safe.

She was safe. And we would remember that.

And then it was clear to me: the truth. It's not the fences that keep us safe, or the science, or the structured way of life. It's us: the Firefly Five.

ACKNOWLEDGMENTS

Sometimes families share DNA. Sometimes they are made of something grander. Thank you to all of the families that made this book possible:

The Bloomsbury family, the best in the business: Cindy Loh, Cristina Gilbert, Lizzy Mason, Beth Eller, Emily Ritter, Linette Kim, Brittany Mitchell, Brett Wright, Erica Barmash, Manuel Sumberac, Oona Patrick, Regina Castillo, Donna Mark, and Melissa Kavonic. And most of all to Mary Kate Castellani who edits with grace and humor and more smarts than any author could hope for.

To the teacher, librarian, and bookseller families that embraced *The Firefly Code* and my other books. You bring the books to the readers, and for that I am truly grateful.

To my teaching families at Dyer and Kaler Elementary Schools in South Portland, Maine, and to those at Berwick Academy, Westbrook High School, and the Commonwealth School. To the students at these schools as well, who inspire me every day.

To the families that are related to me and support me by showing up at events, pushing my books onto friends and strangers, and giving me space and time to write: the Blakemores, Frazers, Tananbaums, Pikcilingises, and Faronis.

To the friends who aren't related to me, but should be: Larissa Crocket, Jessie Forbes, Sarah Newkirk, Lindsay Oakes, and Jenn Swift-Morgan.

And to Sara Crowe, my agent right from the start.

Thank you all and thank you to the countless others who make my daybreaks brighter.